Praise for Undeclared

"I loved this book and can't wait to read the next installment in the Woodlands series, the characters, storyline and gushing romance were all wonderfully written and Jen Frederick's writing is extremely engaging—she is definitely an author to remember and this is a book I'm more than happy to add to my favourites list!" *Obsession with Books*

"Noah Jackson was perfect in every way! He was compassionate, considerate and sexy as hell! His old school values mixed with his slight debauchery made him a perfect alpha male and you can't help but adore every part of his character." *Craves the Angst*

"Wonderful, lovely book, and I wholly recommend you read it." *Nocturnal Book Reviews*

Undeclared

By
Jen Frederick

Cathy -
Reading takes you
on a thousand journeys.
Hope you enjoy this one.
Jen Frederick

To my dear husband and daughter
Thanks for being so utterly patient with me.
I have a lot of reading nights to make up for.

Chapter One

Dear Soldier:

Our English composition class project this year is to write to soldiers who are serving in Afghanistan and Iraq. We were given a list of topics to write about, like the weather and our classes. I have to talk about the weather every Sunday at brunch with my family. It's the most boring conversation ever. Even more boring than church sermons.

I'm not going to write to you about the weather or Differential Algebra because I don't want to bore you to death.

I'd like to send a care package, but I'm not sure what you would like the most. I can't send cigarettes, as I am not old enough to buy them.

Very truly yours,
Grace Sullivan

***

Dear Grace,

Thank you for your letter. We are always glad to have mail from home. Most of our time here in Afghanistan is boring, too. It seems like we have boredom in common.

While war might seem exciting in movies, there is actually a lot of waiting around and doing nothing. It's incredibly hot and dry so the idea of sitting and talking about the weather indoors during brunch seems pretty awesome to me.

Definitely don't buy cigarettes. I'm pretty sure your school assignment isn't supposed to turn you into a felon. You don't need to send me anything. Just getting a letter now and then is great. Look forward to hearing from you again.

Yours,

Pfc. Noah Jackson

FYI: Marines aren't soldiers; we are Marines. Only the Army has soldiers.

Grace

"How 'bout you, Grace? Who's your perfect man?" Amy Swanson, my cousin Lana's sorority sister, stood with Lana and a couple of other Alpha Phis exchanging tidbits on who did what to whom over the summer.

"I'm not getting married. I plan to live a life of bachelorette-hood. I'll be eccentric, have nine cats, and wear blue eye shadow and fur in the summer," I said, trying to sound flippant. But based on the weight of Lana's disapproving glare, I think I slid too far into snarky territory.

Whenever I was asked about why I hadn't had a boyfriend, ever, I always responded in this manner. I knew I was unreasonably sensitive about my non-existent dating life, but the truth was more embarrassing than any story I could make up.

Other than a few drunken hookups, the closest I had ever come to condoms was finding a packet of them lying next to my brother Josh's gym bag. In high school, I had an unhealthy attachment to a Marine with whom I had corresponded for four years, and Lana continued to harp on that even now. "Self-fulfilling" and "self-destructive behavior" were among the many therapy-speak phrases that Lana enjoyed whipping out. At first, these were terms she learned in her own therapy sessions. Now they're from classes she takes as a psych major.

I offered a snarky response to give people some small, delicious detail to focus on so everything else faded away. It was all in the perspective.

Swiveling in my chair, I turned to view my favorite expanse in the library. The reference and circulation desks sat on a balcony above the library's entrance. The distance was just enough to provide the perfect perspective. I stood up and tilted my head down to peer through the viewfinder of my camera. I always set up my tripod when I worked. Some people studied. Others gossiped. I took time-lapse images, shrinking scenes into miniature, shutting out the peripheral noise, highlighting the minute details, and making everything seem unreal and toy-like.

I felt a nudge at my arm. "Let me see," Lana was there, offering a silent olive branch. She knew I was still smarting from her disapproving stare, but I knew I should be the one apologizing. I moved away and she peered through the lens, careful not to touch anything. Lana knew how particular I was about the setup of my camera. She stood up and huffed, "I never get to see what you do." It was a compliment. Lana was good for my ego. She was good for everything. Too bad I was straight. And then there was the whole "cousin" thing.

Shrugging, I looked down again. Two guys had entered the lobby and paused at the monitor's desk. Their heads suggested diametric appearances. Great contrast. One was blond, the other dark-haired. Both were tall. I quickly moved the camera up the rails and retilted the lens. I took one photo and then looked again. The dark one had knelt down to tie his shoe—make that his boot—while the other waited patiently. The composition made them look like toy soldiers, particularly with the uniformity of their jeans, the dark, plain T-shirts, and the heavy-soled boots. I took three more pictures in rapid succession.

"So Grace," Amy called from behind me, "are you still coming over tomorrow to take rush photographs?" Her voice must have carried, because through my lens I could see the dark-haired guy's head jerk up. My heartbeat stuttered, and I moved my hand up to spin the focus on the zoom for a close-up, just as the blond guy bent down and obscured my view. I heard my name again but didn't move, my eyes glued to the scene in the library entrance below.

I felt something sharp in the region of my heart at the sight of them. I lifted my hand almost unconsciously and pressed a fist against the upper curve of my left breast, as if I could physically press the pain away. I thought I had finally stopped envisioning every brown-haired soldier as my Marine. This wasn't Noah Jackson, my pen pal of four years, and his blond-haired best friend, Bo. These were just two random college guys. Probably on the lacrosse team, by the looks of the muscles on their arms. I blinked rapidly and resolutely turned away, walking the short distance between the desk and the railing. Between reality and make-believe.

I cleared my throat and deliberately focused on Amy. "Yes, I'll come over tomorrow."

"What time?" Amy was one of the rush chairs, and she wanted a photograph of the Alpha Phi house to put on the rush invitations. I pulled out my phone to check the weather app. I preferred cloudy days, because sometimes sunny days made the photos look washed-out from overexposure in the light. The weather app suggested 10 a.m. would be a good time. But I had class at 10.

Peering over my shoulder, Lana suggested, "What about after lunch?" Then she added under her breath, "It's just for the sorority."

I made a face at her. I didn't care about much, but I did like my photographs to look good. "Have you guys talked to the Delts?" For the photograph Amy wanted, I'd need to be high up, and the fraternity house across the street was four stories. If I were at the highest level, I'd probably be able to get a halfway decent photo, sun or not.

"Yup. It's all cleared with Jack," Amy said, waving her hand in front of her face. I couldn't tell if she was indicating he was hot or smelly. At my lack of response, Amy clarified, "Jack's the president of the Delta Tau Deltas." I guess the hand movement indicated hot.

"She doesn't care," Lana said, forestalling more painful examination of hot guys and their absence in my life.

I gave her a little push to start her moving around the desk. I needed to send the photos I just took to my laptop. Not because I wanted to magnify the images of the two guys but just to see how they turned out.

"I'll come to the house after lunch," I said. With that, Amy and the other Alpha Phis wandered off, but Lana remained behind. I didn't want her watching me as I looked at the photos. "I'm going to study," I told her in an effort to get her to leave, but my attempts to shoo her along were met with a skeptical glance.

"Right. One week into classes and you're going to study." Her tone was flat and disbelieving. "What is it that you're going to do that you don't want me to know about?" I fought the urge to look at my camera, at the balcony. I wasn't sure what she had noticed as I took the pictures.

"Unhealthy realities can be constructed out of imaginary occurrences as a coping strategy disguised as wish fulfillment," Lana said. She had definitely clued in on my preoccupation with the two guys downstairs.

"I only understood every third word of that," I muttered.

"It means get real," Lana said. "See you at home." She turned, her blonde hair swinging out behind her as she caught up with her sisters.

I forced myself to wait until Lana had walked off the balcony before I rushed over to the camera. In my haste, I fumbled a bit with the controls and almost knocked the tripod over before I was able to email the images to my account.

The time that it took the images to load on my laptop was excruciating. Glaciers moved faster. When the photos finally appeared in my inbox, I zoomed in quickly to see if I had captured the brunette's face with any clarity. But in each of the pictures I had taken, his face was averted or blocked. I couldn't even see a chin profile. I switched to the blond's image. Was that Bo? I squinted, zoomed in, zoomed out. I couldn't decide. I had deleted the scanned photo of their unit off my drive at the end of last semester, right before Lana and I returned home to Chicago. It was part of the process of trying to "get real," as Lana had admonished earlier, so I had nothing to compare to these current photos.

Frustrated, I slammed the top of my laptop shut and laid my head down.

Why was I doing this to myself? Last year had felt like actual torture. My heart jumped into my throat every time I saw a tall, dark-haired guy. I wanted so much for him to be Noah, like I could will his presence from his base in San Diego.

Lana wanted me to go to therapy, worried that I was developing a nervous disorder. It took me a week into the first year of classes before Lana had been able to convince me that Noah Jackson wasn't now or ever going to be attending Central College.

If I was going to be looking at photographs, I should've reviewed the selection for my entry into the art department. I had put that task off during freshman year, scared away by the horror stories. The dean of the School of Fine Arts had managed to make more students cry and want to drop out than when the on-campus Starbucks shut down for three days after a water leak.

I picked up my battered college course catalog. If I wasn't going to get up the nerve to apply to the Fine Arts program, I needed to pick a major, something to focus my attention on, so that the rest of the world became blurred-out background noise. It was all in the perspective, I reminded myself.

***

"Anything wrong, Grace?" I started at the sound. Mike Walsh stood leaning against the circulation desk, holding his ever-present red Nerf ball. Mike maintained that he needed the ball to avoid strangling some of the more obnoxious students, who generally wanted the library staff to do their research for them.

"Nah, just not ready for classes to start again. How was your summer?"

"Can't complain." He tipped his head toward my dog-eared course catalog. "Worried you haven't picked a major yet?"

Mike was my student supervisor and all last year he had watched me page through this course catalog at least once a week. "Kind of. I'm getting so tired of saying 'undeclared' to everyone who asks me about it."

"Just make one up. No one knows the difference anyways."

"No one except the students who are actually in that major," I pointed out with what I hoped sounded like wryness. I wasn't good at lying. For the longest time, I thought Lana was just super-perceptive, until she told me that every emotion passed across my face like a parade of black ants on a white picnic blanket.

"So, you hear the gossip?" Mike leaned closer, his eyes bright with mischief. Mike was known for two things: his red ball and sourcing more gossip than TMZ.

"Is someone sleeping with their professor already?" That was about the only kind of gossip I figured was juicy enough to account for the eager look on Mike's face.

"Nope. We've got some celebrities in our midst this year."

"Like movie stars?" I hadn't heard anything about this, and you'd think that Lana and the sorority girls would've been all over this.

"No, mixed martial arts fighters. Two guys who transferred from some junior college in California."

If my heart had stuttered before, now it completely stopped. All the blood drained from my face, and I may have ceased breathing for a moment.

"Grace, you don't look so good," Mike said, leaning back as if he were afraid I was going to infect him.

"No," I croaked. "I don't feel so good." I pressed my fist against my heart again.

"You should go home. There's nothing going on tonight."

I nodded my agreement. I needed to go home, and not just to the apartment I shared with Lana, but all the way home to Chicago. Instead, shaking inside, I packed up my tripod and camera with little conscious thought, muscle memory taking over. Mike may have even helped me;

7

I don't remember. I felt like my head was filled with cotton. All I could hear was the name Noah, over and over, thumping with each beat of my heart.

Noah

"Tap your Goddamn pencil one more time, and I'm going to snap your fingers off along with it," Bo muttered to me. I looked down at my hand, not even realizing it had been in perpetual motion. "Just go and talk to her."

"Can't. She's working," I said. But she hadn't been working two hours ago, or the many other times I had spotted her during the past week. The truth was that I was a coward. Facing Grace Sullivan after nearly two years of no contact was more terrifying than the first time I was on patrol in Afghanistan. At this point, I'd rather face down ten angry insurgents than one 5' 6" girl I could probably pick up and toss with one hand.

But back then, I had been through ninety days of basic training and was surrounded by my buddies, all of us armed to the teeth while we were deployed. Here my only weapons were my lackluster verbal skills and the knowledge that she had written to me, once a month, for four years.

I justified the two weeks since classes started by telling myself I first had to do some recon. No mission is undertaken without good intelligence.

I had to find exactly the best time to not exactly ambush Grace, but at least find the right way to let her know I had landed back in her life.

I found out she had all early classes and was done by noon every day. I learned she lived in a swanky house two blocks away from campus. Bo had chatted up some chick down at the library desk and learned that Grace did her required weekly hours of service on Thursday nights and Sunday afternoons. The one thing I hadn't managed to obtain was her cell phone number, so I resorted to stalking her around campus.

"If I told the guys that the idea of meeting Grace has turned you into a quivering pussy, they wouldn't believe me," Bo mocked smugly, leaning back in his chair and folding his arms behind his head.

"Half those guys would give their left nut to be me right now," I shot back.

After a few months of regular care packages, Grace had become our unofficial mascot. When the boxes from Grace arrived, the unit hovered around me like vultures and would randomly grab stuff out of the box. They weren't jackasses enough to take the letter, though. Everyone knew that was hands-off. But I had made the mistake of showing Bo her prom picture, and then everyone wanted to see "their Grace." My CO even made me pin the picture up, as if she were some kind of community property.

I suspected more guys jacked off to that picture of Grace than to the chick on the cover of *Juggs*. I guess I was doing my part to benefit unit cohesion, but fuck me, the next picture she sent I kept for myself.

About two years into my service, all the young, single guys and some of the attached ones had begun to view Grace as something of a myth. She was faithful and generous and, after the inclusion of her prom picture, we knew she was, hot, too. She was curvier than the average coed, but I liked that. In her prom dress, she looked like a '50s pinup model, with her dark hair curled and a flower pinned near her forehead. While it could have been the padding of her dress, I suspected that she was stacked.

You couldn't tell the color of her eyes from the picture. She said they were hazel, a mix of yellow and brown that changed depending on what she wore. I may have fantasized a few times about what color they would be when I went down on her or when she was stroking me off.

I looked back over at Bo, still leaning casually back in his chair. "After she's done working," I told him, not sure if I was trying to convince him or myself. I'd wait until she was off work and then walk her home. Sit on the swing that hung on the big wraparound porch of the house she lived in, and try to explain my complete silence for the past two years. Automatically, I wondered what color Grace's eyes were when she was angry.

I hadn't ever been good at explaining myself, and I knew this time wasn't going to be any better. I was, however, good at doing. Only this time, when I went to the circulation desk to actually do something, Grace was gone.

Chapter Two

Dear Grace,

Thanks for the care package. It was awesome and really, really big. I appreciate you not sending me the extra bottles of nail polish that you and Lana received from your Uncle Louis. I'm not a big fan of nail polish myself, but you can make a pretty good incendiary device with it. Don't paint your nails near a fire, or maybe even a candle.

Today was hot—like yesterday and the day before. I don't remember what 60 degrees feels like. It's either brutally hot (day) or freezing cold (night). I can handle the hot. I'm from Texas after all. It's the huge swings in temperature that are hard to get used to.

We've been going on a number of walkabouts that are essentially a bunch of guys going from hut to hut in a small village looking for insurgents or handing out aid. I always think that it's ridiculous to be handing out paper and pens and candy while we are carrying assault rifles, but everyone here treats it like it's normal.

Yours,

Pfc. Noah Jackson

P.S. You can just call me Noah.

Grace

Lana and I lived in this amazing apartment just two blocks off campus. One thing about going to a pricey and old private college was that the surrounding apartments weren't run-down shitholes owned by slum-lords. We lived on the top floor of a renovated Victorian.

It had high ceilings and oversized doors. The lights were reproductions of late 19th Century Victorian decorations, made out of iron and frosted orbs of glass, according to the apartment rental sheet. It was altogether too beautiful to be housing college students, but I guess when the annual tuition at Central was more than the price of a luxury car, the landlords expected a higher caliber tenant. Those were silly expectations. We were college students.

When I came home from the library, I forgot all those things and treated the apartment door like it was the entrance of a flophouse, throwing the heavy wood structure open with a bang, not caring that the newly plastered walls might be dented by the antiqued brass doorknob.

"Lana!" I called as I burst through the doorway, placing my padded backpack holding my camera and laptop on the floor. She shot up from the sofa as if electrocuted and a caramel-brown head of hair immediately followed. I groaned inwardly when I saw it was Lana's boyfriend.

"Hey, what is it?" she asked, smoothing her hair out of her face. I waved my hand in front of my chest to indicate that her shirt was unbuttoned and her camisole askew, and then averted my eyes while the two proceeded to right themselves. Too bad I couldn't cover my ears to avoid the sounds of zippers and snaps. It's not like I'm a prude, but I just didn't like Peter. He didn't treat Lana right, and I didn't like knowing they exchanged body fluids. She deserved better.

Thankfully, my interruption of their intimate moment managed to stop the cycling of crazy thoughts in my head. I felt almost foolish over the panic I had gotten into at the library. Looking down at my hands, I saw they were still trembling. I pressed my palms together as rational thoughts began filtering through my thick head.

I went to the kitchen to grab a water bottle. I busied myself and tried to block out the kissing noises from the entryway that indicated an extended goodbye.

"Even God rested on the seventh day," I told Lana after she closed the door.

She grinned unrepentantly at me and then laughed outright when I screwed my face into a fake offended expression.

"Sorry, I figured you'd go out with the library crew tonight," Lana said. My library crew consisted of my student supervisor Mike and two others. Ordinarily, I'd meet up with them to have a post-work drink and complain about all the dickheads who needed help in the library. I think a whole set of other library students drank on another night. I didn't have a fake ID yet, so I was limited to early hours at a diner that also just happened to serve liquor. "Or be hanging around to find out if the brown haired muscled guy is your fabled Noah." Obviously Lana had noticed my reaction to the guys in the library.

"It's crazy, right?" I needed her reassurance. "I'm just imagining things."

She nodded slowly. "I would think so. What makes you think it was him?"

I dragged myself over to the living room and sank into a side chair.

"At first I convinced myself that it was just another pair of guys who looked like Noah and his buddy Bo. But later, Mike told me there were two junior college transfers from California who were fighters. Noah once wrote that he was interested in fighting after getting out."

"So you added up two guys, one blond, one dark, plus fighters from California, and got your Marine from high school?"

The skepticism in Lana's voice was exactly what I needed, and I mentally leaned into it, relaxing for the first time since I had spotted those two guys in the library.

"I know, honestly. Only I could come up with such a thing," I tried to make it sound like a joke, but I knew my tone was wrong. More hopeful than mocking.

"Oh Grace," Lana sat down on the edge of the chair and put her arm around me. "Don't you worry that you aren't open to new things here?"

Was that what I was doing? Were my hopeful imaginings just a way to keep myself from getting close to others? Even if I could wish Noah into existence here at Central, I couldn't make him love me. And if he had loved me, he would be here. Or I would be with him. I rubbed my forehead. I couldn't even stand to think about all that now. Time to change the subject. "Have you talked with Amy about the picture?"

Lana played along, sparing me any more potential humiliation. "Yeah, we want you to do one of those miniature pictures."

"The tilt shift?"

Lana nodded. "That the kind that makes everyone look like little plastic figures or models?"

I took out a pencil and paper and sketched out the front of the Alpha Phi house. "What do you want me to focus on? Are you going to stand outside and hold hands and sing?" I asked.

"Not sure." Lana was an apathetic sorority sister. "I'm going to be the photographer's assistant and make sure the Delt's house doesn't swallow you whole."

"I thought you wanted me to be swallowed by a Delt," I teased.

"I think I said last year that a cure for one man was another. It was in an attempt to get you over the Noah phase."

"Thanks, Dr. Lana."

"I'm just a psychologist-in-training. I promise to give you free therapy sessions if I mess you up too bad during college."

"I'm holding you to that," I said. "Guess I lucked out when we Sullivans came to live with you guys."

"I think it was kismet," Lana replied, smiling at me, probably relieved I hadn't started crying again.

"Kismet doesn't sound very science-y."

"Still in training, Grace. Still in training."

Noah

Bo's left cross glanced across my chin, and I stumbled back against the ropes.

"Fuck me," he swore. "What's wrong with you this morning?"

As if he had to ask. My trainer, Paulie, jumped into the ring and bustled over to me.

"I only get you for two hours in the morning and this is the effort you're giving? Fuckin' ingrate," Paulie muttered, pulling off my gloves and protective facemask.

Getting hit in the face is probably my least favorite part of mixed martial arts. I could take a body blow or three, but the other guys at the gym joked about my glass jaw. Paulie has tried to beat that out of me. On a regular basis, he and a few other guys punch me in the face while I wear a protective mask. The goal is to make me so accustomed to getting a fist to the face that I become like a comic villain, always getting up again even after the good guys thought they'd killed me.

Taking a blow to the head or the ribs is one thing. What separates the winners from the wannabes is the ability to think. If you're hit with the left cross, that usually means the right side of the fighter's upper body is open. Only the most disciplined fighters always keep their right side protected, and Bo isn't a disciplined fighter. He's fast and he has hammers for fists, but he's lazy, which is why he's only my sparring partner and not competing professionally. This morning, though, my reflexes were coated with tar. Gym chum could take me down this morning.

Bo sensed this, and apparently Paulie did as well. "Get over there and do chest crawls. Twenty five times," Paulie instructed. Holding the upper rope up and pushing the lower rope down, he gestured for me to get going. Bo helped by shoving me in the back.

Military crawls? I could do those in my sleep. I tried not to look grateful at being released from sparring. Pulling my body across the gym mats, one forearm and knee at a time, required no thought at all. By the tenth one, my mind was completely blank of everything but the abrasiveness of the rubber weave of the mats cutting into my arms and legs. By number fifteen, I wasn't feeling anything but a burning sensation in my abdomen. *Pain is weakness leaving the body*, I repeated in a loop. By twenty-five, I felt like liquefied rubber.

My effort didn't quite meet Paulie's standards. When I stood up, he looked at me grim-faced. "Took you two minutes longer today. You're a worthless schmuck. Go run and get the fuck out of here. When you come back tomorrow, your mind better be in the game. We have a fucking meet in four weeks. Do you want to get on the card or not?"

I nodded and took the water bottle that appeared at my side. Gulping down some much-needed hydration, I went over to the bench where my running shoes were. I pulled them on and nodded to Bo. He always ran my cool-down with me.

Every morning I got up at 5 a.m. to train with Paulie Generoli. When I had decided to come to Central, I figured that fighting would've to be shelved or put aside entirely. I wasn't broken up about it. Few fighters ever made any money, although with new network television contracts, and increasing interest in pay-per-view events, the sport was making everyone richer.

Even with the influx of new money, though, the likelihood of fighters making a real living out of it was low. The goal was to get on a television fight card. You do that and you get a pretty nice payday. I played high percentage shots, like saving all my money while deployed, instead of buying new trucks, bikes, or boats. But the lure of getting paid big money for beating the shit out of someone was too enticing to pass up.

My trainer in San Diego begged me not to leave, but when it became clear that I wasn't going to change my mind, he hooked me up with Paulie, a former Olympic wrestling coach. I was lucky to have him and even luckier not to have to pay Paulie for his training services, only for my gym membership. But if I could win something—anything—then

Paulie could use me to bolster his gym's reputation. It was a mutual back-scratching arrangement that could all go to hell if Paulie found out that I was messed up this morning because I couldn't stop thinking about a girl.

Never a big equal rights supporter, Paulie had become increasingly angry toward females after so many colleges began eliminating their wrestling programs. He viewed women as good for only one thing, and Paulie was perpetually single because he couldn't keep his opinions to himself.

"I'm going to talk to her after her last class today," I told Bo as we ran along the nearly deserted downtown streets. Traffic would pick up in about fifteen minutes, but we'd be close to done by that time.

"Where?"

"Outside her classroom."

"Sounds like a terrible idea."

"It's not," I denied. I had debated this all night. It was why I couldn't focus this morning. "Or it might be, but it's the best I've got. I've let it fester too long. It's time to pull the Band-Aid off."

"What was the Band-Aid, exactly? The Dear John letter you wrote to her?"

"Was I supposed to show up at her door with my rucksack and say, 'I'm a fucking mess. I can't sleep. I jump at loud noises. I'm likely to strangle your cat if you have one'," I retorted. When Bo and I separated, I'd spent three months wondering if I had made a big mistake by getting out. I wasn't suited for anything but being a Marine, but time and multiple visits to the VA helped calm me down.

I had wanted to separate, get Grace, and start a new life together. Instead, I sent her a letter telling her she reminded me of someone's little sister and friend-zoned her. I didn't want to think about the anger I would've felt getting that kind of letter from her. The guilt wore me down sometimes, but I didn't want to present a fucked-up version of myself. I'd spent the year putting myself back together, physically and mentally, and another year making sure I could not only get into Central, but pay for it.

If it took another year to win Grace back, I would do it. I'd hate it, but I'd do it.

Grace

When I left class, my first thought was that I was still in bed dreaming, because Noah Jackson was standing there, leaning against the interior brick wall next to my classroom with his backpack slung over one shoulder. Even slouching, he was still taller than many of the other students passing him.

I let out an involuntary cry and swallowed it back, but it was too late. His head popped up and, as he straightened and looked right at me, I got my first full view of him. I wasn't even surprised I recognized him. I couldn't delete his image from my memory like I could from my hard drive.

Noah was older than most of the students. He had never revealed his birthday, even though I asked repeatedly. His excuse was that I would try to do something too extravagant, and he would feel guilty. But based on his years of deployment, I knew he had to be around 23. It wasn't just his age that set him apart from my classmates, but the way he held himself.

I drank him in, mesmerized by the sight.

Even standing silently near the wall, he had presence and an innate confidence. He didn't shrink in on himself, but he stood there comfortably, arms loose at his sides. The crowd moved around him instead of the other way around.

He was shorter than my brother, Josh, who stood at 6' 5, but was more solid. Dressed simply in jeans and a dark gray T-shirt, his body had not lost any of the muscle he had gained while in the Marines. If anything, he looked bigger than he had in the one picture I possessed.

I could see the veins prominently displayed under the skin in his forearms and biceps. Like the arms of a drummer in the marching band. Strong. Powerful. Capable. His eyes were deep-set but in perfect symmetry to his mouth and angular nose. His cheekbones were sharp and high, reminding me of a manga character. But where those characters had rounded baby faces, Noah's jaw and chin were squared off, as if the sands of the desert had hewn that portion of his face out of rock.

I tried to move back into the classroom, but the collective force of the exiting students continued to push me outside. We stood there for a moment, just a few feet away; the distance seemed at once yawning and stifling.

I should've said something witty, like "where have you been all my life" or "long time, no see" because really did he expect he could show up and I'd fall at his feet? But my actual thinking capabilities were currently somewhere on the hallway floor.

It was like fate, or life, or karma hated me. I needed to be in a men-on-their-knees outfit, not dressed in my brother's flannel shirt, baggy boyfriend jeans, and battered canvas Chuck Taylors. I hadn't even showered today because I overslept, spending most of the night tossing and turning.

I wanted to run away before I broke down and completely embarrassed myself in front of my classmates. I turned away from him to head out the opposite end of the building. I couldn't hear the sounds of dozens of students going from one class to the next. Nor could I see.

Anger, resentment, and, if I was being completely honest, joy filled my head and clouded my gaze. I moved down the hall by rote memory. I could see the rear entrance of the square building. The light filtering through the doors seemed like some kind of salvation, and I hurried toward it.

"Grace."

I heard his voice behind me. I sped up. I may have been running. People moved out of my way.

I hit the metal release bar on the back glass doors with the flat of my hand, and the metal clanked loudly, I noted with satisfaction. I wished I had five more doors to bang through, but I guess that would've impeded my stomp toward my apartment.

Ordinarily, I would meet Lana for lunch at the campus café. Today I was going home and hiding in my apartment until I could decide what I was going to do. Like transfer out to another college or figure out how to avoid Noah for the rest of the time he was here. Problem was, I didn't know why he was here or for how long. Transferring might be the best option. I could go to State University, where my brother Josh went. It was only three hours away.

I had reached the edge of campus and could see my house just two blocks away. I was convinced that if I reached the porch of the old Victorian, I would be safe, like when we were kids playing tag. As I stopped for traffic, I felt Noah behind me, his big body throwing a shadow that swallowed my smaller one. Out of the corner of my eye, I could see his hand hover over my shoulder. My whole body tensed. I didn't know what I would do if he touched me, but it wouldn't be good. He sighed softly and dropped his hand away.

"Grace, you're mad. I get it. But can we at least talk?"

I had never heard Noah's voice before. We never exchanged voicemail messages, never Skyped. We had just written to each other—World War II-style. I thought our decision to write only was impossibly romantic. Plus, I didn't want him to see me over the Internet and decide I wasn't attractive enough to write to anymore. I still had those damn letters in a carefully-preserved state in an archival box designed, I think, for scrapbooks. But I had imagined what he would sound like. Low, because it seemed manly, and maybe a little gruff, because of all the sand in the desert. And look, I was right. His voice was low, gravelly, and panty-dropping sexy.

Who was I kidding? The panties probably came off even if he didn't talk to a girl. He could smile or just acknowledge her presence and she'd swoon into his arms. I needed to avoid him, if only to preserve my dignity. I was too afraid that I'd throw myself at him and beg him to take me in all the ways that a virgin could dream of and then some. I kept moving toward my apartment, trying not to race, trying not to look tragic.

Once we reached the front of my apartment, I was stymied.

I had just let Noah know where I lived. Plus, I doubted I could get behind my security door before he put his big foot in and prevented it from closing.

As if he could read my mind, he said, "I already knew where you lived. You aren't showing me anything I didn't already know." I still didn't turn around. I could feel the tears I had tried to keep away begin to well up. Any minute now, I was going to start crying, and he so did not deserve to see me cry. That asshole.

This time, I felt his hand on my arm. I wanted to shake it off, but I didn't move. I didn't want him to know he affected me at all. Or at least more than he already knew. His hand slid down from my elbow to my palm, and I felt a piece of paper being pressed into my hand.

His body crowded mine for a second and I thought I felt his lips touch my hair. "Read this. It's how we've communicated best in the past." With that, he let go slowly. I wanted to just let his note drop to the ground, but as his hand released mine, I felt my fingers curl up involuntarily to crush the note in my palm. He squeezed my now-closed fist and walked away. I heard his footsteps fade, felt the warmth of his body dissipate.

I didn't look back but instead went into the house and walked up the stairs. My feet felt like they had cinder blocks attached. By the time I reached the apartment door, I was shaking. It was hot outside and even hotter on the third floor, but my internal body temperature was telling me I was freezing. Maybe I was going into shock.

I dumped my stuff right inside the front door. I vaguely heard the chirps of my phone, informing me I had unread texts. Ignoring them, I walked into my bathroom, turned on the shower and stripped. Inside the glass cube, with water as hot as I could get it shooting out of the showerhead, I let go.

I wasn't even sure what I was crying about. My own stupidity. My years of not dating, because I was so sure that Noah was my happily ever after. My lackluster freshman year. My inability to gather up the courage to submit my portfolio to the Fine Arts School. My certainty that no one would ever love me. All of it, I guess.

I cried for what seemed like hours, not noticing anything until the water shut off. I looked up and Lana was standing there, her eyes wet and concerned. She held a towel in her hands. I stumbled forward and she hugged me, wrapping me inside the terry cloth. I allowed her to lead me to the bedroom where the shades had been pulled and a towel placed on my pillow.

She held up the covers and I crawled inside like a five-year-old. Once she pulled the covers up over my body, Lana left the room quietly, closing the door behind her. The crying jag, the darkness of the room, and the weight of the covers dragged me into a dreamless sleep.

Hunger woke me up. I glanced at the clock—I had slept for three hours and it was nearly dinnertime. My hair was mostly dry, but I wrapped it up in a towel anyway and shrugged on a robe. I heard the television in the living room. Lana was on the sofa with a textbook in her lap and the remote beside her. Two Diet Cokes were open on the table. I knew she was dying to ask me what was going on, but she managed to stay quiet for the moment, at least.

"Should we have ice cream for dinner?" Lana asked as I walked over and took a long drag from her Diet Coke. I was parched. Dried out. I had no liquid left inside me after all that crying. And I was so shook up by Noah's appearance two thousand miles from San Diego that I actually sat on the sofa, which I ordinarily avoided since Peter and Lana seemed to spend so much time making out on it.

"No," I put the now half-empty soda can on the table. "But I'm hungry."

"I was thinking of ordering in."

"Good call." And then knowing Lana needed an explanation, I told her, "He was waiting outside my Poli Sci class."

"Did you talk?" Lana was matter-of-fact, as if she knew I needed steadiness, not sympathy.

I shook my head. "No, but he gave me a note."

"Like you're third graders? What did it say?"

"I don't know," I admitted. I turned toward the entryway where I had dropped all my stuff, including the note, but Lana had cleaned it up.

"Oh!" She popped up. "I saw it and stuffed it in your bag." She brought my backpack over, and I rooted through it to pull out the folded piece of lined notebook paper.

The note felt combustible. I was afraid to unfold it. I shoved it back into the bag, as if I could hide the whole situation away without having to deal with it again.

"What does it say?" Lana leaned toward me, peering into the bag.

"I don't care. What could he say?"

She shrugged and pointed out, "You don't have to guess. The answer is right there. Want me to read it for you?"

In all the years that Noah and I had been writing, no one else had read his letters to me. They were my private property, and I had hoarded my stash like a dragon guarding her gold. But for the very first time, I was afraid of what one of Noah's letters said, so I reluctantly handed it over and covered my eyes.

I heard the crinkle of paper as Lana unfolded the note, and then silence. Impatient despite my fear, I lifted my hand and peeked over at her. I could see the pen marks through the back of the lined paper. The note was short. Without even thinking about it, I grabbed the note back and read.

Dear Grace,

I thought about how to introduce, or should I say re-introduce, myself to you a million times. In all of my scenarios, I looked like a douche, but

I don't feel right explaining the last two years to you in a letter. But I need you to know that your letters to me while I was in Afghanistan were the only things that kept me sane. I don't want to lose the friendship we built over those four years. Meet me and let me make amends for what happened. I have an explanation. Whether it is any good, whether you forgive me, is all in your hands.

Text me at 619-867-5309. I'll meet you. Any time. Any place.

Love,

Noah

"Love?" He had never written those four letters before. I had. Like an ass, when I wrote to him and told him I wanted to meet him, I signed my letter "Love, Grace." I wondered if that was partly what set him off, what made him decide he couldn't meet the teenage freak he'd conned out of forty-eight care packages and letters. I crumpled the letter into a ball.

"Are you going to meet him?" Lana asked, leaning over and prying the ball of paper out of my hand. She tossed it onto the coffee table. I immediately reached over and started smoothing it out. Even now, after everything he had done, I couldn't help myself.

"I don't know," I mumbled. Why was he here? Was he a student? He had a backpack, but that could mean anything. It must have really been him in the library the other day.

"Let it go for tonight. Come to the party and enjoy yourself." Lana looked at her watch. "We can toss back a few drinks here and then go to the Delt house."

The mention of the fraternity reminded me I had promised to take rush photos for Amy and the other Alpha Phis. I groaned in dismay and embarrassment. "I totally forgot about the photos. Is Amy furious?"

"Nah, I called her right away and said that you weren't feeling well. She said tomorrow would be fine."

"Lana, if you weren't my cousin, I would kiss you on the lips."

"It's only the cousin thing that is stopping you?" she teased me.

"You're the finest piece of ass here at Central, but I have to resist your charms. It's the law."

"If you're making jokes, I pronounce you sufficiently recovered to go and get shit-faced and leer at the Delt rush candidates," Lana proclaimed.

Lana went to make some calls, and I sat on the sofa and tried to stop all the crazy thoughts I had from racing through my mind.

Noah

Bo was lounging against my truck when I returned from Grace's apartment. He was chatting up some blonde chick who looked like all the other girls he'd ever been with. They were interchangeable to me, and likely to Bo, too, since he called them all "babe."

I figured I would know if he ever fell for a girl when he called her by her first name instead of some random endearment.

"That was a clusterfuck, eh?" he asked as I approached.

"Yup," I climbed into my truck and threw my books into the back. I revved the engine a couple of times to signal that I wanted Bo to get in the damn truck. He could pick up chicks another time.

"At the risk of sounding like a girl, do you want to talk about it?" Bo asked when he finally got into the passenger seat. I threw the truck in reverse and peeled out of campus parking lot.

"No, Bo Peep, I don't," I bit out.

So much for being good at doing.

"What were you thinking?"

"What part of 'I don't want to talk about it' did you not understand?"

"Are you giving up?"

"What?" I swung my head toward him. Bo threw up his hands. "No way." I looked back at the road.

"Then let's strategize."

"I've already made every strategic mistake possible. I left too late last night to catch her. I surprised and maybe embarrassed her after class. If I see her at a party and spill beer all over her, my trifecta of stupidity would be complete."

"So now what?"

"Now, it's time to regroup."

"You want to fight or drink tonight?"

"Both."

Chapter Three

Dear Grace,

I'm luckier than most. There are plenty of guys that are homesick and haven't seen their kids or wives or girlfriends for months except over the Internet.

I don't have much to miss back home, but I'm here with my best bud, Bo Randolph. We've been friends since we tried to beat the piss out of each other in seventh grade. Served two weeks of suspension and found out we had a lot in common.

Bo's my battle buddy. This means wherever he goes, I go, and vice versa. You never go anywhere without your battle buddy, including (or maybe especially) the bars.

Yours,

Noah

Grace

"Calm down, jitterbug," Lana said for what seemed like the fiftieth time. She handed me another glass of Vodka and pink lemonade—the lazy college student's version of the Cosmo.

"What's up with you, anyway?" Amy asked. We were pregaming at our apartment, drinking just enough to feel good before we hit the frat party. Knowing when to show up was just as important as knowing which keg to drink from. The keg in the backyard would be cheap and watered down. Kegs kept in the kitchen or interior bar, surrounded by all the brothers in the house, would be more expensive, although not always better tasting.

"I'm sorry about this afternoon and the photo shoot," I told Amy. "I'm totally on board for tomorrow."

Amy waved her hand dismissively. "It was fine. Lana called and said you had eaten something bad at lunch. Why are you two still eating at the café?" She gave a little shudder. "Tomorrow is perfect. More of the house will be there."

I threw Lana a grateful look, and she just patted me on the back. "You'd do it for me," she murmured so only I could hear.

"So are you thinking junior college transfers or freshman targets tonight?" I asked her as I finished applying my makeup, pretending like I was interested in finding a hookup.

I didn't want to answer questions about Noah. I didn't want to think about him at all. If I pretended to be interested in other things, then perhaps I could make that happen. It was worth a try, anyway.

"Depends on what you're looking for. One night hookup? Freshman. Some date potential? JuCo transfer," Lana said, sorting through tubes of lip-gloss. "And can I recommend we do away with lumberjack couture for the night? Your wardrobe suggests that you're gearing up to haul logs out of the forest. If you're aiming for Paul Bunyan, then your collection of plaid shirts is a great start—otherwise choose something that isn't flannel," Lana said.

I looked down at my plaid shirt. "I thought the thrift-shop, country-girl look was in."

"Maybe at State, where Josh goes. In fact, isn't that Josh's shirt?"

I looked away guiltily. It was Josh's shirt. I'd stolen a few things from him this summer. He either didn't notice or didn't care, because he never said a word. But Lana had already seen my expression and started to wrestle the shirt off my shoulders. Lana is thin but strong. It must be all the yoga she does. I stood there in my thin, ribbed tank top, and Lana looked at my reflection in the mirror, quirking one eyebrow at me.

"Let's just say the guy-who-shall-not-be-named is there. Do you want to look hot? Or like you just got back from a gold dig in Alaska?"

"Hot," I mumbled.

"Super." She proceeded to drag me into her room and throw a silky blue shirt at me. "Put this on with your denim skirt and take off your sneakers."

I looked at the shirt. I wasn't even sure how to put it on. There were long straps and a sheet of fabric on one side. "Are you missing a piece, like a camisole that goes underneath?"

"No," Lana snorted and pulled my tank up over my arms. Surprised, I let her manipulate me like a doll. The blue satin turned out to be a halter top with a low scoop back and ties around the neck. It had an elasticized waist that helped keep it in place. I grudgingly admitted to myself that this was actually a good style for me.

The shirt had a low back, so I couldn't wear a bra. Unlike Lana, I had a generous C cup. Not wearing a bra made me feel like I was completely naked. Plus, everyone would be able to tell if the temperature dropped just by looking at my chest.

"Lana, I can't wear this. I feel like a small breeze will reveal all my worldly goods."

"You'll wear it and stop complaining about it," Lana instructed, handing me some silicone rubbery things that connected in the middle.

"Is this supposed to be a bra? It looks like two uninflated balloons connected by plastic."

She reached out to grab it back from me. "Works for me. I'll be sure to stare at your tits to see if I need to bring a sweater."

I hugged the balloons to my chest. "No, I'm all for hiding defective birthday favors under my shirt."

"Well?" she asked after I had attached the sticky silicone to my skin.

"It fits."

"I'm mentally translating that into 'my God, Lana, your taste is exquisite.'"

"My God, Lana, your taste is exquisite," I repeated dutifully.

Lana quickly tied the knot around my neck and spun me around. "I bought the shirt for you last weekend."

I could feel the ends of my hair tickle against my bare back. "I still don't feel comfortable about the back."

"We can tape it just in case," Lana brought out some double-stick tape and adhered the folded seam of the blouse to my back. Double-stick tape was Lana's answer to every fashion emergency. She carried strips of it in her purse and her messenger bag. If I was ever looking for reasons to join a sorority, learning how to avoid visible panty lines, exposed bra straps, and wardrobe malfunctions would be as good as any.

"There," she said slapping my back lightly. "Ready to go."

I went to slip on my tennis shoes, but stopped when Lana gave me the stink eye and held up a pair of low-heeled strappy sandals in the same sky blue as my blouse. "No way," I said.

"They match," Lana replied.

"I won't wear heels, but I'll wear my ballet flats." I would be the only one. Lana's feet were shod with pencil-slim stilettos, and Amy had on cork wedges. Thankfully, I was slightly taller than average and didn't feel like I was standing amongst a tribe of Amazonians.

Without allowing Lana more time to launch a shoe offensive, I scurried to my bedroom and pulled out a pair of silver flats. The parts of my body that I had always liked, no matter how much I weighed, were my calves, ankles, and feet. They were so nice that even strangers noticed, and I tried to focus on them now, when so much of me was feeling exposed.

One time Lana and I drove down into Chicago to shop, we stopped at a shoe store a classmate had raved about. A shoe clerk had stroked my instep and stuck his phone number in the shoebox. I was creeped out and never returned to that store, but I always remembered that event with confused pride. *Hey, some stranger thought my feet were a turn on. Yay!* Quickly followed by, *Eww.*

I saw my reflection in the full-length mirror that hung over the back of my door. Lana was right. The color of the blue top looked perfect with my late-summer tan and brown hair. It brought out the green in my hazel eyes. The blousiness at the bottom of the shirt meant I could stand without worrying that my pooch of a belly would be hanging out.

And my skirt was long enough that it hid the worst part of my legs—my thunderous thighs—while showing off the best part. If Noah was there, I definitely wasn't going to be embarrassed by what I was wearing. All my fantasies and the letters I had sent, yes. My clothing, no.

"You look great," Lana's voice shook me out of my reverie. I saw her leaning against the doorjamb.

"Thanks for buying this for me."

She shrugged. "I can't keep buying clothes for myself. Don't have enough room."

I wanted to ask her if I could borrow some of her confidence along with the shirt. Maybe they sold that at the Gap next to the jeans and T-shirts. Instead, I returned her compliment. "You look awesome too."

She did. Her hair was extra shiny tonight, like a Pantene commercial. She wore Capri leggings and a sheer peasant blouse than hung below her waist. It was a look only a thin girl could carry off. At one time, Lana's thinness was a cause of great concern and worry, but she was healthy now.

"Too much cleavage?" I asked, noticing that the front of the blouse hung rather low.

"No, in fact, you should wear a necklace to draw attention to your girls," Lana pointed to my bare neck. I was already as far out of my comfort zone as possible. The girls would have to go unadorned.

"Are you coming home or staying with Peter tonight?"

Lana made a face. "The frat house? No thanks. Plus I'm kind of mad at Peter."

"Why?" I tried to inject some disappointment in my voice, knowing I was probably failing miserably.

"Oh stop. I know you don't like him." She pursed her lips to one side. "This will only make you big-headed, but I heard over at the house today that Peter has been bragging about hooking up with a girl in London this summer."

"Oh my God, why didn't you say anything?" I turned to her in distress. "It's not all about me, you know."

"You had the Noah thing, and it's all rumors right now. I don't want to get worked up over nothing."

"Are you going to ask him about it?" I asked. "I've been waiting for an excuse to kick his ass."

"I know you have." She dabbed her lips with some lip-gloss, whatever feelings she had about the rumors not showing on her face. Lana and I were true opposites.

"I don't think he treats you right. He's always making plans and then breaking them at the last minute, and his fraternity seems more important than you," I pointed out.

"Eh. I can't always expect him to be at my beck and call."

If I had unrealistically high expectations of guys, Lana's expectations were way too low. She basically required them to breathe and know her name. But maybe when you didn't expect much out of them, you didn't get disappointed.

"The cure for one man is another," I reminded her.

She pinned on a big smile, which might have been fake or real, and said, "Yup. Let's go find our cures, then."

***

By the time we got to the fraternity house, the party was in full swing. You could hear the music from the end of the street, and it only got louder as we approached. Other houses appeared to be hosting smaller parties, but the crowd around the Delta Tau Delta House was already straining the structure.

The guys at the door seemed to know Lana and nodded as we passed through, not even glancing at the list attached to a clipboard. I think one of them trailed a finger down my spine, but I wasn't sure. I didn't dare look back to verify.

There were tons of people inside the house and dozens more in the backyard. Two kegs were set up on a back patio and some guys were doing keg stands. Being held upside down by your legs while someone pours beer right into your mouth seemed like a quick way to be sent to the vomitorium. I stood and watched for a minute; it was such a spectacle.

Someone else was doing beer bongs from a second-story window. When one girl tried it, the beer came out her nose and mouth. Everyone jeered, but she seemed unfazed. Her pregame drinking must have been hardcore.

Lana grabbed my hand and I grabbed Amy's. The three of us linked together and threaded our way to the dimly lit kitchen in the back. A makeshift bar had been created by placing a plywood board on cinder blocks, and we were offered keg beer, the good kind. Lana refused and instead waved a guy over to her.

She whispered something in his ear, and he returned with three bottles that he opened right in front of her. Smart rules for drinking at a house party included always being present when your glass was filled or your bottle opened.

Lana passed around bottles. As we turned to leave, the guy grabbed Lana's arm and leaned down, saying something to her that I couldn't hear over the din of the music, laughter, and general talking.

I watched as his hand that held the bottle opener curled around her side. Lana didn't move away, and I wondered if maybe this guy was her cure for the night.

I didn't recognize him, but his ease in the kitchen spoke of familiarity in the fraternity. He must have lived in the house because, before I knew it, we proceeded in a line upstairs and into a bedroom at the end of the hall.

The doors were almost all closed except another one at the end of the hall that looked to be a bathroom. At the sound of our steps, the door slammed closed from the inside. Occupied, apparently.

Lana introduced our beer supplier as Jack and closed the door behind us once we had all trooped inside. "Jack the president?" I mouthed to Lana as Jack's back was turned. She grinned and waved her hand in front of her face. This time I understood that she meant hot. He was nice looking. He had that easy movement I associated with athletes, but his body wasn't overly developed.

Jack gestured for us to sit. I looked around. The room had two beds on either side of a large coffee table but no chairs, except two that were stationed in front of identical desks at the far end of the room.

Jack and Lana sat down on one bed and Amy and I sat on the other. Jack proceeded to pull out a bottle from under his bed and then revealed lime wedges and a saltshaker in his hands.

Oh no, tequila shots? I didn't think I was ready for this. Lana rubbed her hands together, and Amy bounced on the bed with little squeak of excitement. I looked at the bottle with dread. I was already in a sucktastic mood and doing tequila shots wasn't going to lift my spirits. Chances were, with my luck, I'd probably start sobbing in this strange boy's lap.

"I'm going to sit this out, Lana," I told her. "I'm afraid I'll get sick and then I'll be the worst party pooper ever. Not to mention the fact that I'll probably ruin my new blouse."

"Are you sure, Grace? I'll come downstairs with you," Lana offered immediately.

"Go downstairs and sit in the second windowsill on the right side," Jack instructed. It was clear he didn't want Lana going anywhere. "It's got a deep sill and you can enjoy the party without being crushed. If someone is there, go to the kitchen and grab a pledge. They'll have a green wristband. Tell him Jack said that seat is reserved for you."

"Thanks." I closed the door behind me, grateful to get out of that room.

I went downstairs and sought out the second window well. It was occupied by two guys with green wristbands. I repeated what Jack had said, and the two jumped up like he was there giving the order personally. It was good to be president, I guess. One even offered to get me another beer, but I turned him down.

The window maybe wasn't the best place for me to sit given my backless top. Lana was right about the shirt attracting a lot of attention. After sitting there for just a few minutes, more than one cold beer bottle had been dragged down my exposed spine. My shivers were definitely the result of the chill and not excitement.

If I was interested in a hookup, this would be the place to find one. There were people of both sexes scoping each other out, flirting, and engaging in pre-mating behavior on the dance floor. It made for excellent people-watching, if nothing else.

"Mind if I sit here?" a voice asked. I looked up and saw a curly-haired guy with broad shoulders smiling down at me.

"Not at all," I scooted over. He sat down in the sill, sideways, one leg drawn up and the other stabilizing him on the floor.

"Kyle Briggs," He offered his hand.

"Grace Sullivan," I clasped his hand and shook it once, but he didn't let it go.

"Haven't I seen you in my Poli Sci class?" Kyle asked, still holding my hand in his. I wriggled my fingers a little and he released me.

"Don't think so," I shook my head. I didn't remember him from class. Granted we had only had six of them so far. I knotted my fingers together on my lap so he wouldn't find an excuse to hold them, but that was a mistake, because he just placed his large hand over both of mine. Either he was coming on to me or he was super touchy. Both made me feel uncomfortable. He leaned closer and I could smell the yeast from the beer on his breath. I was trying not to feel overwhelmed, but it was difficult.

"I've seen you somewhere, though, and it bugs me that I can't remember where because I almost always remember the good-looking ones."

"Do you always use bad pick-up lines or just when you're drunk?"

"You're going to make me work for it," Kyle nodded to himself. "I like that in a girl."

I tried to move backward but was blocked by the window frame. Unfortunately, I couldn't stand up with this Kyle guy pressing his considerable weight onto my hands. He took my reply as a challenge; I could see it in his eyes. He thought I was flirting with him and was probably too intoxicated at this point to see a difference between the girl wanting to get away and the girl trying to get in his pants.

I pushed my hands upward, not wanting to leave his big sweaty palm lying across my skirt, close to the juncture of my thighs. "Listen, Griggs, I don't think my boyfriend would want me sitting so close to you." Josh had taught me to never insult a drunken guy, because you didn't know if he was a mean drunk or a happy one. Just try to compliment your way out of a negative situation. Saying I had a boyfriend was an inoffensive way of making sure that Kyle would not be offended by my lack of interest.

Unfortunately, Kyle was denser or drunker than I thought because he only grabbed my hands in his and drew me closer. His other arm came to rest around my back. "Oh ho ho," he cried when his hand met my bare back. I froze and arched away from his hand, but this only pressed me closer to his chest wall. This was going to get ugly if I had to struggle to get away.

The window, which seemed like a promising escape from the crowd, now turned into a prison, and I was boxed in. I looked around frantically for Amy or Lana, but could see almost no one's face. It was just a mass of legs.

"Let go. I'm not interested." The time for soft, deterring compliments was past now. I tugged on my hands and tried to slide sideways, but he threw out a leg to forestall that movement. His face came close to mine.

"You don't need to play hard to get," he said. "I'm yours for the taking."

"I'm not interested," I repeated firmly. "Let me go, or I'll make a scene."

"I'll make one for you." I heard another, familiar voice above me. I looked up at Noah's face and nearly cried with relief.

Kyle wasn't quick enough to realize he was in jeopardy and instead said, "Shove off, man, I've tagged this one."

Noah reached down and in one motion pulled Kyle's hand off mine and me to his side. "She's not a deer." His voice was flat, but I could feel the rigidity in his body. While I wasn't a psych major like Lana, even I could read anger in Noah's stance.

Kyle stood and held up his hands. "Hey man, she was coming on to me."

Noah speared him with a glance, and it must have penetrated because Kyle turned on his heel and left.

The little scene went by almost unnoticed. The crowd kept on dancing and drinking. I felt unbalanced, though, and sat clumsily back down on the windowsill.

Noah remained standing, towering over me. He had definitely kept up with an exercise routine since he got out. Even through the cotton of his dark T-shirt and the dim light in the room, I could make out the definition of his chest muscles. The skin was taut across his high cheekbones, and his eyes were dark and piercing. I felt more exposed under his stare than when I had first donned this backless top.

Anger and resentment began to well up in me, and I wanted to throw a beer bottle straight at his face and mar the perfect handsomeness. Although, as I stared at him more closely, I realized he had a bruise forming under his right eye. I wonder if he had fought tonight and with whom. I wanted to know everything, a whole two years of everything. I bit my tongue to keep the questions inside.

Maybe he was white-knighting himself at all of the campus parties, choosing which damsel he would take home. But it wouldn't be me. I couldn't place my heart in jeopardy again. An entire year had been lost while I tried to deal with conflicting feelings of sorrow at the loss of him in my life, humiliation at believing he could love me, and anger that he had strung me along. I didn't know why he was here. While not knowing was terrifying, I didn't want to suffer more rejection at the hands of Noah Jackson.

I rose. The party was losing its appeal. I should run up to the fourth floor and take a quick picture with my phone and then go home and block out placement for the Alphi Phi photo. But mostly, I felt like going home. I tried brushing by Noah but he caught me by the arm.

"I've been waiting for you to call me." Impatience was etched on his face.

"You'll wait a long time, then, because I threw your number away."

"Will you give me a chance to explain?" He rubbed a hand through his hair and settled it at the back of his neck. He leaned forward. "Can we get out of here?"

"You had a chance. You had two years of chances. I don't know why you're here, but it has nothing to do with me." I tried to leave again, but the hand on my arm was immovable. He wasn't hurting me, but he wouldn't let me go either. I was never sitting in a window again.

"It has everything to do with you," he said, his face intense, leaning down to make sure I heard him. An involuntary warmth began to spread through my body, and I tried to beat it back.

"Really? I don't believe you." I knew I sounded petulant, but I didn't care. I just wanted out of there before I let him convince me otherwise. I suspected that if I gave him enough time, Noah could get me to believe pretty much anything.

"I know," he replied. He sounded frustrated, and I could feel myself weakening again.

We stood there, staring at each other. The crowd of people streamed past us, now just streaks of color caught on low-speed film.

While the crowd had felt oppressive before, it now seemed a safe harbor. Within the mass of people, perhaps I could lose Noah or, even more importantly, myself. I just wasn't equipped to deal with him right now. Since my previous attempts at disengagement had been unsuccessful, I tried a different tactic.

"I can't deal with this now."

"When, then?"

I felt like I was being interrogated, and the sense of injustice threatened to choke me. I wasn't the one in the wrong. I should be asking the questions, setting the limits, defining our boundaries.

"I don't know. Two years from now," I said. Snideness creeping into my tone. Probably a guy who looked like him and kept a girl on the line for four years expected her to lie down and beg to be walked over. I looked down pointedly at his hand still encircling my arm. "You can let go anytime now."

He released me immediately, and I headed for the stairs to collect Lana or maybe drink myself into oblivion with tequila shots.

I felt Noah's body heat behind mine. He wasn't going anywhere. But I could ignore him.

But a clearly tipsy Lana and an every drunker Amy were coming down the stairs as I reached the first landing. Jack was nowhere to be seen. New plan.

"You two ready to go?" I asked. Lana was wide-eyed and mouthed, "He's right behind you" to me. Correction—Lana wasn't tipsy. She was drunk.

"I know," I said, "and you aren't invisible to him. I'm sure he can see you."

"Yup," Noah affirmed.

"Oh no!" Lana said "What about your cure?"

"Are you sick?" Noah asked. He came up to the landing and looked at me intently.

"Not that kind of cure, silly," Lana said before I could open my mouth. She was feeling no pain. She stumbled down the stairs dragging Amy behind her. "Cure for heartache." *Thanks Lana*, I thought, *as if I hadn't been humiliated enough before.*

"I'll drive y'all home," Noah said. "My truck is out front."

"You can't park on the street," Lana said, poking one long fingernail into his chest. When her poke found no purchase, she began patting. "Wow, this is like marble. Amy," Lana turned and held up their joined hands, "feel this." At which point both girls proceeded to pat Noah's apparently very hard chest.

He, at least, had the grace to look embarrassed by this. I had to hustle Lana out before her drunken state revealed something even more humiliating, although at this point, I wasn't sure what that could be.

I pulled their hands down. "Come on, let's go."

Lana tugged back. "No, there's another house party over on Forest. Let's go there."

This night was fast becoming a farce. I couldn't shake Noah. I couldn't get Lana to come home with me. Part of me wanted to just sit down on the floor and cry like a toddler, but I had already done that earlier today.

I let out a frustrated breath. "Where's Jack?"

Lana and Amy turned in unison to look up the stairs. We all waited for a heartbeat but the upstairs hall remained empty. No help from that quarter.

"My big sister is at the party on Forest," Amy offered. To the Forest party it was, then. Amy's big sister in the sorority could watch over them.

I turned to Noah. "Guess we're taking you up on the ride offer."

He nodded and didn't smile like he had won, which made the situation only slightly more acceptable. As we walked behind him, I noticed how the crowd just seemed to melt away from us, like he was Moses parting the Red Sea.

Outside, Noah stopped briefly beside the blond guy I'd seen with him in the library, who was now talking to three girls. This must be the infamous Bo Randolph. Noah didn't introduce us, though, and instead shepherded us toward his truck sitting in the driveway of the fraternity.

I'm not sure how long the vehicle had been there, and its presence surprised me. "Are you a Delt?" Only members of the fraternity got to park in the driveway.

"No," Noah shook his head. "Just know someone."

He opened the passenger side doors and helped all of us into his dual cab pickup.

"There's a lot of space in here." I had never ridden in a pickup before and was surprised at how roomy it was. The vehicle smelled new.

"You just get this?" I asked him as he climbed into the driver's seat.

"Smell give it away?" He honked twice to get a couple of people to move out of the driveway and then backed up.

"Hard to hide that new car smell."

"I got it this summer. Bo told me he was done ferrying my ass around," Noah said. I remembered Noah telling me once that they were always being counseled to not spend their entire earnings on a new car or a motorcycle or a boat when they were back on leave or just returned from deployment. Noah must have listened to them.

"So you didn't spend all your money on new wheels the moment you separated?"

"Nope, had other plans."

I refrained from taking the bait to ask more information, even though I was dying for it. After a few beats of silence, Noah said, "Not going to ask me about my other plans?"

"Not interested," I lied, looking out the window. He made a couple of turns and then headed down Forest. Noah navigated the campus streets like an upperclassman and not some new transfer who had been in town only two weeks since classes started.

"You seem to know this area pretty well."

When his answer wasn't immediate, I knew he was going to tell me something that would make me angry again. By his sheepish tone, he knew it too.

"I've been here since June," he admitted.

"In town?" I could hear the high-pitched screeching tone of my question and tried to swallow down my mounting emotions.

He nodded. He started to say something but then slowed the vehicle.

"I don't see any house party." He turned slightly and called to the back, "Where to on Forest, ladies?"

Lana didn't respond. When I turned around, I saw both of them had passed out. They must have had a lot of tequila shots.

There was nothing to do but to take them—and Noah—home.

Noah

Grace's body was rigid in the passenger seat of my truck. She was strung tighter than a garrote wire.

The Marines had taught me a lot. I learned all the delicate pressure points on a man's body. I learned to walk a hundred miles in full battle rattle, carrying a pack and ammunition heavier than the two girls in the back seat. I learned how to start a fire in the desert out of nothing more than a soda can, toothpaste, and the sun.

But the Marines had not taught me how to win over a girl whose heart I had broken. Most of the guys in my unit were the ones who had been cheated on. Sure, some of the guys may have forgotten their hometowns when the Air Force chicks or supply personnel arrived at a forward operating base, but most of us were lonely bastards.

I admit that the few times I imagined Grace and me getting together, there was a lot less space between our bodies. When I played this moment out in my mind, I figured I'd calmly explain what happened, and she'd listen intently. I'd apologize and then take her to a movie or two before showing her exactly why she should be with me. In bed.

Right now Grace would probably rather climb in bed with a rattler. I grabbed the back of my neck and squeezed the tight muscles there in frustration. Maybe I should've taken Bo up on his offer to strategize, but his relationship experience was as non-existent as mine. Getting advice from another Marine on how to handle a relationship was like asking another orphan how to handle your parents.

Ironically, the one person in my life who I felt comfortable enough confiding personal shit to and who might give me halfway decent advice was sitting in the passenger side of the truck, doing her best to ignore me.

I wrote stuff to Grace that I would never say out loud. Communicating with her had never been an issue before. But we were writing then. Letters only. Old school style, we agreed early on. I cast around for a reasonable explanation, one that didn't make me out to look too much like a loser. My previous explanation, "I had to get my shit together," didn't seem like it would cut it.

I glanced at her in her shiny blue top with its bow I'd like to untie with my teeth. Her brown hair looked incredibly soft, and I wanted to dig my fingers into the thick strands. She looked expensive, like the china Bo's mother used for company. Totally above my pay grade.

I was right to have waited and gotten everything in order before coming here. Grace had sent me *The Odyssey* once during deployment, writing that we could experience her English lit class together. As Odysseus fought his way back to Penelope, his faithful wife, he had to overcome obstacles from sirens to monsters.

Homer never said whether the obstacles were all in Odysseus's mind, created from too much war, too much time at sea, too much time away from reality. But they could have been.

It's a cliché among fighters that they are all trying to beat back their shithole childhoods. The military is full of guys whose dads were deadbeats at best and abusive monsters at worse. My own old man fell in between. He never raised a hand to me. Too lazy. His preferred method of punishment was making sure I understood that I had ruined his life.

My dad was mad at the world and had been since I killed my mom by being born. He hadn't called me Noah since I was probably eight or nine. *Shithead* was his preferred name for me. *Worthless* was his favorite adjective. When he was drunk, which was as often as his measly paycheck allowed, he liked to string them together with a few curse words. *Noah, you worthless shithead, you're not going to amount to anything more than knocking up some trailer park trash.*

The Marines may have made me a man, but Grace made me human. No matter what I told her in my letters, she accepted it and wrote me back something funny or sweet. She made me realize I could have more if I wanted it. And I wanted more *bad*.

Chapter Four

Dear Grace,

I don't think you'll ever see me on YouTube, but there is shit-all to do around here, so guys will memorize songs and videotape each other performing. I have zero twerking ability. I guess if there's ever some music video involving marching, I could participate in that.

I think the higher-ups like these videos because they make A'stan look fun, which it isn't. But it's good PR.

Some guys from MMA were here to entertain the troops. I talked to one of the managers, who said that a guy could earn six figures a year for beating someone else up in the ring. It's not really boxing skills that matter, either, because a lot of the skills are kicking and hand-to-hand combat, which is something that we're taught here.

It's kind of a cool idea. Yeah, there are worries about concussions, but I think the pros outweigh the cons. Bo isn't interested, but he doesn't need to be either. He's got plenty of family money. He told me that we both should go to college after we get out and that I could use the GI Bill to pay for everything.

What college did you say you were going to? Central? Mail me something about it the next time you send a care package. I think I should check it out.

Yours,
Noah

Grace

Noah navigated us to my apartment without asking for directions once. He parked in the small drive behind the house. Before I could open my own door, he jumped out and came around to help me out.

"How about I carry them in?" Noah asked, opening the back seat of the cab.

"We live on the third floor, Mr. Macho." I wondered for the millionth time why we didn't live on the first floor. Lana always said it was good exercise, but she never had to practically drag my drunken body up two flights of stairs.

He looked at the girls dubiously. "I don't think you're rousing them. I've carried heavier things over longer and rougher terrain, so I think I can manage two girls who each weigh about the same as a feed sack."

Even with some heavy jostling and the promise of comfortable beds, I could not manage to wake Lana or Amy. Noah gently pushed me aside. "Keys?" I pulled out my apartment key and handed it to Noah. He hefted Amy in his arms and disappeared inside the house.

"Lana, I think I'm in trouble," I whispered to her passed-out form. "I don't know how much longer I can resist him. He's going to be in our apartment. I'm afraid I'm going to attack him or something. I wish you were awake to protect me from myself." Lana moaned in response, and I stroked her head.

Noah returned and wasn't one bit out of breath. He hoisted Lana onto his shoulder, and I shut the doors to the truck. The truck's headlights flashed, and a mechanical beep signaled that Noah had locked the doors. He motioned for me to go first, but I felt really self-conscious that my big butt would be waving in his face. When he refused to move until I did, I heaved a big sigh and climbed the stairs. I hoped he liked juicy round ones.

Noah had placed Amy on the sofa when he came back for Lana, so I led him to Lana's room. He set her on the bed and went to get Amy. When the two girls were lying side-by-side on the bed, I shooed Noah out of the room and proceeded to take off Lana and Amy's shoes. I wiped Lana's face down with a wet wipe so she wouldn't have to wake up with makeup on tomorrow. I tended to Amy the same way, taking my sweet time.

I sat down on the side of the bed, stalling. I was pretty sure I couldn't handle Noah alone in my apartment with no buffer. My biggest fear was that I would break down in front of him, followed closely by the mortifying image in my head of dragging him to my bedroom.

I listened for the front door but it didn't open or close. Instead, I heard sounds of life out in the living room. The faint buzz of the refrigerator filled the air momentarily, and I could hear water rush into the kitchen sink.

Finally, past the point of being rude, I took a deep breath, rolled my neck on my shoulders like a fighter ready to start the match, and went out to face my opponent.

He was leaning against the kitchen counter drinking a glass of water. "Do you mind?" he asked, tipping the glass toward me.

I didn't mind that he was drinking my water or using my glass. I did mind a million other things. I shook my head, walked into the living room, and sat down in my chair, grateful to at least be in my own space.

He came over, almost hesitantly, and I watched with perverse enjoyment as he sat down on the sex sofa. But maybe he didn't care. He probably had his own sex sofa where he brought the girls he'd strung along for years. I felt a twinge of something like disappointment that I hadn't even warranted an invitation to Noah's sex sofa.

He didn't say anything and neither did I. Instead I stared at his hands and the complicated wristwatch on his arm. I didn't know anyone who wore a watch. We all kept time by our phones.

Noah's watch was thick and had multiple dials and faces. I idly wondered if it kept time or helped him travel through time.

"What—" my voice cracked as I broke the silence, "what is it that you want?"

"That's a loaded question. A lot," he said after a pause. "For now, though, to be friends again."

"Were we ever?"

"When I was three years in, I made E-4. It's this weird position where you aren't the lowest person on the totem pole anymore, but you don't have much real responsibility. The goal for most everyone, I guess, is to make E-5, but you only make E-5 if you re-up or if your commitment is longer than four years. The idea was always to get in, get eligible for the GI Bill, and get out," he paused. I still hadn't looked at him, but I heard him lift the drink and take a sip.

"Grace, please," he touched my hand. I realized he had moved to the edge of the sex sofa, and his body was now only inches away from me.

I was being childish, I knew, by refusing to look at him, by pretending I wasn't paying attention. Of course I was. I hung on every word. I was embarrassed. So I turned my head and stared at his hand, which was still lightly touching mine. It was enough, I guess, because he continued.

"But I enjoyed being in the Corps. Remember the letter that you sent where you explained that you kept going to parties with Lana but you never felt like you fit in, even after years of being with the same kids?" I looked up, surprised he remembered that, and nodded. His eyes were pinned on me, his face serious. I felt his hand tighten on the top of mine and I didn't move away. Not an inch. I couldn't.

"And I wrote you back and told you how the Marines made me feel like I fit?" I nodded again, knowing he was reeling me in but unable to stop it from happening.

"I kept thinking that maybe I didn't want to get out, that this was the right place for me, forever. Only, there were two things that made think maybe a career in the Marines wasn't for me." He paused and took another drink. He was now holding my hand in his, and I was letting him.

There was something almost dream-like about sitting in my apartment where Noah was so close I could smell him. His scent was clean and woodsy, like he had rubbed against a pine tree in the morning. I, on the other hand, smelled like stale beer and a mix of pot smoke and cigarettes from the party. He must have just arrived when we ran into each other.

His hand felt rough but steady, but his brown hair was mussed, as if he had run his fingers through it multiple times. Some of the ends stood up. Rather than looking awkward, it invited a touch to smooth down the strands. I dug my fingernails into the palm of my free hand to prevent myself from doing just that.

His forearms were dusted with dark hair and his biceps stood out in relief against the T-shirt, muscled and thick. His jaw and cheeks showed signs of late evening growth, and I wondered if they would feel scratchy or soft against my skin.

My eyes traveled across his jawline up to his lips. They looked soft, but slightly chapped, as if he had been exposed to too much sun or wind.

I was glad my hand was palm down. I suspected that it was sweaty, and I could feel that my pulse had picked up.

Each millisecond I was taking a mental photograph. *Click. Click. Click.* No matter what happened, I knew I would take these images out and look at them again and again. I met his eyes, and they were searching. Crinkles were forming at the corners. He was smiling at me.

I had lost the train of our conversation, but Noah easily picked it up again.

"Anyway, when I read your letter, I just wasn't sure what I was going to do and I felt..." he paused and looked away from me. I knew what he was going to say. He felt that I was too emotionally invested to merely be friends. I grimaced and tried to pull my hand from under his. He gripped it tighter.

"I know what you felt." I couldn't keep the accusatory tone out of my voice.

"Do you? Because I was really confused at that time and could've used some enlightenment."

I tugged again and this time he released me. His hand went through his hair again. A tic, then. A giveaway that he was frustrated. By the look of his hair, he must have been frustrated at least a dozen times today.

I knew I didn't want to hear whatever lame excuse he could come up with about why he hadn't wanted to meet me last year. I wanted to know what he was doing here and why he was haunting me around campus.

"Why are you here, at Central?" I specified so he wouldn't respond with something lame, like "because I drove you home."

"It's the Harvard of the Midwest?" Noah countered. The statement sounded more like a question, like he was asking if I bought his response. I didn't.

"What about 'Bo won't move north of the Mason Dixon line,'" I countered.

"I may have lied about the weather to Bo and suggested it was a lot warmer than it really is."

"He bought that?'

"He'd never been here before."

"What's going to happen when it snows? Or the temperature falls below freezing?"

"I may be looking for a new place to live come November, when Bo figures out that the temp gets fairly low. Got a couch?" His smile turned wry, as if he knew I was going to say no, but I didn't know what to make of this question. It was probably just rote flirtation, no different than washing your hands by habit after using the restroom.

"Yes, but it's very hard. The couch has seen a lot of activity."

This time I gave him pause.

"I don't want to know, do I?" His tone was rueful but not accusatory. I didn't elaborate.

Perhaps sensing I was reaching my limit for small talk, Noah said, "I remembered you telling me that it was a great school, Ivy League quality but without the East Coast... What did you call it?"

"Ancestry bias."

"Right, more focused on attracting new blood than maintaining old lines. I couldn't afford four years, but I could swing two. So here I am. Fresh out of junior college and ready to get my Finance degree."

Everything he said made sense, but I still felt like he was leaving something out.

I cocked my head to the side and considered him. He wore a calm look on his face, but the skin around his eyes was tight and drawn. If he had been older, maybe he would've had furrows in his brow. The light smile he wore didn't seem to fit the rest of the expression on his face.

"Okay," I said.

"No more questions?"

"Why lie in wait for me after class today?"

"Ah, well, it took me a week of recon to figure out your class schedule. Last class of the day, last day of the week seemed to make good sense at the time. It wasn't until I was there and all the other people were around that I realized I had made a shitty decision."

"Smooth."

"Yeah, not my best."

"What about the library?"

"I didn't want to bother you during work hours, but when I came down as the library was closing, you were gone."

"Why seek me out at all?" I asked, remembering how I left in a hurry that day, thinking I had seen a figment of my imagination.

"I think you may have figured out from my letters that I don't have a lot of family. You were the only one who wrote me for my entire deployment, and any good memories I have of those four years are all tied up with you, Grace. How could I not come here?"

There was only one response to this, but I left it unsaid. He knew he was breaking me down, but I wasn't out yet. If he had truly felt this way, why not meet two years ago? He had talked around the issue, so I let it go. I felt exhausted, like I had run a triathlon or some other extreme physical activity that wears you out so much even your teeth ache from tiredness.

I dropped my head and stared at the coffee table, counting the faint grain lines under the layers of lacquer. If I ran my hand across it, I would feel slight imperfections in the coating as if the lacquer had clotted up in places or an air bubble got painted into the surface. That was our conversation, smooth on the surface but lumpy underneath.

"So now what?" I asked, turning my head to the side to peer at him. Not bothering to sit fully upright, I was unwilling to let him think he was completely off the hook.

"Now, I..." he paused, ran his hand through his hair.

I finished for him. "Friends?"

"Friends, sure."

I wanted to know what that meant. Like, would we eat lunch at the café whenever our schedules permitted like Lana and I did? Would we go out for drinks on Thursday after the library closed? Or would we just say "hey" on campus, and shoot the breeze during a party if we happened to be standing next to each other?

"Friends" encompassed a wide range of relationship interactions, and frankly, it didn't give me much to work with. But I was too drained from everything that had happened in the past twelve hours to press the issue right then.

Instead of asking more questions, I stood up, withdrawing my hand from his, signaling I was done with the conversation.

"As your friend," Noah stood, "can I take you out for breakfast?"

"I guess. When?"

"This morning. Nine o'clock."

I pulled my phone out of my pocket and looked at the time. 12:10 a.m. I had four unread texts. One voicemail. I stuck my phone back into my jeans skirt. "Nine o'clock?"

"I'll pick you up," he said, taking my statement of time as confirmation. I could have turned him down, and we both knew it. I walked him to the door. He opened it and then turned toward me, holding out his hand. "I'm so glad to have finally met you in person, Grace."

I shook it and replied faintly, "Nice to meet you, too." He didn't release my hand, instead pulling me a little closer, so close that my breasts were a hairsbreadth away from his chest and I could feel the warmth of his body like a blanket. His neck was eye level and part of me wanted to reach up and smell him up close. With effort, I refrained. His free hand came between us and tilted my chin up.

I stared at him. I had fantasized about this exact position a million times. Being in the circle of Noah's arms. What would happen when I was there? But nothing prepared me for the reality of this moment and everything that preceded it. His head dropped, and for a breathless moment I thought he might kiss me. Instead, he lifted his head slightly and pressed a kiss to my forehead. He mouthed something indistinct against my temple and then let me go. Just dropped both of his hands and stepped one pace back. He tucked his fingers into the front pockets of his jeans, and for the first time since I had laid eyes on him that day, he looked uncertain.

"Tomorrow, then."

I guess we were friends who had breakfast at 9 a.m. on Saturdays.

"Tomorrow," I said and let him out.

Even though I was fatigued, I lay in bed and could not sleep, my mind replaying each minute of the night, flicking through images and recounting each morsel of conversation. I started fantasizing about walking to class with Noah, holding his hand. As I drifted off, I was aware of a sense of dread at the idea that I was pacifying myself with a picture of Noah once again.

Noah

Walking out of the apartment felt like a mistake, but I couldn't come up with a good excuse for staying. I had hinted at sleeping on the sofa, but Grace chose to ignore me. Her suggestion that she had used it for something other than studying and watching movies wasn't lost, either.

I had barely restrained myself from dragging her into my arms and laying her down across the cushions. She didn't seem to notice how the thought of her on that sofa with anyone else made my fist tighten in resentment.

I've never been very good with girls, but I never had to be. In high school, there were always girls who wanted a taste of the other side of the tracks. When I was a Marine, there were no shortage of women at the base bars looking for a similar thrill. I perfected the art of standing still, which was about all it took to find myself some random company.

I didn't need a relationship. In high school, I never wanted to connect with someone, because I was leaving town as soon as possible. In the Marines, there was never any time to develop a relationship. It was basic, then deployment. And then Grace happened.

When she first wrote me, I only wrote back because our CO told us we had to, but then I realized I looked forward to getting her letters. If it wasn't for Grace, I wouldn't have received anything from home. Any care package items would've been cast-offs from someone else. It's not like everyone had family or a girlfriend or someone back home. There were plenty like me whose unit was their family.

So maybe my initial responses to Grace were driven by self-interest. At some point, though, Grace's letters took on a greater importance. With each letter and each care package came the knowledge that the person behind those letters cared whether I made it home.

But I still had no finesse, and after I separated from the Marines, I fumbled Grace's pass. And then I talked myself into believing that she'd just wait around until I was ready to come and get her.

I needed a new plan. It was a good thing I only needed a few hours of sleep. My nights would now be spent figuring out how to get a woman I cared about into my corner, rather than the best way to take an opponent to the mat.

Chapter Five

Dear Grace,

My biggest fear, huh? I don't think I ever told you about my recruitment experience, did I? So the AF reps show up at high school on career day. Bo had skipped and gone somewhere to drink the day away. Lucky bastard. I would've cut class that day, too, but I had too many skips and was warned that if I had any more, they would withhold my diploma and make me go to summer school. That wasn't going to happen.

Anyway, I end up talking with the Army and Marine recruiters. Their spiels are pretty similar. They ask me about my interests, and I tell them getting the hell out of Nowheresville is my priority. The Marine recruiter nods and says he felt the same way. He tells me I can earn money, get my college paid for, and make a lot of friends. The first one sounds interesting, the second intriguing, the third I could care less about. Turns out the last one is actually the biggest benefit of joining.

Later, the recruiter follows up with me. Gives me a huge laundry list of awesome things about joining. I tell him he doesn't have to sell me anymore, that I'm ready to sign. Only I'm debating between the Marines and the Army. Then I make my biggest mistake ever. I admit that I'm not a fan of water. The Marine recruiter laughs and says, "You'll be infantry, son," and I sign.

When I get to boot camp they tell me the Marines are a branch of the Navy. The Navy, Grace. The Marine recruiter must have noted that I had an aversion to water, because every punishment I ever received was water-related.

The moral of this story is that I can't go around telling people my greatest fear, because someone will use it against me. It ain't water anymore.

~Noah

Grace

A soft knock on my bedroom door woke me up the next morning. I sat up, disoriented. The sun was filtering through the sides of my curtains. I grabbed for my phone, but I had forgotten to plug it in last night. The dark screen stared up at me mockingly. It was dead. Crap. What time was it?

I scrambled out of bed and opened the door to find Lana standing with her hand raised.

"Knock, knock," She lowered her hand. Her expression was unreadable and that was sufficient to alert me that something was wrong.

"What time is it?" I looked at her bare wrist. "Why don't we wear watches?"

"Because we have phones?"

"My phone is dead! I'm supposed to meet Noah for breakfast at 9 a.m."

I heard a cough from behind Lana. Noah was standing in our living room, waving to me. He was dressed in jeans and another dark T-shirt. Sunglasses hung from his collar. He wore a watch, only I couldn't tell the time from here. I smiled weakly, gave him a half-wave. I grabbed Lana's arm and dragged her into my room.

"How long has he been here?" I asked, running to the bathroom attached to my bedroom.

"He just got here," Lana said.

"My God, what should I wear? Do I have time to shower? How could I have overslept?"

"Yes, take a shower, but don't wash your hair. We'll put it up. It kind of looks like sexy bedhead."

I screamed a little when I looked at myself in the mirror. I had a pair of boxers on and one of Josh's old shirts. My hair was matted on one side and stuck up about four inches from the top of my head. I couldn't believe Noah saw me like this.

"Go out there and tell him I'm sick," I instructed Lana as I turned on the shower and waited for the hot water to climb four stories from the basement.

"Sick with what?"

"Sick with bad hair." I attacked my hair with a brush. Sexy bedhead, my ass. I looked like a drunken housewife. I only lacked the raccoon eyes.

"While you and I may think that's an illness worth staying in bed for, my guess is Mr. Hard Body out there isn't going to fall for that."

"Pick something out for me to wear and go stall him."

"Are you two dating now?" Lana called as I jumped in the shower. I washed all my parts in the quickest shower known to womankind. I tried to keep my hair from getting wet, but the ends were dampened. After toweling off, I pulled my now-combed hair into a low ponytail.

"No. We're 'friends.'" I curled my fingers into air quotes.

"Ugh, the worst." Lana laid some clothes on the bed and went out to entertain Noah.

I grabbed some lip gloss and mascara and headed for the bedroom to see what Lana had chosen for me. On the bed were the shortest shorts I had ever seen. I swear she hides random outfits in her closet that she trots out right when I can't refuse to wear them. I pulled on the bright blue shorts and a racerback bra lying next to the shorts. A white floral racerback tank completed the outfit. It was dressier than I would ordinarily wear, but the loose fit of the tank made up for the brevity of the shorts.

Ten minutes after jumping out of bed, I walked out of the bedroom. Lana was ensconced on the sofa and Noah was in my chair. She was full of smiles, but her eyes signaled to me that we were going to have a long talk about Noah. If only I had answers for whatever questions she'd have.

"Sorry about that, but I'm ready now," I announced, double-checking to see if I had a credit card, my school ID, and keys in my bag. My phone was charging on my nightstand. It was at 5% when I left the bedroom.

Noah stood up and looked me up and down. He opened his mouth and then closed it. His lips curved up slightly at the ends and this time the smile, albeit small, was real, all the way from his mouth to his eyes, unlike last night. "You have some sandals or something?"

I looked down to see my feet were bare. I turned around and ran back to my room, returning momentarily, properly shod. I fiddled with my bag a little to hide my embarrassment. Could I never catch a break around this guy?

Noah turned to Lana and held out his hand. "Great to meet you finally, Lana."

"I'll see you around, I'm sure," Lana shook his hand and grinned at me. Apparently it had taken Noah no time at all to charm Lana. I was right to be wary. Lana liked to play overprotective mother hen, although the kind that finds hookups for her charges, not the kind that separates the girl chicks from the boy chicks. That he was able to make her so at ease in less than ten minutes told me I had almost no chance at keeping a barrier between us.

I jingled my keys.

Noah walked over. Before I could put my hand on the doorknob, he had swept me aside to open the door and waved me through.

"It's the 21st century, Noah. Women open their own doors."

"Not while I'm around." His previously non-existent southern accent showed up as he drawled the last part. "My momma would be turning over in her grave if I let a woman touch a doorknob."

I merely grunted in response, pretty sure he dragged that old line out anytime he wanted to get away with something—as only good-looking guys could do.

I stopped when I hit the porch of the Victorian and blinked like a mole seeing sun for the first time. I felt like I had engaged in a twelve-hour bender and had only two hours of sleep before someone pried my eyes open again. The bright sun turned to dark spots in front of my eyes, and I started to sway.

"Whoa, there," Noah said, setting his hand around the base of my neck, his thumb and fingers wrapped around like a reverse collar. "Let's get some protein in you. The diner okay with you?"

There was a diner on the south end of campus that served breakfast all day long. I nodded again. Noah unhooked his sunglasses and placed them over my eyes, dragging his fingers behind my ears. I suppressed a shiver.

We walked for several minutes without a scrap of conversation. Trying to think of something interesting to bring up reminded me of my early days of writing to Noah, making sure each word was interesting enough to lure him into writing me back.

In retrospect, I probably looked like a fool from the very beginning, a bothersome child who was trying to buy her way into a cool kid's group with treats and expensive toys. I bit my tongue in an effort to not be the first one to break the silence.

"So, weather's nice today," Noah finally said. I nearly stumbled. Was that a reference to my first letter when I told him I wasn't going to ever refer to the weather because it was such an incredibly boring topic, or was he just really bad at making conversation?

"Yeah, nice." Our breakfast was going to feel really long if this was the best we could come up with. After the silence became too much for me, I went for the low hanging fruit—his major.

"What do you do with a finance degree?" I had skipped all the business majors in the course catalog. I'd have to go back and review those.

"Build empires," Noah responded immediately, relief evident in his voice.

I raised my eyebrows behind the sunglasses. "Lofty ambitions."

"Aim high."

"Are you allowed to say that, given that you're a Marine?"

"Probably not. Don't repeat it or they'll take away my right to shout Oorah. What're you studying?"

"Didn't your recon divulge that? You know my class schedule, where I live, and apparently where I was partying last night."

"I admit that I hung out over at the Fine Arts Center for a few days and was surprised I didn't see you or any of your work," Noah said, unperturbed by my recitation.

"Why would I be at FAC?"

He shrugged. "I just thought you'd be majoring in something over there. Like art or whatever majors there are in fine arts."

I could rattle off a few. Unlike the business section, I knew this part of the course catalog by heart.

"Because of my photography?"

"Yeah, I mean the stuff you sent was amazing. It should be in a magazine or a museum or something. You aren't going to do something with that?"

"Um, thank you, but first, my stuff isn't that good and second, photography is my hobby," I said. I didn't want to admit to Noah, who had fought in a war and was likely putting himself through school here at Central, that I was too weenie to submit a portfolio for entrance into the Fine Arts program. Instead, I told him a partial truth. "I don't want to ruin it by having the stress of having to support myself with it."

Noah shook his head. "You can tell you've never had to worry about money."

"What is that supposed to mean?"

"Only people with money ever say money ruins things."

"That's ..." I trailed off. I hadn't had to worry about money, but it's not like money had ever made me happy. It didn't keep my dad from dying. It didn't make my mom suddenly stop being addicted to anti-depressants. It didn't prevent Lana from getting an eating disorder. "I'm undeclared. I haven't picked a major," I finished.

I felt his hand on my head as he turned my head to look at him. "Not knowing isn't so bad. You're young yet."

I stuck my tongue out a little. "What are you, my dad?"

"Is that your kink? I haven't had a girl ever call me Daddy before, but I'm open-minded."

"'Eww' is the only response to that." I shook my head. I couldn't tell if his flirting was just to cheer me up or lighten the mood, or if it was an invitation. I did know I didn't want to talk about money or majors. "How is empire-building these days?"

"Slow, but I've got a plan."

"Are you empire-building by yourself or with others?"

"Others right now," Noah added. "Roommates."

"How many roommates do you have?"

"Four."

"Wow, and they all go to school here? Have I met any of them?" I was letting curiosity get the better of me.

"No, only Bo and me. Finn flips houses and works at his dad's construction company, Adam plays in a band—although technically I think he lives off his trust fund—and Mal," Noah paused, "I'm not sure what Mal does. "

"That's a lot of testosterone in one house."

"Yeah, it can be fun, but also a pain in the ass."

The mile walk along the campus was over before I realized it, and not once had Noah removed his hand from the back of my neck. He opened the door with one hand and placed a light pressure with his other to propel me forward. A huge clock over the reception desk declared it was nearly ten o'clock.

We sat ourselves in a booth and pulled out the slightly greasy menus that I hoped were tacky-feeling because of a cleaning compound and not something else. A waitress came over and took our orders. Noah ordered an egg white omelet with fresh vegetables and wheat toast, no butter. I ordered the number two: eggs over easy, toast, and bacon.

"How did you come to live together?" I picked up the thread of our conversation. From across the booth, I felt Noah's long legs stretch out next to mine, his jean-clad legs rubbing slightly against my bare leg.

"Bo and I went to the Americana bar down on Fifth one night."

"Never been there," I admitted. Lana and I stuck pretty close to campus. I wasn't even sure I knew where Fifth was.

"I'll take you sometime," Noah said, nonchalantly presuming that we would be spending more time together. "Adam was in the band. He tried to crowd-surf an unfriendly crowd for some reason, and we ended up defending him. Not sure why, though. His music sucked that night.

"Ouch. What's the band?"

"No band right now. He couldn't play all summer, so they found a new guitar player. The band he was in was called Ten Speed."

I made a face, and Noah laughed. "I know. I kept telling Adam that he couldn't be in a band called Ten Speed and still hold his head up."

The waitress brought our breakfast, and I watched Noah surreptitiously. I realized that I didn't know until now whether he was right or left-handed. I knew a lot of other things about Noah, like that he and Bo had been friends since the seventh grade, when they got into a fight and were sent to detention together. Noah hated his father and loved tart things like Starbursts and Skittles, but he wasn't much of a chocolate fan.

Four years of letters can make you think you knew someone really well. Sitting across from him for the first time watching him eat bland wheat toast, I wondered if my collection of facts stood for actual parts of the whole or simply random tidbits I could trot out if I was playing Noah Jackson Trivial Pursuit.

"What are you doing after breakfast?" Noah asked.

"I'm taking a picture of the Alpha Phis for a rush invitation."

"Is that a regular photo or one of your special ones?"

"Well, it's a miniature one, if that's what you mean. It's not like I invented the technique."

"Are you going to show me how you do one of those?"

I shrugged slightly. "I guess, if you want."

"I want." He looked at me as if waiting for something.

"Like today?"

"Such an enthusiastic invitation." He made a tsking sound. "Why yes, Grace, I'd love to come and be your assistant today."

"I actually already have one—it's Lana."

"Isn't she a member of that house?"

"Yes, but she's a bad member who's using me as an excuse to get out of her rush duties."

"You know, if you weren't doing it for them, they'd have to pay someone," Noah said.

"Yeah but I'm happy to do it as a gift."

"They think it's good enough to put on their stuff."

"I get that I can make money off of it. I just don't want to."

"I'm just trying to point out that what you do has value."

"Got it." I picked up my toast and bit down hard.

"So, are you seeing anyone?" Noah asked, abruptly changing the subject.

"What?" I choked in surprise on my toast and swallowed an unchewed piece in order to avoid spitting it all out on the table.

"Seeing someone. Dating. Hooking up. Hanging out?"

I wished I could say that I had found someone really wonderful, and that he'd come all the way to Central for nothing. I didn't think my old line about being a cranky cat spinster was going to work for me here. Instead, I asked him, "Are you?"

"Nope. And I haven't been for a long time."

"Since like when?" He was sharing, so I might as well take advantage. I ignored the rest of my breakfast. I was hungry for information. What had he been doing for the last couple of years?

"Since high school."

I sat back, stunned. He hadn't dated anyone since high school. That seemed preposterous, and I told him so. "I don't believe you."

He wasn't offended by this, but instead gave me a half smile that hinted at something more. "Truth. Ask Bo."

He pulled out his phone and shoved it toward me. Handing someone your phone was like giving them the Pulp Fiction briefcase. You couldn't take it and not look inside. I was pretty sure I wasn't ready to view the contents of his phone, no matter how tempting. With great effort, I pushed the phone away.

"Like no dates, hookups, hangouts at all?"

"Like no serious girlfriend since high school. It's not easy to maintain a relationship while deployed, and I didn't have anyone I cared about enough to make that effort before I left."

"You wrote to me for four years," I pointed out.

"I can make an effort when I want to." He looked at me like this was important, but I couldn't get past the idea that Noah hadn't dated any-one seriously since high school.

"But since you've been out?" I pressed.

"Not everyone can just get into Central, Grace. I was busy studying, taking practice tests, and trying to make myself into an interesting can-didate for admission. Girls were the last things on my mind." He wiped his mouth with a napkin and pushed his almost spotless plate away. "But you haven't answered my question."

I didn't want to make it seem like I was sitting around waiting for him, even though I had been. In a moment of panic and stupidity, I lied.

"I'm not dating anyone, but..." I paused intentionally, and took a sip of my Diet Coke. "I'm interested in someone."

Noah's eyebrows raised.

"Who is this lucky guy?"

"Ah... Mike Walsh." Mike was actually the two-year crush of a differ-ent library co-worker, Sarah. She was always looking at him with puppy dog eyes when she thought no one was watching.

"Is he a frat guy? Jock? What?"

"He's my student supervisor at the library."

"So what's the problem?"

"What do you mean?"

"You like him, but you aren't dating."

The thing with making up stories is that people always wanted details. I rubbed my suddenly sweaty palms together and tried channeling Sarah. What would she say? "I like him, but he's never asked me out."

"Isn't this the 21st Century?" Noah threw my own words back in my face." Why are you waiting?"

"I don't think he's interested." Good lord, what was with the inquisition? I felt my cheeks heat up. Lana would know immediately that I was lying. I didn't know how intuitive Noah was, but I dropped my gaze to my half-eaten breakfast to avoid looking at him in the eye.

"How do you know? I think you girls assume that guys are mind readers. Or impervious to rejection."

I thought about this. Why didn't Sarah just ask Mike out? It was obvious to everyone in the library that she liked him.

"I thought I had made it pretty clear," I muttered.

"Call him now and ask him to a movie."

"Now? My cellphone is dead."

"Use mine." He gestured toward his phone still lying face up on the table.

"I can't."

"Why?"

"Because I don't know what his phone number is." I had it programmed into my phone, but I never called him. I never had occasion to.

"Lame, Grace. You like this guy but you don't know his digits?" That did sound bad. But I didn't memorize phone numbers unless they were really important. Your phone did that for you.

"Where is he right now?" Noah pressed.

"Um, I have no idea." I didn't know what Mike did on the weekends. Other than our occasional, Thursday night, after-work get-togethers, I didn't hang out with him. I hung out with Lana and her crew, which usually meant sorority and fraternity people. Mike was GDI—Goddamn Independent.

"You've had a crush on a guy you've worked with for the past year and you don't know his phone number or how he spends his R&R time?" Noah looked at me skeptically. I shrank back into my side of the booth. I promised myself that I would never lie again. I wanted to throw up my hands in surrender and confess all.

"He might be at the library," I said. I didn't know Mike's work schedule, but he was often at the library either working or hanging out.

"On a Saturday morning?" Noah looked at his watch. "At eleven o'clock?"

"Why do you care?"

"I'm your friend," Noah replied and placed his forearms on the table, leaning closer to me. "I want to help you out. Isn't that what friends do?"

"I've never had a male friend before," I admitted. "I don't know."

"Just pretend I'm one of your girlfriends, then."

"Riiight." Because that would be so easy to do.

"Let's go to the library."

"Right now?"

"Yes."

"Don't you have anything to do today?" I tried to think of an excuse to get out of this, but saying you had to study two weeks into the new year wasn't ever believable. Laundry, though, was a good excuse. Everyone had to do laundry. But before I could trot out my excuse, Noah was standing up ignoring my question.

I dug in my pocket and pulled out my debit card. I placed it on top of the wallet carrier that the waitress had dropped off earlier when she cleared our plates. Noah took out his wallet and threw down a couple of bills to cover the total plus a big tip. He stuck my card in his pocket.

"Hey, that's my card."

"Don't make me hurt you, Grace." He fended off my attempts to grab my card back. "I'll return your card when we get to the library."

"But I wanted to pay," I said. "That's what friends do. They pay their share."

"You can buy next time," Noah said and pushed me forward and out the door.

The library was on the south end of the campus, near the diner. It was a quick walk over, and I didn't have time to think up any other plausible reason we should go back to the apartment. Noah's long legs were eating up the pavement, and I felt like a tiny Chihuahua trying to keep up.

"Are we racing?" I asked.

"Sorry." Noah slowed down. "Not used to walking with anyone as short as you."

"I'm not short. I'm above average height for a female." For some reason, Noah's lack of experience walking around with shorter people was kind of pleasant. It fit in with his earlier confession that he hadn't dated any one seriously since high school. Or maybe it just meant he dated really tall women.

We walked into the library, and a girl I didn't know too well was manning the desk. I thought her name was Molly or Marie or Maria or something.

"Hi, Grace," she said. I winced inwardly, feeling like a tool for not knowing her name when she knew mine. Faces, I could remember. Names, not so much.

"Hi. Is Mike around today?"

"Actually, yeah, he just came in and was going down toward Periodicals."

"Great," I said. I was batting negative one thousand today.

I walked slowly down the stairs but didn't dawdle at the door. I knew I should've introduced Noah, but since I didn't remember her name, I left one embarrassment to head to another.

"Not going to introduce me?" Noah whispered.

"I don't remember her name," I admitted.

"Ouch," he laughed.

"Next time I pause, introduce yourself," I instructed.

"Yes ma'am," he said, trying to sound obedient but failing. I could practically hear his smile through the words.

We walked downstairs, turning left toward Periodicals, and sure enough Mike was there, leaning on the desk, flirting with some girl wearing a sorority T-shirt. Her Greek letters were appliquéd in white on the back of her pink tee.

"That's Mike," I pointed out.

Noah stopped and turned toward me. Then looked back at Mike, disbelieving. Mike tossed his hair out of his eyes. Once and then again. "Mike." It was a disbelieving sound.

"What's wrong with Mike?" I asked, faking my indignation. Mike was decent-looking, but he had long bangs and was constantly flipping them out of his face. You couldn't talk with him for more than five minutes without a head toss.

He was on the thin side, which was another negative strike against him. You never date a guy who can wear skinnier jeans than you. I glanced furtively at Noah's thighs. While Noah wasn't heavy, he was big enough that I knew he wouldn't be wearing my pants, ever.

Noah just shook his head at me and walked forward toward the pair. "Hey, Mike Walsh, right? Didn't you come to my house out at the Woodlands before school started?" Mike turned toward Noah and stuck out his hand.

"Dude, yes, it was awesome. You're Noah Jackson right? You fight?" Mike made a little move, like he was ducking and avoiding a fake punch.

"Right. I hear you work with my friend, Grace."

Mike peered around Noah, and I gave him a limp wave and a weak smile.

"So I was thinking about going to the movies tonight. You want to come?" Noah was saying.

"Um, yeah, that would be awesome." Mike looked suitably surprised, as any normal human being would be when some total stranger came up and asked them to see a movie.

"Great. Grace here is going to come, and I'm bringing a friend," Noah emphasized the friend with a wink at Mike. He winked back uncertainly, his eyelid lowering slowly as if he wasn't sure what he was winking about. I wasn't sure either. Noah was bringing a friend? We were doubling?

Then my heart sank to my feet when I saw that Sarah was working the periodical desk and had heard this entire exchange. Her expression accused me of violating the girlfriend code.

I wanted to jump back there and assure her that I didn't have designs on her boy, and that despite the fact that she and Mike were not dating, I considered him off-limits. But I couldn't do that and keep up my stupid fiction with Noah. I'd have to explain myself later, if she let me.

I extricated myself from the situation moments later by saying I had an appointment at noon. I left Noah standing there chatting with Mike about some kind of fighting stance.

Noah

Grace's abrupt departure, while her "man of interest" was throwing a head fake, was more encouraging than anything she had said all morning. When Grace brought up Mike during breakfast, her tone made me instantly suspicious. She drew out the name slowly, like she had to make one up. My first thought was that she was faking. When the name was attached to a real person, someone she worked with at the library, I admit that I may have had a moment of doubt.

But seeing him, I couldn't believe it. While Grace wasn't super-communicative in her letters about her dating life, this guy didn't fit her. He wore jeans that were so tight I wondered if they were from the women's section of the store. I wanted to lop off those stupid-ass bangs of his. I could barely see his eyes. I didn't trust anyone whose eyes I couldn't stare straight into. This guy looked like a stiff breeze might snap him in half.

If I pictured Grace with anyone, something I tried not to do, it would be someone like her brother. A jock. Or, because she loved photography, maybe one of those foreign war correspondents. But not this guy, who looked like he spent more time in front of the mirror than an entire sorority house.

Inviting him and Grace to a movie was risky, but if I was there, I could get a better sense of whether she actually liked him—in which case I'd have to kill him—or whether she was just using him to put me off.

It could be that Grace was just setting up a series of tests for me to pass, like the *Twelve Labours of Hercules*. That was fine. I'd complete each challenge, and then we could be done with it.

Even though my reunion plans were less than stellar, it was all working out. Grace was talking to me. I didn't have to skulk around campus anymore. I was putting together the final piece of my overall plan. Get out of the Marines, get a degree, get Grace.

It was all going to work out fine. I pulled out my phone to text her, only to realize that I still hadn't gotten her number.

Item number one. Get Grace's number.

Chapter Six

Grace,

I'm sorry I haven't written for what must seem like months now. I'm currently sitting on my rucksack with an envelope addressed to you on the bed. I've been writing you back lots of things in my head, but I can't seem to find one minute to actually put pen to paper. By the time you get this, I'm not even sure where I'll be.

I ended up getting two of your packages at the forward operating base. Mail delivery is really spotty of late. We are all cursing and celebrating the supply truck's appearance. Cursing because it never gets here on time and celebrating because of its assful of goodness.

I was the most popular guy for a day when I opened those packages. And yeah, we got a ton of mileage out of hazing Bo with the movie The Notebook. He does kind of look like the guy who plays the lead.

Yours,

Noah

P.S. Weather. So cold I'm wearing socks to sleep.

Grace

I slammed the apartment door open. I'm surprised we don't have gouges in the wall from all the times I've flung open the door.

Lana was lying on the sofa, and Amy was sitting in my chair painting her toenails. Being used to my door dramatics, Lana didn't move, but from Amy's curses, I must have made her mess up a nail.

"What happened?" Lana called as I walked over to the kitchen to pour myself some water.

"Noah just asked me to go on a date with him," I paused, and Lana and Amy started to squeal with excitement. "But I'm going with Mike Walsh, and Noah's bringing a 'good' friend." I held up my fingers to do air quotes around the word good.

The squeals turned to groans of dismay. "No way," Lana said.

"Yes way. Worse, this girl who I work with was there when Noah set up the double date, and she has a crush on Mike. She looked like I had stabbed her in the heart with a fork."

"You kind of did," Amy pointed out.

"How'd this happen?" Lana asked.

"I told Noah I was interested in Mike," I admitted. Groans from both girls filled the air.

"Why?" they both exclaimed.

"Because I didn't want him to think I was some pathetic dolt who sat around waiting for two years for some guy to come and say 'Let's be friends.'" I gave a half-hearted defense of my stupidity.

"Bet you didn't expect this," Amy said, completely deadpan. I almost lunged for her. Lana glared at her, and Amy drew back and made a zipping motion with her fingers over her mouth.

"What are you going to do?" Lana asked.

"Have the best damn time of my life tonight." I stomped into my room and slammed the door shut.

"What about the picture?" Amy called after me. I held back a sigh. I had already bailed on the picture once, and Amy was super nice to let it go. She didn't deserve any blowback for my recent wave of flakiness. I picked up my backpack that carried my camera and my laptop. My phone was fully charged, so I quickly scrolled through my contacts and found Mike's number.

Meet you at library tonight?

Sure, came the quick response.

The campus movie theater, the Varsity, sat on the very edge of the south end of campus, down by the diner. We'd just walk. I didn't want this to appear any more date-like than it already did.

I pulled the backpack on and picked up my tripod. Opening my bedroom door, I said to both girls, "Let's go."

As we descended, I could hear footsteps on the stairs below. Noah's face appeared around the next turn.

"Great. I didn't want to be late for my tutorial," Noah smiled at us. I heard Amy give a breathy sigh behind me.

"I'm the assistant," Lana told Noah.

I muttered, "Fine," motioning him to turn and go down the stairs.

At the porch, Noah stopped me and tugged at my backpack with one hand, grabbing the tripod with the other. For a moment I resisted until I realized how ridiculous we looked, as if we were two dogs fighting over a bone. I let both the backpack and the tripod go.

"Let me guess—something to do with your momma." I rolled my eyes.

Noah shrugged on the backpack. "I had it easier than you, you know."

"I don't think that just because you lost your mom when you were born, and I lost my dad when I was twelve that you had it easier than me," I replied softly. I didn't want Lana or Amy to hear me, but I also didn't want Noah to believe I thought his loss was less than mine. As if sensing I needed a moment, Lana hurried a reluctant Amy along.

"It's true. I don't think you can miss what you don't know," Noah replied.

"Sure you can." I think Noah missed his mother more than he ever would admit.

"I don't have memories of her, but you have twelve years of them with your dad.

"I also didn't have someone blaming me for my dad's death like your dad has."

"Are we going to try to out-horrible the other?" Noah ran a hand through his hair.

"Out-horrible?"

"Like my life is more horrible than yours?" Noah explained.

I shook my head. "Is that what I'm doing? Because I didn't mean to."

"I know it wasn't," he let out a deep breath. "This is too heavy a discussion for a sunny day."

I looked up and squinted. Full midday sun.

"What's wrong?" Noah asked. Maybe I did have a black-ants-on-a-white-blanket face.

"I'm just hoping for a little cloud cover."

"Why is that? I thought pictures needed a lot of light."

"Full sun is great for taking photos of the sky, but it casts hard shadows and makes even really beautiful people look kind of awful. You have to have a lot of experience to take good full sun pictures, and I'm not there yet."

Noah opened his mouth, but I jumped in to add, "And don't say that's why I should major in art, because the best way to become a better photographer is just to practice."

"Fair enough. Tell me about how you create these pictures that look like Bo's old mechanical football game with the tiny plastic guys."

"I'll do better than that," I said. "I'll show you."

After climbing the three flights of stairs to a messy room at the top of the Delt house, I was grateful Noah was carrying my bag and tripod. Lana and I were both a bit winded, as was Jack, who escorted us up. Two younger Delts stood in the room frantically trying clean up, but it was too late. While a path had been cleared from the door to the windows, it still smelled like old socks and pizza boxes. Red plastic cups lay haphazardly on their sides, and the two desks pushed away from the window were piled high with video game boxes, textbooks, and a variety of T-shirts.

"Sorry," Jack said as we entered. He glared at the two fleeing Delts. It looked like someone was likely to get a house punishment later.

I took my tripod from Noah and set it in front of the window. "Can we take the screen out?" I asked Jack.

"Sure." He walked over and peered around the sill. I could tell he didn't know how to remove it. Noah gently nudged him aside and pulled two clips from the bottom, tugged the screen out and set it aside.

I pulled out my camera and clipped the base onto the tripod. Noah stepped closer until his arm brushed mine.

For a moment, I paused. It seemed too unreal that Noah was standing next to me while I was taking a photograph. I wanted to yell at him, and, at the same time, I wanted to burrow under his arm and wrap myself in his scent. I closed my eyes for a moment and took a deep breath to clear my head, but instead my nose filled with the clean, warm male aroma that made me think of parks in mid-spring when all the greenery was sprouting and there was freshly turned dirt in all the flower beds.

"So Lana, you do this stuff too?" Jack's overly loud voice reminded me why we were all here. Or at least why I was here. And it wasn't to sniff Noah's T-shirt and imagine we were running through a field of daisies.

"'This stuff' as in photography?" Lana replied, waving in my direction as I positioned my camera. I peered through the lens and saw Amy signaling me from across the street. I debated whether I should get a stronger zoom lens out.

"Um, yeah." Jack sounded confused by the impatient tone in Lana's voice.

"I told you last night I was a psych major."

"Oh, ah, that's right." Clearly Jack had little memory of the night. Too many tequila shots. "So a psych major. That's like head stuff."

Noah and I looked at each other, and I could read his expression just as well as he could read mine. We shared a private grin. Jack's presidency here at the Delts wasn't due to his big brain. Either that or Jack's ability to think was being short-circuited by Lana's presence. This was a definite possibility. If anyone I knew belonged on a magazine cover, it was Lana.

She was one of my favorite subjects, although she rarely allowed me to take her picture. Her eating disorder left her with a distorted self-image. Though the photographs I took of her showed how gorgeous she was, she never quite believed I didn't use some secret photography trick. I'd given up trying to explain that the distortion happens in her head and not with my lens. But I guess we all had our blind spots. Mine was standing right next to me, so I couldn't judge Lana too harshly.

"Tell me how this works," Noah ordered. I refrained from rolling my eyes and saluting. If I did, it might give him the idea he could give me instructions all the time.

"Most of the time, when you take a picture, you are trying to take a straight-on photograph. With tilt shift, you're tricking the eye into thinking you're seeing something closer than it really is by focusing on a point or object from a distance and then blurring the edges. I have the camera on the rails so it can move up and down," I gestured toward the two thin metal rods on either side of the camera. "The tilt is the pivot here on the lens." I moved the lens and tilted it up and down to show how it hinged at angles away from the body of the camera. "Some real pros can do it without all this equipment, and some just use computer hacks."

"So is it like the opposite of a rearview mirror?"

"Kind of, but imagine the rear-view mirror being able to shift up and down and then tilt."

"Do you have to be high up to make it look like a model toy town?"

"Not always. Some people are able to take ground level shots, but I'm better at taking them up high and at a distance."

"Is it harder with people?" Noah seemed really interested, and I could talk about my hobby all day long.

"No, people make it great. They give it scale, actually. This type of thing is really well-suited for having the girls against the backdrop of the house."

I made a few more adjustments and then turned to Lana. "I think I'm ready."

She texted someone. A few moments later, the Alpha Phis began streaming out of their house. They were all wearing red shorts and white-and-red T-shirts with their Greek insignia on the back. As they formed a line, I took a few pictures. Action shots were the best. Like the one I took of Noah kneeling in the library when I thought he was some random lacrosse player.

"Have them move around some more, like in a circle or something," I called to Lana. She must have relayed the message, because the girls on the lawn moved into a round formation and started walking in unison. I motioned for Noah to look through the viewfinder. I noticed that he was careful not to touch anything, like Lana always was. Most people would've put their hand up to the lens or bumped the tripod. I held the remote in my hands and took several photos while Noah was looking.

He stepped back. "That's pretty cool. I want to see the bigger versions, though. It's hard to get the full effect with the tiny viewfinder."

"I always tell Grace that I can't see what she sees," Lana interjected.

Noah nodded in agreement. "Yeah, I mean I kind of see it, but it's not the same as the prints Grace sent me."

"What ones did she send you? My favorite is the football one with Josh," Lana said. I let the two of them chatter about their favorites while I raised and lowered the camera and adjusted the tilt, taking several photographs.

The Alpha Phis had gotten tired of doing circles and were breaking into small groups. A few sat down on the stairs of the house and some others stretched out on the lawn. The different body positions gave the image so much more composition. *This* was the photo. I would still review them all, but this one spoke the most to me, and I just knew that when I scrolled through the images this would be my favorite.

The sisters might choose something else more polished, but the relaxed and conversational nature of the scattered crowd would be the best image of the set.

"I'm ready," I said, straightening up. I rubbed my neck a little to ease the slight ache that had gathered from bending over the camera. I felt a warm hand push mine away. Large, strong fingers cupped the base of my skull and flexed against my neck, gently but firmly massaging me. I closed my eyes for a moment and allowed the pleasure to wash over me.

The room was utterly silent, but I could feel Noah's body, the heat and mass of it, next to me. I wanted to place my hands on him, stroke that marble-hard chest that Lana and Amy had patted down last night. But I knew that would be an invitation I wasn't prepared to extend.

I curled my hands into fists, and the sting of my nails in my palms brought me back. I opened my eyes to find Noah staring at me, his hand still on my neck. His brown eyes had darkened and the skin over his cheekbones was pulled tight. He looked hungry and more than a little predatory. I shivered, a matching hunger building inside of me. It would be so easy to drop my defenses and tumble into his arms, but what would happen when he let go? I didn't think I'd recover from the fall.

His fingers tightened for a minute and then dropped away. I took a deep breath and turned to dismantle my equipment. "Thanks for your help. I'm going to go over to the house for a little bit and look through the photos. See which ones they want."

Noah understood that this was a dismissal. "I'll walk you over."

He carried everything for me, down the four flights of stairs, across the street, and into the front reception room of the house. The girls fluttered around him like butterflies trying to alight on the same flower. He didn't talk or flirt or even acknowledge them. He set down my things and then hooked his hand around my neck again, turning me so I was looking directly at him.

"I'll see you tonight," he said.

I only nodded my response.

It took longer to fend off questions about Noah than it did to pick out a picture. The consensus of the rush committee was to use the image that had them circled around the Alpha Phi sign on the front lawn. It was one of my least favorites, but with a little processing, I could make it acceptable even for me. I ended up eating dinner at the sorority house, so I had little time to get ready for my date with Mike. And Noah. And whomever Noah was bringing.

***

"What's showing?" I asked Mike when I met up with him at the library.

"Some movie with subtitles. I never thought Noah Jackson would be into this sort of thing. Who do you think he's dating?" Flip went his hair.

"Dunno," I mumbled. This thought had tormented me all afternoon, and by dinnertime I had stoked my anxiety into anger. Mike seemed nervous, and maybe if we were on a real date, I would be nervous too. Instead, I was kind of angry, and anger burned away nervousness and made me feel stupidly brave. Anger: the sober student's high.

I broached the Sarah subject with Mike, figuring this might be the only time I'd have alone with him before the movie started. "We should've invited Sarah."

"Why?" Mike asked, this time pushing his hair back with his hand.

"Because she's a cool girl, and I think she'd have liked this movie."

"Really? I got the impression she didn't like movies," Mike said.

"How so?"

He shrugged, shoving both hands in his pockets. "I asked her to a few, and she always had excuses not to go. Maybe she just didn't want to go with me."

Good lord. Was it possible that Sarah's unrequited feelings were actually returned, but through a series of miscommunications, Sarah and Mike each thought the other didn't return their feelings? It was like a classic romance novel, where I could play the adorable Cupid matchmaker, doing something productive for once. In the book, however, I'd have tangled red curls. I always loved the heroines with red hair—and so did their male counterparts. Before I could ask any questions, though, we arrived at the theater.

Noah was already standing there, and Bo was standing right next to him. There were three theater students, all beautiful, talking to both of them. One of them had tangled red hair. The universe hated me. Was this like a multiple couple thing, a sextuplet? An orgy of moviegoers? Noah broke away from the group when he saw us arrive.

"Which one's your date?" I asked, bracing myself. Please don't let it be the cute redhead, I prayed.

"Bo's my date," Noah smiled, turned and gestured for Bo to extricate himself from the others.

"You two are dating?" Mike asked, mouth agape. Apparently, to Mike, Noah Jackson liking movies with subtitles was less astonishing than Noah liking men. I could only sigh in relief that I wasn't in competition with some gorgeous romance book heroine with red hair.

"Nope, just needed some bro time," Noah said, and he turned and bumped fists with Bo.

"Bro time at a foreign, subtitled film?" I asked, skepticism heavy in my tone.

"Sure. Aren't we here to be better educated?" This was from Bo. He handed out tickets to Mike and me.

I stared at Bo and Noah's smiling faces when the reality of the situation struck me. Noah hadn't brought a date. He'd brought his best friend and battle buddy. Most importantly, he had brought a guy. I felt guilty at all the angry thoughts I had directed at him earlier while having dinner with the Alpha Phis. I felt even worse having used Mike as a defense against my feelings toward Noah. Neither one of them deserved that.

"Thanks," Mike snatched his up. He didn't offer to reimburse them.

"What do we owe you?" I asked. Bo looked offended, and Noah shook his head in mock dismay.

"Bo's momma is still alive, but hearing that her son didn't buy a girl's movie ticket might send her to an early death," Noah said, drawing out his vowels to exaggerate his Texas accent.

I rolled my eyes, but Mike just shrugged. When we got inside, Bo said, "Why don't you and Noah grab some seats, and Mike and I'll field the refreshments."

"Why don't you and Noah go get the seats, and Mike and I will get the popcorn and stuff." I wanted to speak to Mike about Sarah some more before the movie started, and being separated wouldn't provide that opportunity.

"Since you paid for the movie," Mike added. I realized that Mike's silence on the tickets wasn't him being a cheap jerk, just picking his battles. Maybe I had misconceptions of Mike too. This made me want to work even harder to get him together with Sarah and make up for my jerkiness.

I left Noah, Bo, and Mike debating who was going to buy popcorn, soda, and water (the latter being Noah's drink of choice), and found an open section a quarter of the way down the auditorium-style seats. The Varsity Theatre was old and the royal blue velvet seats hadn't been updated for at least a couple decades. The cloth was worn through on the arms, and some of the springs' resilience had been weakened, so when you sat in them, the seats kind of collapsed.

A movie here was about the cost of a soda. I don't even know why I argued about paying my way. If I really meant for Noah to be deterred, I should act like I didn't care. Arguing over everything and ignoring him were obvious signs that I was trying too hard. I resolved to try to be friendlier and less bitchy. I wanted to project an "I don't care" attitude, not an "I'm so hurt that I can barely stand to look at you, yet I don't want to be away from you either" message.

Looking around, I was surprised by the number of people in the theater for a Saturday night early on in the year. I figured everyone would be at some house party, or over on Greek Street, or in one of the campus bars.

I leaned over to a girl next to me. "What's the movie?"

She looked at me like I was crazy. "Lust, Caution."

"That doesn't sound very French."

"It's not. It's Chinese. Directed by Ang Lee," She bit out each word as if I was five years old.

"I thought it was a French film with subtitles," I couldn't let go of the fact that it wasn't a French film.

"You got half that right. It's got subtitles." With that she turned away and resumed her conversation with her friend. I think it had something to do with half-wits and how they shouldn't even come to subtitled movies if they weren't serious film students.

I pulled out my phone to do some quick searching on "Lust, Caution," but I heard a commotion and saw the three guys at the aisle, trying to get through to the seats I had picked out.

Mike led the way, followed by Noah and then Bo. When Mike started to seat himself, Noah grabbed his arm and pulled him upright.

"No, you sit over there," Noah directed Mike to the seat I was in. "Grace, sit here." And then, as if he thought his orders would sound better, he added, "Please." I wasn't planning on moving, but Mike stood there uncertainly, with Noah's hand still gripping his other arm.

"Move, girl," I heard from behind me. "The movie is about to start."

I let out a loud and ungrateful sigh and moved one seat over. Everyone collapsed in their chairs, and I heard a "finally" behind us.

Now I was in the worst position I could imagine, in a dark theater sitting next to Noah, so I leaned into Mike as far as I could without making it seem like I wanted to get intimate with him. I tried to portray a certain nonchalance over the fact that I was going to watch a Chinese-subtitled film with Noah Jackson. I probably looked like I had overused the distortion or blur tool on my computer photo-editing program right now.

"The film isn't French. It's Chinese," I felt responsible for dragging Mike here, so I tried to impart what little knowledge I had.

"Oh yeah? I just heard that it had subtitles and assumed it was French," He whispered back. I gave him the *I know, right?* look. Then he offered me a drink of his soda. I moved away and gave a mini-shudder. I wasn't going to suck on the same straw he had in his mouth. Who knew what kind of backwash Mike sent into the soda? Now, Noah's drink? A couple of years ago I'd have paid money to place my lips around something he had touched. Cripes. Who was I kidding? I wanted to suck on that water bottle of his until you couldn't tell where his DNA started and mine began. I sunk lower in the seat.

The nearly three hours of sitting between Mike and Noah in the dark watching an extremely erotic film was possibly one of the most uncomfortable situations of my entire life. The movie was about a female spy sent to seduce an opposition leader. It was scene after scene of sexually explicit and forbidden love. The first sex scene was fairly violent, and I could see Mike shift restlessly beside me while Noah was stoically unmoving. I could feel myself dying of embarrassment. I tried to look at it from a filmmaking point of view, separating myself from the action on the screen and examining the angle of the shots and the placement of the shadows. It didn't work.

As the movie played on and the love scenes became increasingly graphic, I stopped watching. I was acutely aware of Noah. At one point, he propped his arm on the armrest, and I could feel the warm cotton of his sleeve and the soft tickling sensation of his hair against my arm. I wanted to rub up against him, place my cold nose into his throat. I wanted to pull his arm around me and drape his hand on my thigh. But I remained in my own space, arms tucked close to my sides as if I was afraid that one movement might send to me lurching into his lap to try and act out some of the scenes on the screen.

A strange tension began to seep into my body as the movie ticked on. I imagined Noah lifting his hand from his own thigh and placing it on mine, moving up and down my bare leg in long sweeps, higher with each pass, until his fingers tucked right under the fabric of my skirt. The thought of Noah's hand between my legs made me shift. Discomfited by him, I crossed and then uncrossed my legs.

My inability to sit still didn't go unnoticed. Mike looked at me impatiently and moved away, as if I were adversely affecting his enjoyment. I clenched my hands in my lap and closed my eyes, which only made it worse, because now all I could hear were sounds of the rustling sheets, the fall of the cloth onto the floor, and the crescendo of sounds, both human and instrumental. The air felt thick and heavy around us, like I was breathing underwater. Each breath felt labored and sounded harsh to my own ears, and I wanted to stop taking in air altogether.

At the moment I thought I would explode out of my seat and flee the theater, I felt a large, warm hand cover mine. Noah's touch was completely unexpected, and I froze. But instead of this development causing me more anxiety, Noah's hand soothed me. I unclenched my hands. The block in my throat dissolved, and I was able to take a few deep, calming breaths. Each muscle that had tensed up seemed to unknot and relax.

The movie went on, but I noticed little of it. Instead, I focused on the tendrils of warmth that curled outward from the hand in my lap like vines on wall. The hand never moved, not throughout the entire movie. I glanced to see if Mike had noticed, but he wasn't paying any attention to me.

The heat, the dark, the sudden cessation of panic—it all made me drowsy. Noah shifted and I felt his shoulder close to my head like an invitation. I looked at him, but his eyes were focused straight ahead. It was like his arm was detached from his body. Perhaps it was mine now.

I rested my head tentatively against the shoulder that was in my space. No one moved. I stopped worrying about what Mike would think and allowed my eyes to drift closed and my thoughts to wander into nothingness.

The noise of dozens of spring-loaded seats being snapped back in place woke me up. I jerked upright. Noah's hand was no longer in my lap. I straightened and tried to look like I hadn't spent the last half of the movie sleeping and holding hands with him. Too late, though, as Mike was standing up and looking down at me with a puzzled expression.

At least he didn't look angry that he'd found his "date" asleep on the shoulder of another guy. I wiped the sides of my mouth as surreptitiously as possible and stood up. To Mike I said, "So do you want to go to the CoffeeHouse?"

Mike looked surprised, and I heard a choked-off noise behind me. I ignored both reactions and smiled as widely as I could. Having not practiced this in front of the mirror, though, it could have looked like the joker's grimace.

"Sure." Mike was either baffled by my behavior or intrigued. Either way, he was willing to place himself in my company for at least another hour.

"Great," I heard from behind me. "I'd like a coffee."

I turned then and looked at Noah. "I'll call you tomorrow." I was deeply embarrassed by my actions tonight. I needed to make things right with Mike and then figure out what I was going to do with Noah.

I turned back to Mike and motioned for him to exit the theater. When he didn't move right away, I pushed him slightly and his inertia dropped away.

I don't know where Noah and Bo went, but when Mike and I exited the small theater, they weren't behind us. We began the twenty-minute walk through the heart of the campus to get to the coffee house on the other side.

Summer was refusing to release its hold, and the night air was sultry instead of cool. Tall, wrought iron lampposts lit our way, interspersed with emergency call boxes.

"That's probably the weirdest date I've ever been on," Mike broke the silence as we wandered down the sidewalk bisecting the east and west sides of the campus. "Did you ask me out to make that other guy jealous?"

"No!" I exclaimed and then confessed, "I might have said I thought you were cute, and he thought he was trying to help me out."

"So what was with the hand-holding and snuggling during the movie?"

Had I really been snuggling? "I was having a panic attack, and Noah must have known it. He was just trying to calm me down. I wasn't snuggling. Honest."

Mike shrugged. "I didn't think you were interested, so you kind of surprised me."

It was now or never. I placed a hand on Mike's arm and stopped him. "The situation kind of got out of hand. Noah and I go way back. But I do think you are missing out on someone. Just not me."

"No?" Mike looked adorably confused now.

He hadn't been whipping his hair out of his face for at least ten minutes, which seemed like a new record. When he wasn't in a group, he wasn't insufferably trying to make himself seem more attractive by hitting on every female in a twenty-foot radius. Maybe Sarah spent a lot of time alone with Mike and this was the guy she was attracted to.

"Why aren't you dating anyone, Mike?"

This question clearly caught him off guard, because he stammered before he defensively replied, "I've had hookups."

Ugh, classic Mike response. "So are you only interested in hookups?" I needed to feel him out without throwing Sarah under the bus.

"No," he replied slowly and then swung his hair out of his eyes. "I asked a girl out a few times in my first year, but it didn't go anywhere. Hookups are easier, you know. Less pressure."

I did know. My few college experiences had been drunken make-out sessions with guys equally drunk, but I didn't think anyone truly enjoyed those experiences.

"What about Sarah?" I offered up in what I hoped was nonchalance.

"Who do you think I asked out in my first year?" He laughed but it wasn't a funny sound.

"Really?" I was completely surprised by this. Sarah looked at him so longingly but maybe it was with regret, not unrequited love?

"Wait." Mike caught my arm. "This isn't a bad idea."

"What isn't?" I hadn't proposed anything yet so I wasn't sure what idea he was talking about.

"We can pretend to be interested in each other, and we can make Noah and Sarah jealous at the same time," Mike sounded enthused by this.

"That never actually works out in real life," I pointed out.

"It was just an idea," Mike muttered. We walked a little farther and then he asked, "So what's the story with you and Noah?"

"I haven't had nearly enough to drink to divulge that. How about you and Sarah?"

"She seems to only like me when other girls are into me. If I'm not dating or hooking up with someone, she has zero interest," he said, bummed.

"Sounds like a mess." Was I really thinking I could play Cupid or something? That wasn't in my skill set. This night was officially a disaster. I'd fallen asleep on Noah's shoulder, possibly drooled, and now made Mike go from enthused to sad in five seconds. I was the opposite of Cupid. Instead of shooting love arrows, I shot depression arrows.

"I thought she might have put you up to this," Mike confessed, sounding almost hopeful.

"I wished she had," I replied sullenly, "but instead she gave me the evil eye, so you might want to go to the library tomorrow and strike while the jealousy-iron is hot."

"See, we should carry this on for a while. It'd be good for both of us."

Mike was trying to be encouraging, but I had seen the light. "I have enough dysfunction in my life," I told him.

We were closing in on the CoffeeHouse, but I wasn't in the mood to go there anymore. I wasn't going to orchestrate any big love connection between Mike and Sarah. I wanted to go home. "Do you mind if bail on you?"

"Nah, I might as well go home anyway." We changed course and Mike walked me to my front door, just two blocks away from the Coffee-House. He gave me a big hug. "Thanks for the effort tonight, Sullivan."

After saying goodnight, I slipped inside. It was early yet and the apartment seemed huge and empty. Lana was at her sorority house and might not be back anytime soon. I pulled out my laptop and crawled into bed. Only nineteen and I was already staying home, alone, on a Saturday night. I might as well start my cat collection.

Noah

I'm not sure how being around Grace managed to fuck up my decision-making process so much. I felt like I was pushing the shoot button on my Xbox controller every time I wanted to jump, resulting in stupid, self-inflicted casualties.

Bo had to physically restrain me from following Grace out of the theater. I fought back the urge to tackle her, throw her over my shoulder, and escape through the back exit. I'd take her to my truck and we'd drive to San Diego. Or maybe South Carolina. There had to be someplace within the eight thousand acres of Marine property on Parris Island where I could stash her.

"I think you're supposed to take your girlfriend to an erotic film, not your best male friend," Bo commented. "Unless you're trying to tell me something, in which case I have to tell you that I'm flattered, but I play for the other team."

My only response was to bare my teeth at him. I thrummed my fingers on my jeans while staring after the empty space left by Grace and her "friend" Mike.

"You don't really think she's interested in him, do you?" I turned to Bo.

"Nah. Chick doesn't hold your hand during the entire movie while being into the other guy," Bo assured me.

"But she left with him." Self-doubt was creeping in. Success had no room for self-doubt. I checked myself. Was I starting to sound like a creepy motivational poster?

"I'm thinking you got hit too many times in the head last night," Bo said, gently knocking me in the back of the head and pushing me forward at the same time. "This is Grace. She sent you a care package every month for four years."

That was the mantra I had held onto since getting out. After reading *The Odyssey*, I had convinced myself that Grace was Penelope and would wait for me until I had finished my battles and returned home victorious. Why else would she send me that book?

"It's early yet. Let's go down to Mick's," Bo suggested. Mick's was a seedy bar on the South Side that was frequented by angry townies. It was a good place to get drunk and get in a fight, something Bo enjoyed doing on an all-too-regular basis.

The transition from Marine to civilian hadn't been easy for either of us, but Bo seemed to particularly miss the adrenaline rush of always being in danger. While going to a bar populated by guys hopped up on steroids and nursing a hard-on for Central college kids wasn't exactly the same as being on patrol, it was something.

"You should go put on a polo shirt," I told him, nodding my acceptance of his offer. The T-shirts we had on weren't quite the right look to incite the type of antagonism that would rid us both of pent-up frustration.

"Nah, we'll just hit on one of the girls there, and that should be enough."

Bo was right. Three beers and five numbers later, we were thrown out of the bar for breaking a bar stool and roughing up some town toughs.

"I shouldn't have let the last guy land that blow to my face." I looked in the truck's rear view mirror. My lip had been cut by a punch to the mouth. No mouth guard meant my inner lip was lacerated too.

"No kissing for you tomorrow," Bo said, checking out the bruise that was forming under his right eye.

"I'll tell her that I had to fend off your advances after the movie."

"You wish." He turned and grinned at me.

It wasn't the way that I wanted the night to end, but it was better than sitting in my truck all night behind Grace's apartment.

Bo blew a kiss to the bartender as we peeled away.

Chapter Seven

Dear Grace,

I didn't realize it was the anniversary of your father's death. That had to be hard. My mom died when I was born. I have no memories of her. I guess she was a saint because my father is a jackass. Only a saint could ever spend time with him willingly.

You have to wonder what shitty thing I did in a past life to have my mother die while that mean-ass son of bitch lives. The good really do die young. You certainly see it here all the time. The most rancid, lazy, selfish motherfuckers live through it all, while the guys who care most about their unit step on an IED and die. Sorry for cursing.

We're always told that when they die, they go to a better place. I hope so for all our sakes.

Yours,
Noah

Grace

Every Sunday I worked a six-hour shift at the library. The library was situated in the middle of campus and was one of the more stately buildings, with its wide-tiered steps framed by large, two-story pillars. Its brick facade looked like it had been standing there for at least a century.

Every student at Central had to work ten hours a week somewhere on campus. Nearly all the student jobs allowed you to read or study, so I wasn't sure if this system was designed to create a more egalitarian environment or just force us to do our homework.

During the first hour of my shift, I kept worrying that Noah would show up. I hadn't called like I had promised because I hadn't come to any conclusion about what to do. Noah wanted something with me, and I wasn't so stupid to know it wasn't just friendship, but I hadn't dated anyone before. My feelings for Noah were too strong for a casual relationship, and I had scared him away once before.

Finally too antsy to sit, and hating myself for keeping one eye on the entrance, I asked permission to shelve the returned books. I hadn't even unpacked my camera tonight. My confusion over Noah was becoming all-consuming, and I liked that least of all.

No one really enjoyed shelving, and I was sent on my way with a grateful glance from the girl working the reference desk.

I stuck my earphones in and maneuvered my cart full of books in and out of the rows of shelves, keeping myself busy until I heard the soft chimes warning that the library was closing shortly.

I'm not sure where Noah had been all day, but he was waiting for me on the porch swing of the Victorian when I got home from the library.

He stood as I walked up.

"Stalking me again?" I asked, unable to keep the sarcasm out of my voice. Inwardly I winced.

"No, stalking would've been waiting in the library for the past—" he looked at his watch, "six hours."

"Why are you here?" I asked, allowing him to lead me over to the swing. He took my messenger bag from my shoulder and placed it on the floor, urging me to sit down.

I sat. He gave the swing a little shove with his feet and we swayed gently.

"I think we just need to get to know each other again." His voice was steady and clear in the night air. I felt like Jell-O on the inside.

I refrained from pointing out the obvious. You couldn't read nearly forty letters from someone and not get to know them a little.

I ran my eyes over his face, trying to read some expression, and noticed his lower lip was scabbed. My hand was up and hovering like I could make it better with a touch. "Ouch," I said.

"Yeah, it only hurts when I smile or laugh."

"Or kiss," I added, and then mentally kicked myself.

"The person I want to kiss isn't really feeling me right now," he half-joked. His eyes were warm, and I knew I was courting danger here. The old Noah wound healed up over the last year, and now I was threatening to slash it open and pour salt all over it.

I started to draw my hand back, but Noah grabbed it and pressed it against his lips. I could feel the ridge of his scab, a hard contrast to the soft portions of his lips. Against my will, I rubbed my fingers across the uninjured parts. That tiny touch had set up a riot in my stomach like a battalion of butterflies was trying to beat its way out. I didn't heal him with my touch, but from the softening of his lips I could tell he liked it. I stroked him slowly and his mouth parted. His breath felt hot against my fingers, and I felt something coil inside me in response.

"I'm really glad to see you made it home safe and sound," I admitted. My words sounded breathless. I had prayed so hard for that outcome. Even when he hadn't wanted me, I was so happy that he was alive and unharmed.

"I missed you, Grace. More than you will ever know."

He smelled delicious again. I wanted to press my nose into the well of his throat and breathe deep, imprinting his smell onto my memory banks. It would make my nighttime fantasies slightly more real and vivid. I forced myself to drop my hand.

"I—" I cast around for the right words to say. I wanted to explain myself in a way that still preserved my pride but conveyed I wasn't a toy to be discarded and then picked up whenever he felt like playing with it again. "If you truly want to be friends, Noah, I can do that. But nothing else."

His face remained unchanged, which made me falter. Maybe he did just want to be friends, and I had misread the entire situation. I gave him an uncertain smile and said, "I'll see you around campus then?"

"Don't friends hang out?"

I nodded my head. Yes, but we weren't really friends. We were some weird, undefined category where we had some shared intimacy, yet were not in a real relationship.

"How about we study together at the library on Wednesday?" Noah offered.

I shrank back, tears at the back of my throat. I was right to be cautious. He wanted to just be friends, like his kiss-off letter said. He had referred to me as a little sister. I cleared my throat to make sure I sounded as easy going as he did. "Sure. I have Stats & Methodology that day, and I always need to review my notes after that class. Meet you there."

I stood up then and walked to the door that led up to my third floor apartment. When I looked back to wave, Noah was standing there with one hand on the back of his neck and the other at his hip. He looked frustrated, managed a slight smile, and then nodded in return. I went upstairs, as confused as I had ever been.

***

I had three classes on Mondays, Wednesdays, and Fridays. They started at 8:00 a.m. and ended right after noon. I usually met Lana for lunch at the Quad Commons Café, the one place Amy says we should never eat. Lana rarely got up before eleven and scheduled all of her classes in the afternoon. Lunch was about the only meal we shared together on a regular basis, and it was usually the first of the day for her.

We had two choices on campus. The dining hall, which served a variety of cafeteria food, along with a salad and dessert bar, or the Quad Commons Café, where you could get deli sandwiches and light grilled items. On Tuesdays, we would meet at the dining hall, because they had

Taco Tuesdays, but most days we met and had big prepared salads from the QC Café.

Lana had already purchased everything and was sitting at a table unwrapping her salad.

She was wearing sunglasses, which I tipped down when I arrived at the table. She allowed me to see her swollen eyes before pushing the glasses up and waving me to my seat.

"Peter?" I queried. She mhmm'ed and I waited. She pulled out her phone and showed me a picture of some blonde in front of a mirror, wearing tiny panties and her shirt pushed above her bare breasts. They were rather large and obviously fake. Not Lana.

"You're getting hit on by a stripper?" I guessed. Lana made a buzzing sound.

"Wrong. Peter forwarded me this charming selfie."

"Intentionally?" I gasped in horror.

"No, I think he meant to send it to Luke Larson, his frat brother, but the phone auto-filled 'Lana' instead," she explained in a careful monotone, as if any expression of emotion might break a dam she'd built.

"Done in by autocorrect." I handed her back the phone. I wanted to delete the photo. It wouldn't do any good for Lana to keep it on her phone. "What did you do?"

"I replied back 'nice rack.' He called me immediately asking what I was talking about. He tried to say that it wasn't anything, just a pledge prank. The lies were so weak that I figured he wanted to get caught, forcing me to be the one to break up with him."

"Did you?"

"I didn't give him the satisfaction. He wants to break up to pursue other girls, then he needs to man up and do it. I'm not going to make it easier for him." Lana picked up her fork and started rearranging spinach leaves. Her disinterest in eating worried me, but it was only one day.

"I'm surprised you shed any tears over him."

"Oh, closure, you know." She gave an uncaring wave of her hand, but her actions revealed that she liked him more than she had let on. Sometimes it was hard to know where you stood with Lana. She was too busy protecting herself. If you weren't persistent, she never let you in. Even I found Lana hard to read, despite living with her since I was twelve. But I knew her tough exterior hid a very big heart. We may be cousins by blood, but we were sisters of the heart.

"We Sullivans are bad at relationships," I informed her. "You and I need to start following Josh's playbook." Josh didn't date. He hooked up exclusively. Currently, he seemed to be trying to burn his way through the female population up at State.

"Of course we are," Lana said. "We're merely exhibiting patterned behavior learned at an impressionable age. We don't know anyone who has a healthy and loving relationship, so we are unequipped to develop our own."

"So essentially we are doomed," I said wryly. Lana's parents were married, but Uncle Louis was hardly ever home, too busy golfing or out on his boat. I guess I understood because no one liked being around Lana's mom. She was mean to everyone but hardest on Lana, constantly criticizing everything about her. Lana wasn't ever thin enough. Her blonde hair had too much brown in it. Her grades weren't good enough. She didn't speak well enough. It was amazing that the eating disorder was the only thing Lana developed.

She shrugged and moved a few more pieces of food around her bowl. Not one piece had made it to her mouth yet.

"Do you ever think part of our problem, Lana, is that we spend more time talking about boys than anything else? How is this different than high school?"

"The guys are better looking?" Lana asked, more of a statement than a question. "When we were in high school, you never talked about boys."

"I didn't?" I thought back to our many discussions, and they all seemed devoted to who was dating whom. If only we got tested on the social status and habits of our classmates. I'd have aced that test.

"Nope. It was always Noah for you. You weren't interested in anyone else. It's no wonder that the real Noah is screwing up your head big time."

"Do you think I shouldn't spend time with him?" She hadn't said a word of warning, and I had been waiting for one or a dozen.

"No, actually I think spending time with him is a good idea. It's like the pictures you take in rooms with too much light."

"Overexposure?"

"Right. It will show you how real and flawed he is, and then, when he dicks you over again, you will finally give up on this fantasy and move into the real world."

"Ouch," I said. I knew Lana was hurting, but I didn't need to be a passive punching bag.

"I'm not trying to be mean here."

"No?" I loved Lana but she had a little of her mother in her, and sometimes, when she was hurt and angry, it leaked out. I braced myself.

"No. It's just that…" she paused to look up from her food, "…it's easier to have a relationship with someone who isn't there than someone who is."

"How did this discussion become all about me?"

"Because it's easier for me to talk about fixing you than fixing myself," Lana admitted.

"All right. If subjecting myself to your amateur psychoanalysis is going to make you feel better, get it out," I motioned for to continue. "Just eat a few cucumber slices between criticisms, please." Lana made a face but took a whole mouthful of food. After she had swallowed, she deliberately wiped her mouth with her napkin before continuing.

"You haven't picked a major because you're afraid to commit to any-thing. You won't take classes at the FAC because you're afraid to admit how much you love photography. You won't date. You've only had a few hookups and with guys you don't even really like. They are safe for you."

I felt like I was being dissected right there on the QC Café table. I was cut open from throat to stomach, and all my insides were laid bare. I looked around to see who was staring at the trainwreck happening at my table, but the crowd was oblivious to how Lana was wielding her psychological scalpel.

I wanted to place my hand over her mouth and tell her to be quiet.

"I'm the same way," Lana admitted. "I keep picking guys who are bad bets because they do what I expect them to do: screw me over. That way, it's never my fault when the relationship fails."

"I'm not sure what the practical application of your discoveries is," I said, hurting for both of us. I wished I could make our lives as bright, colorful, and delightful as my tilt shift photographs.

"Well, if I knew that bit of information, I wouldn't have to go to school for six more years to be a licensed psychologist, would I?" Lana said.

"Thanks for nothing. I'm supposed to meet Noah at the library to study."

She shrugged. "It's all part of the desensitization plan. More time spent with the real Noah will inevitably result in disappointment and then cure."

We spent the rest of the lunch eating in silence. Apparently Lana's analysis of me made her hungry. I guess I could suffer through some hard truths if it meant Lana would stay healthy.

***

Noah was waiting at the library entrance, his backpack slung over one arm. Cecilia, a tattooed pixie of a girl, was languidly waving people in. I wondered if she lived there, given how often she was in that chair. She definitely exceeded the ten hours of mandatory service.

"Hey, Grace."

"Noah." I realized I was more than a little frustrated with him. He was making me confused and off balance with his determined pursuit but talk of friends only.

"How was your Stats and Methodology course this morning?" Noah asked. I was surprised he remembered but then he knew my entire schedule.

"I didn't realize that there was so much math involved in psychology," I told him.

"It is a science course."

"I know, and apparently there is a lot of statistical analysis of raw data and stuff. I think I need a degree that has no math."

"English literature," Noah said.

I grimaced. That sounded almost more painful that math. "Do you have an answer for everything?" I asked. There was no heat in my question, and I knew the response; he held himself with such utter confidence.

"Yes," he replied, but gave me a wry grin to signal I wasn't to take the answer seriously.

"Do you have a place here you like to read?" Noah asked me.

I did, but I wasn't ready to share it with Noah. It was a retreat. "Not really. You?" I asked.

"Definitely." He took my hand. "Follow me."

I let Noah lead me through the library. He seemed to know several people, bumping fists, nodding his head, and giving hearty pats on the shoulder to guys that would've left a bruise on me. Given that this was Noah's first year here, the breadth of his acquaintances surprised me, but maybe some of these guys had been to his house or one of his fights.

He led me to a reference section that housed architectural and design books. I rarely came up onto the third floor. It was usually noisy and occupied by students there to socialize rather than study because there was a lounge area with four upholstered chairs and two short sofas arranged into a cozy square. A guy with short reddish-blonde hair, wearing jeans and a white cotton button down, was already sitting there, with a huge stack of books and a contraband cup of coffee. He looked up as we approached.

"What took you so long?" He stood and slapped the back of his hand against the back of Noah's. "Who's this?"

"Grace, meet Finn. He's one of my roommates."

"Nice to meet you," I said. Noah still hadn't released me, and I could only do an awkward wave with my left hand. Noah drew me down on one of the sofas next to him.

I settled in next to Noah and pulled out my psychology book. Noah grabbed his laptop, crossed one foot over the opposite leg and stretched out his arm on the back of the sofa, which was so short that his fingers were right behind my hair again. I wondered if the ends of my hair were seeking out his fingers, like little sentient beings searching for warmth. I wanted to lean back and rest my head against his hand. I remembered the comforting weight of it as we had walked to the diner and the sure strength when he had massaged my neck at the Delt house. Lana's theory about overexposure wasn't working. I tried to focus on something other than my growing physical response to his presence.

"What're you studying?" I asked Noah.

He grimaced. "My CFA Level One."

At my look of mystification, he elaborated, "It's a finance certification exam with three levels. My first one is in December. When I pass, my next one is in June, and the third is in the following year."

"Noah's a finance whiz," Finn interjected, taking a sip of his contraband liquid. He looked at ease, like he had sat in the chair a hundred times before.

"Finn, are you a student?" I asked. I didn't recognize him, but he might be an upperclassman.

"Nope, just looking at stuff."

"Finn's a house flipper," Noah explained. "But really, he's a frustrated wannabe architect."

"Noah's only partially correct," Finn said. "I look through these design books to get ideas on how to make our houses more interesting for buyers. You don't happen to have your real estate license, do you?"

I shook my head.

"One of our roommates dated my last realtor, and now she won't talk to me," Finn said glumly. "I hate the realtor side of flipping."

"I don't know anything about real estate. I didn't even know you had to have a license." I admitted.

They didn't ask me any more questions, and we all settled in to study. A few minutes into reading, I felt Noah's fingers combing through the ends of my hair. I wasn't sure if he was doing it absently or on purpose, but it was distracting. My physical interactions with other guys may have been limited, but I knew friends didn't stroke each other's hair. The hairs of my neck stood up and I felt goose pimples rise on my neck and chase down my arms. Noah noticed my little shiver and pulled out a sweatshirt from his backpack, offering it to me.

Shrugging it on, I tried not to be too obvious about sniffing the fabric. The clean, spring scent that I had associated with Noah floated around me, interfering with my ability to focus on my pages. It took a masterful effort to shut out all the Noah influences and read.

We had all been silent for some time when Finn stood up and said, "I'm hungry. Let's go eat." He stretched and his T-shirt rode up, showing some nice solid abs. Did all the guys in Noah's house do a thirty-minute ab routine? Was that a prerequisite? Like on the application, it asked if you had a steady job, could afford the rent, and oh, by the way, can you do one hundred sit ups in one minute?

"Hey, eyes up here," Finn said, teasing me. I tried to beat back the blush that I could feel heating my cheeks. I wasn't even ogling him. His shirt had pulled up and I couldn't help noticing. Finn had dark markings under his shirt, a tattoo of something winged.

"Wear longer shirts," I said, but my attention had fixated on Noah. I hadn't seen him without his shirt off, and his arms were bare of any ink. I wondered if he had tattoos somewhere that I hadn't yet seen.

"Ooh, I'm being disrespected because of how I'm dressed," Finn said, interrupting my fantasies of Noah disrobing.

"Knock it off," Noah shook his head with mild impatience. "I thought you were hungry." He picked up his books and stuffed them in his backpack. Then he grabbed mine and held it open. I looked at him in confusion, and he shook the bag. Apparently he was going to hold it open while I put everything in.

Noah zipped up my backpack when I was done and took both bags, slinging them over his shoulder. He gestured for me to walk in front of him and they filed in behind me.

"Where do you want to eat?" Noah asked Finn.

"I've got Bo's card," Finn replied. "We can eat on campus."

"That okay with you, Grace?" Noah asked.

I nodded. All this time spent with Noah was going to go to my head. I knew I should probably head home, but I wasn't sure how I'd be able to pull my backpack off Noah's shoulder. We walked down the stairs, and, as we were headed to the doors of the library, I saw Mike standing behind the reference desk. He stared at me with raised eyebrows, and I gave him a little wave. I didn't have an explanation for Mike about Noah and me because I couldn't define the relationship myself.

Outside, Noah walked beside me, and Finn walked backwards, facing us. "What's your superpower?" he asked me.

"My super-what?"

"Your superpower," Noah said, smirking. "This is how Finn determines whether he can hang out with you. He classifies people according to their response."

"Wow, that's a lot of pressure," I said. Rearranging my face so it looked like I was deep in thought, I pretended to contemplate the question and then answered, "Invisibility."

"Not X-ray vision?" Finn teased, I guess referring to my faux pas of staring at his exposed abdomen.

"What's the point? You're already walking around flaunting yourself," I shot back. It was easy to engage in conversation with Finn. There weren't any emotional stakes. "Anyway, what about you?"

"Flying," both of them said in unison and then high fived.

"Really? Flying?" I asked. "Invisibility is so much cooler."

"It's not bad," Noah conceded. "But the ability to fly is the best superpower ever. Why do you think Iron Man's suit has rockets?"

"Iron Man's suit has everything."

"Spiderman wishes he could fly. It's what puts the Super in Superman," Finn declared.

We then debated the value of various super powers. Apparently my chosen superpower passed Finn's internal test because I wasn't told to go home.

When we arrived at the QC Café, I realized I was pretty hungry. Instead of pretending that I loved lettuce, I followed Noah to the grill. I ordered a burger, assuming he would too, except Noah didn't order a burger. He ordered a plain grilled chicken breast and even asked for extra vegetables. Finn detoured to another part of the café altogether, but we met at the check-out line.

"What is that plate of food?" Noah asked Finn as we paid. It was clear from Noah's expression he was offended by Finn's selection.

"I think it's cheesy tamales," Finn replied. "Not all of us have to maintain our girlish figures."

"Get your food, you clown," Noah replied, shaking his head a little, and giving Finn's tray a little push. Noah led us to a table on the far side against windows overlooking the North lawn and residence halls. The Café wasn't very full, as it was still fairly early. We sat down and spread out our trays and set to eating.

I decided that eating a burger in front of Noah was right up there with trying to manage spaghetti. Only dogs in cartoons looked good eating spaghetti. Ditto with hamburgers. Eating a hamburger wasn't sexy, but I also feared that using a fork and knife would be ridiculous. I sighed internally. Who cared about sexy? *Friends didn't worry about being sexy*, I lectured myself. I ate my hamburger and made liberal use of my napkin.

"How are your cheesy tamales?" I asked Finn.

"Terrible," he admitted with a chagrined smile. "But probably more flavorful than the cardboard Jackson's eating right now."

"Jackson's insides are shriveling at the thought of eating your mystery plate," Noah replied.

"Then stay away, because you really can't handle more shriveling, or someone might mistake you for a girl."

"Your sister had no complaints last night."

"That would actually be an insult if I had a sister, but I'm not surprised your little brain couldn't form a better insult. Small brain, small—" Finn wiggled his eyebrows.

The two continued to exchange insults, each more vile than the last.

Noah seemed in no hurry to leave after he'd eaten his food. He got another drink and returned, moving his chair so it was farther away from the table. The rearrangement of his chair put him closer to me, and he slung his arm across the back of my chair and stretched out his legs.

"I'm running on campus in the morning, want to have breakfast afterward?" he asked me.

Before I could answer, Finn interjected, "Did you know that Noah and Bo can run for 12 miles with packs weighing 150 pounds, while simultaneously doing jumping jacks and shooting guns, all before the sun rises?"

Finn must not know that Noah and I corresponded for four years while Noah was a deployed Marine.

"She knows," Noah replied before I could respond. "Grace and I were, ah, friends, while I was deployed."

"Oh, you from Texas too?" Finn asked.

"No. From Chicago. I wrote to Noah as part of a class project."

Finn looked from Noah to me and back again. "What year are you?"

"Sophomore. And no, before you ask, I don't have a major."

"That makes you nineteen?" Finn hooted. "I think you are too old for her, old man."

"Is that true?" Noah asked, looking at me. "Am I too old for you?"

"What?" I tried to laugh but it sound like a nervous giggle. "Of course you aren't too old to be my friend."

Noah made a noise like a hum at the back of his throat. I wished for Lana's perception skills. They were almost like a super power in my estimation. I would've given anything to know what that noise meant. Finn thankfully made no comment.

A guy I didn't know came over and clapped Noah on the back of the shoulder hard enough that Noah almost spilled his drink on me. "Jackass," I heard Noah say under his breath, and I swallowed a smile.

"Braaaa," the guy brayed like a donkey. His shirt, emblazoned with three Greek letters, looked stylishly faded, and he wore loud plaid shorts and flip flops. Noah knocked the fraternity guy's fist and received a slap on the upper arm in return. I wondered if learning to shorten every word to three letters was part of the secret rituals that took place on Greek Street during pledge week.

"Marco," Noah replied in greeting.

"I hear you all are having a little get together on Friday to welcome back the ladies. Any chance of an invite?" Marco said.

"First I've heard of it," Noah responded, a non-answer to Marco's query.

"Let me know, and I'll help you tag the hot frosh buns." He laughed at his own terrible joke and moved to sit down at the empty chair at our table. Noah must have thought that the guy would talk to us all evening if we stayed, so he stood up and said, "We've got to run. Nice seeing you, Marco."

"Yeah, man, I will see you around campus." Marco turned to Finn and added, "And Finnster, man, we will see you at your party."

"Indeed," Finn intoned and picked up his tray.

Noah grabbed our backpacks and slung them over his shoulders, so I picked up both trays and his cups and made toward the clean-up conveyor belt. I thought for a minute that Noah would fight me for them, but I raised an eyebrow at him and he backed away.

"You know," I said to Noah, "I can carry my own books."

"I'm sure you can," came his laconic reply, "but why should you?"

I didn't have a non-confrontational answer. I wondered if friends were invited to parties, but neither Finn nor Noah brought it up again. They walked me to my apartment, where Noah finally handed over my bag and said he'd see me in the morning.

Noah

"Could it have killed you to give us a minute of privacy?" I groused as we walked to campus parking, where I had left the truck.

"Yes, actually," Finn replied. "After hearing from Bo how inept the great Noah Jackson is with this girl, I had to stick around."

"I hope we put on a good show for you."

"Nope. I kept waiting for you to put your big-ass foot in your mouth. Sadly, nothing," Finn let out a loud belch.

"Goddamn, that reeks," We stopped at the truck and I made Finn stand outside for a good minute before I unlocked the doors. "I told you not to eat anything that they smother in cheese at the dining hall," I said after we had finally gotten into the cab.

Finn responded with another, smaller belch. I rolled down the windows.

"Are we having a party this weekend?" I asked Finn.

"Why not?"

"Just wondered when this was decided. But whatever, I'm on board." I tapped my fingers absently against the steering wheel. Getting Grace in my own territory might be a good way to move our tentative dance from one between friends to more. I didn't like the idea of her going to fraternity parties looking for something I could and wanted to provide. Whatever that was.

"Post-party hookups can be dangerous," Finn warned.

"Sure, but I need to get her in my territory and away from campus."

"Isolate your prey and lure her into your cave? Does that work?" Finn asked.

"We'll see on Saturday night."

Chapter Eight

Dear Grace,

We aren't supposed to be sent out on a raid again for thirty-six hours. I'm not holding my breath. The base has a bunch of new Air Force personnel. Bo tells me that the Air Force girls are better-looking than in any other branch of the Armed Services, and so he has left me to my letter-writing. He'd know. I think he's tried them all out.

Tonight, after I finish this letter to reassure you that I'm just fine but worn out, I plan to lie down in my bed and read the book you sent me. The Odyssey? I know you think I'm doing heroic deeds, but I'm not. Or if I am, they are the same things being done by millions of other soldiers from around the world.

I'm ready to be done with this deployment. And Sgt., if you are reading this, I mean that I'm excited for this deployment to be done so I can re-up. (Not really, Grace, but just in case.)

Yours,

Noah

Grace

I didn't see much of Noah after breakfast, which ended up being a hurried and unsatisfying affair given that Noah had to run off to do something. Mike had me reshelving books for the first hour, and during the second, I sorted through old journals that would be sent out to be bound. Finally, I was told to go to the reference desk where Mike was still working.

"So you dating Jackson now?" Mike asked me, almost before I could sit down.

"No, we're just friends. Why do you ask?" I said, trying to keep the moroseness out of my voice.

Mike shrugged. "Saw you holding hands the other day."

"Oh, he just drags people around if they don't walk fast enough."

"Have you been to one of Noah's fights?" Mike asked in his gossip reporter voice.

Mike wasn't looking at me. He was throwing his red ball up in the air. I grabbed at it on its way down. "Hey, I was playing with that," Mike yelped, but settled back in his chair when he saw me glaring at him.

"Tell me about the fight," I encouraged.

"It's mixed martial arts. They use their—"

"Hands and feet. I know. They fight in an Octagon. Josh loves that stuff. Tell me about Noah's fight," I ordered impatiently.

"It wasn't a sanctioned fight, and they held it in some warehouse downtown this summer. I couldn't see very well, but I heard he broke some guy's eye socket in three places," Mike said excitedly.

I couldn't reconcile the picture of Noah pummeling someone's face into tenderized meat with the guy who opened doors for me and carried my backpack.

"So he's never brought it up?" Mike asked, curiosity coloring his voice.

"No, not a word." If I sounded disgruntled, who could blame me? I felt like I was supposed to know him better than anyone, but here was Mike, a stranger to Noah, who knew secret things about him that I didn't.

"Weird," Mike replied. "It'd be the first thing I would bring up if I was hitting on a girl. He's like a mini-celebrity in town. I was here over the summer, and when he walked into The Circus, the DJ announced him." The Circus was one of a couple dance clubs downtown. I didn't ordinarily go there because it required someone to be the designated driver, and I hate driving.

"There isn't anything going on between us," I insisted and tossed Mike's ball back to him.

Bothered by Noah's silence on the subject of his fighting, I turned away from Mike and picked up my book. After a few seconds of fruitless reading, I asked, "Mike, when did you pick your major?"

"Sophomore year. I took French Revolutionary History because I didn't want to have any Friday classes, and it was the only one that worked out with my schedule. I ended up getting hooked on history."

"What are you going to do with a degree in history though?"

"Teach, I guess. I'm going to grad school, and then I'll do my doctoral dissertation on peasant munitions during the 18th century."

"All that from one class?" I gaped at him.

"Yup. Are you worried you haven't picked a major yet?" he asked, tossing the ball toward me.

"Kind of. My Uncle Louis, who pays for this gig here, told me I had to have a major picked out by Thanksgiving or else," I said and threw back the ball.

"What's the 'or else?'"

"Dunno. I'm not sure I want to find out."

"Are there any classes you're taking this semester that you enjoy a lot?" Mike asked.

"No. I kind of dislike them all," I confessed.

"Brutal," Mike said tossing me the ball. I fumbled it a little but managed to hold on. "What about your pictures?"

I groaned, "Taking pictures is a hobby, not a vocation."

Mike moved back several paces and motioned for me to throw him the ball again. "Okay, then, what about being a reference librarian?"

"Because look at us. I don't want to throw a little red ball around all day in between shelving and sorting journals," I whined.

Mike just laughed. "I don't think real librarians spend all day throwing balls around."

"I guess I just feel no passion for this. What if I committed to it and then it didn't work out?" I had to stop myself before I sounded like I was a whiny six-year-old.

"So you do something else, then," This time, when he threw me the ball, the velocity had increased, and I missed it. The ball went sailing over the brick half-wall and into the common area below. We both rushed over to see where it had landed.

Noah was holding it and looking up.

"Nice catch," I said weakly. Mike and I both pushed off and went back to our chairs.

"At least we didn't break anything," Mike said, rooting around in his bag.

"What are you looking for?"

"Something else to throw." He brought out a power bar. "How about this?"

"Mike, seriously. A power bar?" I shook my head.

"What?" He looked at it and then shrugged and ripped it open. "Want a bite?"

Why not? He held the bar out, and I took a small bite. "My God," I said, spitting the pieces into my hand. "That's like cardboard chopped up and glued together with raisins!"

He took a bite and said, "Mmm, delicious."

"I'm going to read now, you fool." I pushed his chair with my foot and he rolled about five feet away, chewing on his cardboard bar.

Finally determined to focus on my book, I heard someone clearing his throat and looked up to see Noah standing there, a grim look on his face.

Noah

Had I completely misjudged the two of them? I thought that Grace had less-than-zero interest in this guy, but here they were playing games and eating food together.

"Hey Noah," Grace looked a little flushed. Was she turned on by this guy? Embarrassed I had seen her eating his power bar? I couldn't read her face.

"Hey," My greeting came out shorter and curter than I wanted. She looked down at my hands fisted on the counter. I forcibly made myself relax and spread my fingers out. *See*, I tried to convey, *I'm harmless.*

"Um, something wrong?"

Yeah, I thought. You're eating food from some other guy's hand. Some guy you said you were interested in. But Grace had pushed the friend thing pretty hard yesterday. I didn't want to crash and burn in front of this guy in case there was anything remotely going on between the two of them. Never appear weak in front of the enemy.

"Do you have a minute?" I wanted to talk to her alone. Separate and isolate the target. She looked over at Mike, who waved her away.

"I can handle this," Mike said.

Grace grabbed her cell phone and walked down the long counter to the exit. I followed her. "Where to?" I asked.

She walked toward the stairs and up to the first landing. There was a door there, but I had never opened it. I always assumed it would be locked, but Grace opened the door without a key and stepped inside. I followed.

"What is this place?" There were ordinary light bulbs instead of the hard fluorescents that lit the main library, and row upon row of metal shelves, some empty and some full. The place smelled old and looked abandoned.

"It's the stacks. Old books out of circulation are put in here," Grace said softly.

She walked down a small pathway until I saw a metal desk set into a nook. There were two lamps and two rolling chairs. The chairs looked like the ones in the study carrels. I raised a questioning brow toward her.

"The library crew sometimes studies in here during finals or midterms. It's super quiet, and no one else ever comes in here."

Studying is likely the last thing I would do in a place like this. For college kids, this is an ideal place to have semi-public sex. I wondered how many people had done the deed in here, and I wondered if Grace was one of them. I corralled my thoughts before I got too worked up. Imagining Grace having sex on these chairs or the desk with someone other than me would be unproductive. I liked to envision her as untouched, although that was highly unlikely. She was too pretty, too smart, and too interesting to have not dated or at least had a few hookups. Either that or all the guys at Central were blind and dumb. I'd like the latter to be true, but I wasn't placing any money on it.

Grace sat down and motioned for me to sit across from her.

"We're having a party this weekend. I want you to come," I told her without preamble.

"I can't. Josh has a home game, and he arranged for me to come take some pictures." Her response came quickly, as if turning me down didn't require much thought.

My plans for the party instantly changed. The guys could host it without me. It's not like they included me in the planning stage anyway. Maybe I should've waited for an invitation, but you make your own opportunities.

"Can I give you a ride? I wouldn't mind seeing State play."

She nibbled on her lip. This time I did wait for a response. I needed assent here. I couldn't really just show up at her apartment and throw her into the cab of my truck. Or could I? Even for me, that might be a touch too controlling.

I tried to look as non-threatening as possible while inwardly urging her to cave. Having her to myself in a vehicle for several hours, schmoozing her brother, and staying overnight with her someplace was better than bringing her to a loud, out-of-control party. I'd even honestly answer the "Have you killed anyone?" question that every civilian asks a returned soldier instead of my usual smart-ass response of "not tonight, but it's still early."

"No," she said finally. "I've got a ride." She didn't look at me. Her eyes were aimed at my hands, which were clenched together between my legs. Clenched together so I wouldn't drag her onto my lap and force her to acknowledge that what had built between us for four years just needed some physical manifestation to make it all real and permanent.

"Who?" I asked, as if I had the right to know. If it was Mike, I was going to go out there and make it physically impossible for him to walk for three days, let alone drive a couple hundred miles.

"Don't know. Friends of someone who knows Josh, I guess. He arranged it."

I couldn't believe this. She was going off with some strangers in their car? "How do you know that they aren't going to try and make a skinsuit out of you?"

"Um, because they are Central students." She looked at me as if I was insane. Maybe I was. Being near Grace and not having her was turning me inside out. "I'm pretty sure Josh wouldn't send me off with a couple of 'Natural Born Killers,' but I promise that if one of them looks even remotely like Woody Harrelson, I won't get in the car with them on Saturday."

She patted my leg like I was five. I wasn't going to be able to see her until she got back from the game on Sunday, then. Thursday night I was scheduled to meet with some scouts from a fight management team who were going to watch me spar a guy from a neighboring gym on Friday. There was a lot of potential money riding on the outcome of this week, and I couldn't afford a Grace-like distraction in the gym.

"I should get back," Grace said and stood up. I followed her out of the stacks. I cast around for some excuse to see her before she left.

"Hey, do you mind if I use your shower in the morning? I want to run on campus before classes."

Grace turned to me with a skeptical look on her face. "Why not just use the locker room?"

"Grace, do you shower in the locker room at the Phys Ed Center?"

She made a face and conceded my point. "Sure, I guess. That's what friends are for, right?"

"Right. When are you done?" As soon as we're done here, I'd go and find the dictionaries and start defacing the word "friend." I hated it and worse, I was the first to use it. I felt like I was getting slapped in the face with that stupid, shit-ass letter I wrote two years ago. Should I just come out and admit what a fuck-up I was? The whole point of waiting to come and see Grace was to present a non-fucked up version of myself.

"I close." Her face was down. I couldn't see what she was feeling. I wished I was better at reading people or, really, just at reading Grace. Instead, I nutted up and said, "Cool. I'm going upstairs to study, and then I'll come down at closing and walk you home." We were almost back to the reference desk by then.

"No need, man," Mike called. "I'm closing, too, so I can walk Grace home." *Like hell you will.*

"I need to walk Grace home," I said slowly. "To drop off the clothes I'm going to be storing in her closet." Mike's mouth opened as if to say something, then it closed. Yeah, what could he say to that? Grace turned to me, beet red, her mouth slightly open as if she was shocked. Did she really care if this guy thought we were sleeping together? I didn't. I wanted him to spread the word far and wide so that no one else would think it was okay to hit on her.

Grace turned toward Mike. "Oh, Noah just keeps clothes in my closet so he doesn't have to drag around the extra change of clothing he needs after he's done showering." I hid a smile. That was a poor-ass explanation if she was trying to make it seem like we were just friends.

"So," I said, turning back to Grace and dismissing Mike. "I'll come down when the library closes. If you have a break, I'll be in the same place where we studied before."

Grace just nodded, and I reluctantly left her. I heard Mike say, "I thought you were just friends."

Her response was, "It's a long story." One she hadn't shared with Mike.

When I came down after the warning bell sounded, Mike was gone, and Grace was alone. On the walk toward her apartment, I asked, "Is that guy hassling you?"

"Mike?" she asked, looking confused. "No, not at all."

I was unconvinced. "He seems like a punk."

"A what?!" she laughed.

"Am I going to have to take him out back and teach him some respect?" It was more of a literal question than a hypothetical one.

"Mike's a good guy. There are a lot of girls who work there, and I think he just feels responsible, like a dad."

"Or a lecher." Dad, my ass. Mike probably stroked one off every night he worked with Grace. That's what I'd do. After nearly an hour of unproductive studying, I had decided that I was going to play it straight with Grace. No more of this friend shit. I was going to mark my place in her life, and she'd come around.

She smiled. "Lecher? That's very 1800s of you, Mr. Jackson." My new tactic seemed to be paying off. Grace was flirting with me. I returned her smile with one of my own.

"Punk didn't seem to break through for you so I'm trying different descriptive terms until I find one that sticks."

"I like 'lecher,'" she said, holding her hands behind her back. "It's got a certain resonance. Do you really have clothes to drop off?"

"Nah," I said. "I'll bring those in the morning. I just wanted to make sure Mike got my message."

"What message was that?" she asked with what sounded like a little giddiness in her voice. She might protest that we were just friends, but I was starting to think she liked my show of possessiveness. I'd try to keep to only small doses until I built up her tolerance for me.

"That if you need company on your way home, it'll be me," I said firmly. It wasn't exactly like I was peeing on her leg, but kind of. While she was going off this weekend without me, I felt like we were turning a corner to someplace better. Hopefully a place that had a bed and lots of nudity.

Chapter Nine

Dear Grace,

I think what you feel on my letters is dust. I'm bummed that it is on my letters to you. They say it's sand, but it's finer than that. It's like the particles that make up the sand, and it is everywhere. When you get home on leave and wash for the first time, you have to stand under the water for at least twenty minutes, all the while watching the black dust collect and pool at your feet, creating coffee-colored water that swirls down the drain.

I don't think you can ever fully erase the dust from your belongings. It sticks with you no matter how long you let the water wash over you or how many times you wipe it away. Like the tension I have in being weaponless and exposed back home, the dust is one of the many things I'll carry with me when I'm out.

I'm sorry that it is invading your space now through my letters. It's like I'm spreading a contaminant. Am I Patient Zero, or are you?

I probably shouldn't have volunteered for a third tour, but combat pay is hard to turn down. After three years here, though, I feel like I am a loosely contained conglomerate of those particles of dust.

Yours,
Noah

Grace

I got a text that my ride would arrive in fifteen minutes. I rushed around and threw together a change of clothing and toiletries, which I stuffed into a backpack that wasn't full of my camera equipment. I pulled on a pair of jeans, flats, and my State T-shirt. Over that, I wore a State replica jersey that had my brother's name and number ironed on the back. I wrote a quick note for Lana:

Off to see Josh play today. Won't be back until tomorrow. ~ G

My ride was a couple. They had agreed to drive me in exchange for tickets to the game. I wasn't sure if they were Josh's tickets or someone else's. The girl told me she was hung over and planned to sleep the entire ride, which sounded like a pretty awesome plan to me. Alone in the back seat, I closed my eyes and was out before the car even left the city limits.

Once we got there, they dropped me off at the gate and went to park.

Not a skin suit yet, I texted impulsively to Noah. I almost wished I had taken him up on his invitation to come with me.

I received an immediate response. *They could be saving their gruesome acts until the ride home.*

I took a picture of their license plate. *You know what to do if I don't show up at the library on Sunday.* I sent Noah the picture I had taken.

Don't mock me. Rather have a pic of you.

Like Lana, I had my own insecurities about my body and preferred to be on the other side of the camera. The lens side.

Can't. Never learned how to take selfie.

Noah replied with a picture of Finn and Bo wrestling a keg into place in what must be Noah's backyard. *Party won't be good without you.*

Are you camera shy too?

Nah, just withholding the good stuff 'til I see you.

Absence makes the heart grow fonder?

If that's true, I expect a really warm welcome when you get back tomorrow.

We were flirting. Even a dunderhead like me could pick that up. Giddiness spread through my body, and, while I missed Noah, I realized that I needed this. This small separation reminded me of what it was like when Noah had sent me that Dear Jane letter telling me we should just be friends. I remembered how empty I had felt after that letter, an emptiness that Noah filled when I saw him again on campus. It was easy to be prickly within his steady presence, but now that we were away once more, I realized how much I wanted to be with him.

When I got back, it would be no more games. I would tell him straight out how much he hurt me, how much I wanted him, and how scared I was. Then the ball would be in his court.

I realized then that is what I should do with the art program, too. I needed to stop living the fear of failure. By not submitting my photographs to be reviewed, I was guaranteeing my continued failure, just like Lana had said. Sure it was easy to say that photography was just my hobby or that I didn't want to infect it with money. But I needed to grow up and accept my lumps, whatever they may be. I had survived one break-up with Noah; I could make it through another. I could even survive rejection from the art department.

I guess we'll see tomorrow how warm I can be. I texted back, deliberately provocative. *So brave,* I thought to myself, *when I didn't have to be there in front of Noah.* His response took a minute, but when it came, I felt flushed with excitement and happiness.

Sorry for the delay in replying. Had to adjust myself. Can't wait. Be safe and don't look at anyone but your brother.

Yes, sir. I wished there was a salute emoticon, but there wasn't, so I sent a winking smiley face. *;)*

I headed for the will call booth to pick up my tickets. Inside the envelope with my name on it were two tickets, a lanyard, and a note from Josh.

Come to the Fieldhouse after the game. Someone will let you in. Just wait for me.

The game was a blowout. Everyone was scoring touchdowns for State, and Josh was pulled from the game early in the fourth quarter. I sighed in relief and happiness. Post-game celebratory attitudes were a lot more fun to deal with than the post-game mopes. I had taken some great photographs early in the first quarter and then went down to sit in the friends and family section.

I said hello to the parents I recognized. Nate Levacki's parents both hugged me and said they missed me but promised that they took good care of Josh whenever I missed a game. Nate, who we all called by his last name, was Josh's roommate and the starting tight end. Mom never came to Josh's games, and after the first year, Levacki's parents finally stopped asking about her.

By the time I got down to the Fieldhouse, the team had already changed, as several of the players drifted out toward the exit with street clothes and wet hair. Josh, unfortunately, didn't show up for at least thirty minutes more.

By that time, I had stretched out onto the floor along one wall within the hallway of the Fieldhouse, the painted white brick walls protecting me on one side and my backpack serving as my pillow. I threw my arm over my eyes to protect them from the harsh fluorescents that lit the hallway. I was a little tired from the game and the drive. Josh finally showed up and woke me from my nap by nearly stepping on me.

"Nice bed, Grace," Levacki smirked.

"I wouldn't have had to lie down if you prima donnas hadn't taken time to Bieberize your hair." I referenced his carefully-styled sideswept bangs and stood up.

"I've got to give the ladies an excuse to brush the hair out of my eyes," Levacki replied, swinging his head to the side so his bangs lifted and resettled.

"Guys who wear more product in their hair than a girl are never going to get laid," I said.

"Kids, kids, kids." Josh laid a hand on both of our shoulders and separated us, forestalling any sexually suggestive comeback Levacki might have had. Josh liked to pretend I was still twelve and tried to prevent any male from saying anything that intimated I might know what a penis was or what it was used for.

Another teammate of Josh's came up and slapped him on the back. "Good game. See you at West End?" The teammate peered around Levacki and Josh at me. I gave a little wave. "You can bring the chick. She's hot."

"This is my sister, you asshole," Josh scowled. The reference to my supposed hotness got Levacki's back up, as well, and he pushed the teammate away. "We're not taking her to that hell hole."

The player shrugged and walked off. "Your loss," echoed down the hallway.

"Where are we going?" I asked.

"Some girl Levacki is seeing suggested a new bar that has a battle of the bands tonight."

That did sound halfway entertaining, plus I could tease Levacki about his new girlfriend. We grabbed some food and went back to the guys' apartment, where we all played video games for a bit. Several other of Josh's teammates arrived. Josh pulled me into the kitchen to grill me about why I was staying overnight. Usually I just did a day trip but, this time, I asked Josh to find me a ride that would stay until tomorrow.

"Don't give me this bullshit about missing me, either," he warned. I hopped up on the counter while Josh pulled a beer out of the refrigerator.

I picked at the label of the bottle he handed me. "I just wanted to get away from Central."

"What about this Noah kid?"

Oh, Lana. She had apparently called Josh in a preemptive move, and now he was going to flex his big brother muscle. I rolled my eyes.

"Just some guy," I shredded the label with my fingers, pulling off one soggy bit at time. The bits felt wet and cold in my hand, like used Kleenex. It was kind of gross. I shook the mashed-up label onto the counter.

"Some guy you wrote to for four years showed up on your doorstep out of the blue?" He sounded skeptical.

"How do you know all of that?" I asked shocked.

Josh threw me a disbelieving look. "You *are* my sister. We lived in the same house. Hello."

I shrugged. "You never asked me about it."

"It didn't seem important at the time, but now that he's come half-way across the country to go to same college as you, I think he qualifies as a person of interest." Josh was getting his criminal justice degree. He wanted to go FBI if the football thing didn't work out for him.

"We're just friends," I lied. I wasn't about to tell Josh anything until Noah and I had settled things between us. Maybe it was part superstition, but mostly it was just self-preservation. If I admitted to having feelings for Noah, this lecture from Josh could be unending.

"But Lana said—"

I held up my hand and interrupted him. "It's really no big deal. I can't imagine you want to think about my love life."

He grimaced. "Right. Okay. Well, be careful. Guys suck. They only want one thing. Lecture over."

Thank goodness. I was right to keep my developing relationship with Noah private. After Josh kicked everyone out, he and I piled into Levacki's car and headed to the bar where the bands were playing. Josh had handed me an ID. "It's an old ID from a sorority sister of Levacki's new girl. So remember when we get to the door your name is 'Sara.'"

"Can I keep this?"

Levacki shrugged from the driver's seat. "Why not? I'll just say you lost it or something."

"Cool." Now my own fake wasn't even a fake but a real license with a picture of a brunette who didn't look much like me, though in the dark light of a nightclub it could easily pass as legitimate. This would be useful if Noah and I wanted to go out.

When we got to the club, the bouncer recognized Josh and waved us through without requiring us to pay cover or show our IDs. Josh's celebrity can be a hassle at times, but admittedly it got us a few nice perks. Someone had even set up a roped-off area for the bands that were competing, and a couple of tables were cleared off and set up for Josh, Nate, and the other players who came.

Our corner was right off the dance floor. I could tell that other girls were wondering how I came to be with Josh and Nate. Once they found out I was Josh's sister, every time I went to the bathroom one of them would be there telling me how pretty I was so that I could report back to Josh how nice they were. I wanted to tell them that a) this hadn't worked since I was twelve, and b) there was no way Josh would bring home some girl from the bar when I was with him.

He pretended that he was setting a good example. I guess he never realized how much girls gossiped about guys and sex, because I had gotten an earful ever since he started making the rounds in high school. I kept quiet about it, though, knowing he would be mortified. I certainly was.

I allowed myself to drink heavily. Josh and the others were there with me, so I knew I was safe. The liquor desensitized me, and I became more frenetic as the night went on, dancing and carousing in my little group. I actually ended up having a good time. Josh eventually had enough, though, tired of babysitting me and maybe just exhausted from the game. We left Levacki there acting as the dancing pole for a few girls. He looked happy.

***

Josh saw me off on Sunday. "Be careful down there at Central. Have you thought about joining the chess club? I bet those guys'd make good boyfriends."

I scrunched up my nose. "They have sex in the chess club, too. I hear it's really crazy. The winner sweeps the chess pieces off the table and then just takes their partner right there on the table."

Josh look horrified and partly intrigued and said, "No shit?"

I laughed at him. "I have no idea, but this is the very reason I didn't go to State with you. You'd have been monitoring the dating pool non-stop."

He didn't even look ashamed at being caught.

"Just looking out for my baby sister." Ruffling my hair, he handed the backpack to me and shut the door. Tapping on the front window, he handed the driver some cash for gas, and we headed back to State.

I tossed my phone back and forth between my hands, unable to sleep on the return trip. I wondered whether I should text Noah and when we would meet up again. I wondered what I should wear. I hadn't ever bought sex underwear before, and I assumed that I would be having sex with Noah at some point in the near future.

The thought made me faint with worry and overly excited. I needed to have a long talk with Lana. Were there books I should read on making it good for Noah? Should I be watching some porn? Questions ping-ponged back and forth in my head during the whole trip home. I was relieved when we pulled up to my apartment.

I thanked the two for the ride and asked, "Do you guys need more money for the trip?"

"No, we're good. Text us anytime you need a ride," the guy responded. I nodded and slid out the door. It was time to do some research.

Noah

When I was in high school, we managed to have keggers courtesy of an assistant wresting coach who was old enough to buy beer and young and stupid enough to be willing to supply it to underage kids. While there was a social hierarchy observed at the parties, it usually started with male student athlete rather than rich kid.

I never played sports in high school, even though I had the build. I didn't have money, either. But I did a good job of looking dangerous, which was enough reason for many of the girls to walk over to me while

I stood, holding up a wall at these parties. Friendship with Bo, who was rich and did play football, didn't hurt.

As I leaned against one of the posts holding up the roof over our deck, I couldn't help but be reminded of those days. Present but not quite belonging. Even though I lived here and had more right than anyone—besides my roommates—to be standing where I was, I still fit poorly. I was always just waiting for someone to kick me out.

I took a long draw from my Coors. Glass bottle. Hierarchy at parties like these was established by the quality of liquor in one's hand. Glass bottle meant you were either trustworthy enough the hosts weren't worried you'd break something or in good enough that they wouldn't care if they had to clean up after you. Essentially, glass bottles were for very close guy friends and any girl you wanted to nail. Plastic cups and keg beer for the rest, or the "pogs," as Bo called everyone. It was an insult leveled toward anyone not infantry Marine, but it worked just as well in the civilian world.

"Nice buffet." Bo came up to stand next to me, waving at the college girls we had rounded up from Central. It looked like the beach at Silver Strand, where the West Coast Seals trained. That expanse of beach was strewn with women and their tight bodies, with very little covering them.

The night air was heavy with humidity, and the pool gave everyone an excuse to strip down regardless of whether they had bathing suits. A couple more hours and there would be plenty of nudity, as even the thin scraps of underwear would become too uncomfortable for some.

When I first moved into this house, I thought that the distance from Central would prevent any real partying with the students, and, given that I was a couple years older than most of the seniors, that was okay. That line of thought ended with our first rager, held at the start of summer classes. The debauchery of that night must have spread like a fire through the California forests in summer because we've had to turn people away ever since.

The number of people just showing up was unmanageable. While we weren't gunning to be neighbors of the year, we didn't want to be monumental assholes, either. So we instituted rules. No more than six people per car. Every vehicle had to have a designated driver. Everyone had to be of age. By the end of the summer, though, we still hadn't managed to curtail the migration westward. The last party we held we required people to have armbands that Bo and I handed out on campus.

It made the parties more exclusive to students at Central, which put us in the position of divining the haves and have-nots. It made me uncomfortable.

So yeah, the buffet of girls was quite impressive. While they were all very nice to look at, not one of them was the girl I was thinking about. Which Bo knew.

"Going to try one out tonight?" Bo pressed.

"No."

"You really think you're doing the right thing?"

"In what way?"

Bo gestured again to the pool lined with college girls mixing with guys from the gym where Bo and I worked out and some of the guys that worked on Finn's construction crew. It was a weird mix, but it always seemed to work, even if those Central girls would never date any of the guys here. Central girls, like the girls back home, liked to flirt with the blue collars, but they always went home with the ones who would end up wearing suits and ties. "You've barely sampled the goods here."

"I figure you're doing enough sampling for both of us." I drained the last of my beer and went inside to get another from the fridge. The kitchen was fairly empty. Another sign of belonging. No one goes into the fridge except us. Bo followed me inside, and I tipped my head toward the fridge to see if he needed a new one. He shook his head.

The only furniture we had on the first floor was a very long, battered table, where a bunch of people seemed to be doing body shots off one girl laid out like a sacrifice, and two equally battered sofas around the spot where our big screen TV usually hung.

It made for a good party house. I headed for the stairs. Maybe I should see if Grace texted me. The stairs were taped off with some fake crime scene tape. I hopped over and took the steps three at a time. When I stopped at the landing, I realized that there were people in the hall bathroom going at it.

I hated that. Someone always had to clean up the mess left by drunk people. The vomit was bad enough—but somebody's discarded condom was even worse. I gave the door a loud bang and told them to get the fuck out. I didn't stick around to see if anyone obeyed my orders. Bo was right behind me and banged on the door, too. "I hope you used a condom."

I smirked at him. Our interruptions definitely would've caused a hitch in some guy's stroke.

"What're we doing upstairs?" Bo asked.

"I'm checking my phone." I hadn't heard the phone alert me to any text messages, but it was loud. Maybe I had missed one. I wanted to be in a quiet place if I needed to call Grace back.

"I'm worried, man," Bo said concern tingeing his words. I wasn't really listening.

"Yeah?" I responded, my attention on my phone. No messages.

"Grace was a nice girl to send you all that shit, but you know you don't really owe her anything," Bo continued.

"I don't think I owe her something." I was getting a little irritated now that his words were penetrating.

"I just don't get it. She's not your type at all," Bo said.

"What's my type?" I challenged.

"Someone more driven. Someone who has her act together."

"She's got her act together," I said. I really didn't know if she did, but what did it matter. I knew where I wanted to go. She could just come along with me.

"She doesn't. She doesn't have a major. She almost had a panic attack watching a dirty movie with you. She doesn't have any other interests in her life."

"How do you know that?" I shook my head. Bo knew nothing about Grace.

"Because I can ask questions just as good as you. This girl goes to class, does her ten hours of service, and nothing else. She's not in a sorority. She doesn't do theater. She doesn't volunteer. She doesn't take a ton of classes. She's just existing."

"Sounds familiar," I said, looking pointedly at Bo. I wondered why this bothered Bo so much, since he pretty much described his own life. He looked away for a minute but didn't allow that point to deter him. He pressed on.

"Yeah, but I shot bad guys next to you," Bo said. "You have to be friends with me. And you can be friends with Grace. It's just, why tie yourself to one girl? You should be downstairs taking one or more of those chicks up on their offers instead of up here checking your phone. This is your time to enjoy yourself."

Bo's mantra was to live hard, as if we only had so many years to be able to have fun before real life beat us down. Enjoying life apparently included bedding as many girls as humanly possible, like life was a first-person-shooter game, only women were Bo's targets. He was accumulating life points with each conquest.

"You don't know her," I repeated.

"Tell me, then," Bo said skeptically.

I stared at him in disbelief. "Why're you busting my balls over this?"

Bo looked out the window over the pool and at the mass of flesh below. "Because you're one of the good guys, Noah. The rest of us are a bunch of assholes, but you deserve something special."

"You sell yourself short, bro." I clapped him on the shoulder. I didn't want to argue with Bo over Grace. These two were going to have to be friends. They were going to be part of my life for a very long time. "Be happy for me. I want to look at the world like Grace does, so that even the ordinary things look amazing."

"Just think about it," he warned. "It might even be good for you and Grace. You could make sure that she was right for you by testing out some other options."

"How about I go downstairs and be the best fucking wingman ever," I suggested. Bo shrugged. He'd said his piece. If this spiel had come from any other person, I'd have thought that they were implying I wasn't good enough for Grace. Bo was the opposite. He didn't think Grace was good enough for me, which I didn't get, even though I appreciated the loyalty.

Bo and I were about the only two guys unattached in our unit when we began, but by the end at least half, if not more, had divorced, broken up, or were cheated on. Grace had been more constant than any woman we knew. She was able to cut through all the bullshit and focus. I wanted that, and I wanted to be the object of her focus. There wasn't any reason to sample anything. I knew a good thing when I found it.

 Chapter Ten

Grace

When I got to the apartment, Lana greeted me. She was alone.

"How was Josh?"

"Good. He didn't get hurt much in the game, and I got some cool photos. I think they want to frame one in the locker room." I went into the bedroom and dropped my backpack on the bed. "By the way, thanks for calling Josh and ratting me out."

"You're welcome," she said, completely unrepentant. She came in and helped carry my toiletries into the bathroom. "What'd he have to say?"

"He lectured me for all of two minutes and then the idea of his sister having sex turned his stomach, and we dropped the subject."

"I can't count on Josh for any help in this, can I?" Lana complained, but amusement was lurking in her voice.

"Nope," I placed the now-empty bag into my closet, tossed the dirty clothes into my hamper, and went to stretch out on the bed next to where Lana had planted herself.

"Your desensitization plan didn't work," I told her and braced myself for a lecture on foolishness.

"I'm not surprised," Lana sighed with resignation.

I turned to look at her. "What? No 'don't do this self-destructive thing?'"

"I don't think anyone could withstand a guy like Noah," Lana admitted. "And his steadiness says something about him. Like he's really sorry, and he's serious about winning you back. That's pretty awesome."

"I'm scared," I told her quietly, almost afraid to say it, as if speaking it out loud gave my fear power.

"That's normal," Lana smiled wryly. "I'd be scared too."

I lay back against my pillows and thought of Noah lying next to me on the bed. What scared me was that I wasn't going to be enough for Noah. My limited bedroom experience was bound to show. Maybe we could start off slow and work up to actual sex. We hadn't even kissed yet. I thought of the roughness of his slightly chapped lips against my fingers and suddenly felt very heated. Overly heated.

"God, it's so hot in here. Do you have the air on?" I asked Lana.

"65 degrees," Lana said, "but I don't think it's working."

"Nope, not working," I said. Lana had a light sheen on her forehead from the heat. I'm sure I didn't look much better.

"What do you plan to do this afternoon?" she asked.

"I'm supposed to call Noah, but I'm wiped out. I think I drank too much last night. I need a nap." I ran my hand over my forehead. I could feel a headache coming on, part hangover and part heat-induced.

"I'm going to the house," Lana said, and she got up to escape to her presumably well air-conditioned sorority house.

I drifted off to sleep but woke what seemed like minutes later when the phone rang.

"Did you forget something?" I thought it might be Lana.

There was a pause and then a familiar low voice came on the line. "Missed you last night."

Noah.

"What're you doing right now?" he asked.

"Right now? I'm lying on my bed in an apartment where the laws of physics apparently demand that heat rises," I complained.

"Heat and cold displace each other, actually. The cold sinks and the hot air rises, one molecule at a time."

"I thought you were a finance major. Whatever, I feel like I'm in an uncooled attic. I don't think the air conditioner they installed is powerful enough."

"What if I told you I could solve your problem of being hot and miserable?" Noah cajoled.

"I didn't say I was miserable."

"I used my great deductive reasoning skills," he said dryly.

"Fine. If you can solve my problem of being hot and miserable, I'll give you—" I said, breaking off before I could blurt out something suggestive. I hurried to add, "I'll bake you brownies."

"Great, it's a deal. I'll collect you in twenty minutes, and you can deliver the payment after we make you cool and happy." He didn't mention if he'd have liked something else.

"Where are we going?" I asked, curiosity chasing away my headache.

"It'll be a surprise, but get your swimsuit and a change of clothing," Noah instructed and then hung up.

The idea of a swim sounded great.

Noah knocked on the door at fifteen minutes instead of twenty, but I was ready. Not much preparation was really necessary for swimming. I pulled on my swimsuit and a terry cloth cover-up. A towel and a change of clothing went in a bag with some sunscreen, and I was waiting by the door when he knocked.

"Where are we going?" I asked when we got to his truck.

"Surprise," Noah said, helping me up into the cab.

He drove west of campus in the direction of two of the city malls.

"Are we going shopping?" I asked Noah, worried that I wasn't quite dressed for the occasion. "Because I'm wearing a cover up and flip-flops."

He glanced over at me and said, "You're perfect."

For some reason this caused me to blush, and I tried to disguise my response with another question. He didn't really think I was perfect. It was just a saying. "What's our destination?"

"Casa de Hombre."

"The Man House?" I translated with some amusement.

"Yup."

"You have a pool at your house?" And I thought I lived in swanky college digs.

"Finn's dad is in construction. He was building this house at the Woodlands." Noah said it like I should know about it, but I didn't.

"Never heard of it," I admitted.

"The Woodlands is a gated community. Very rich. The guy who contracted for the house lost his shirt during the downturn, and his financing fell through. Finn convinced his dad to let him finish the house and buy it. We all contribute to the mortgage, and when we sell it we'll split the equity," he explained.

"Sounds all too grown up for me," I said. I couldn't wait to see where Noah lived. This was personal and intimate stuff, and I could barely sit still with my excitement.

Noah stopped at the gatehouse in front of a two lane street and pressed a button on a remote. The gate opened, and he waved at the attendant.

The Woodlands was aptly named. A variety of trees, none of which I could identify, hung over the streets and filled the yards of the houses that dotted the landscape. Each home looked like a private oasis of forest and green grass.

"It's really nice back here. You have parties? Don't your neighbors kick up a fuss?" This area looked too sedate to tolerate a bunch of college or near-college aged kids.

"We invite them or pay them off. You'd be surprised how many people won't call the police if you give them a little money. Plus, other than the occasional party, we're pretty good neighbors. We mow our grass and don't keep the trashcans on the drive for too long."

He pulled into a wide driveway that dipped down and ended in front of a large two-story house that looked primarily made of glass with a few wood beams to hold it up. The end of the drive separated the main house from another smaller structure that looked like a detached garage.

I shook my head. "I guess I understand why there are so many of you living together."

"Yeah, it's a pretty sweet setup," Noah replied with pride.

We walked in the side door. Noah said, "I think Adam is practicing in his studio." He pointed to the detached building across from the house. "Finn and Mal are watching football. The pool is empty and the games are bad."

He led me through the kitchen and out the back door onto the patio.

"Tell me the truth. Finn whacked the buyer so he could get this house." I couldn't believe my eyes. The place was gorgeous. We stopped before the pool, which was laid out in a classic mosaic pattern with an infinity edge. The drop-off made the most of the forested woods behind the house.

"It's possible. You've met Finn. He's totally got that serial killer vibe," Noah joked. Finn looked like a mischievous choirboy, innocent but with a lot of knowledge in his eyes. He probably got away with a million naughty deeds.

"It's obvious from the start what with his illicit coffee cup in the library and his predilection for architectural design magazines. Classic signs of perversion," I snickered.

The pool was spectacular. It had jets in the concrete on one side that arced into the pool. Attached to the shallow end of the pool was a raised, tiled round area that looked like a Jacuzzi. The pool itself was rectangular, with one end framed by a sizeable pool house. A covered deck area contained a brick oven that looked to be in disarray.

Noah led me around the scattered bricks. "Finn and Mal are building an outdoor grill, but it's a project that has taken them all summer to get to this point."

It looked like a mess, as if someone had taken a sledgehammer to a brick wall. If this was the process of reconstruction, I worried about the houses that Finn flipped.

The pool area was empty and quiet. A large fence and barrier of trees on either side of the property shielded us from the neighbors.

"Just drop your stuff on a lounger. You can change in the pool house," Noah directed.

"I've got my suit on already," I told him. "I thought you were against water." I had once asked Noah what his greatest fear was, after sharing that mine was spiders. He had told me it was water, but that the Marines worked that out of him.

"I overcame that fear, remember."

He took off his shirt and jumped into the deep end. When he surfaced, he gestured for me to join him. It felt like a thousand degrees, and I was eager to cool off. I dropped my bag on the lounger, disposed of my cover up, and jumped in right next to Noah. It wasn't the most elegant of jumps, but I didn't care. I wanted to have fun today.

Noah and I played catch with a Nerf football and challenged each other to see who could make the biggest splash. Apparently the games inside were so bad that Finn, the serial killer, came out and challenged Noah to a race. I played the flag girl, which meant I sat at the end of the pool and yelled go and then lied about who won. Noah won every time, but I said Finn did.

After the very exhausting effort of watching two fine male specimens swim, I decided to go lie on one of the loungers. It was, I decided, one of the better afternoons of my life.

Later, Mal came out and fired up the grill. Apparently it worked amidst all the rubble. Adam emerged from whatever part of the house he had hidden in, and we all enjoyed steaks and beer. Bo was conspicuously absent, but I refused to let that dampen my enjoyment. Noah and I made a grocery run for s'mores fixings. I was nearly comatose after all the food.

"Can you just wheel me home and dump me on the porch? I'll sleep there. It'll be cooler, and I won't have to walk up stairs," I asked Noah, who sat next to me on an outdoor loveseat. I wanted to just pull up my feet and lay my head in his lap. I wanted to stay on this love seat replete from chocolate and marshmallows and the heat of his large body next to mine.

"You can't expect me to drive you home," Noah protested. "I'm at least four s'mores over the driving limit."

I made a halfhearted slap at him and reminded him that of all of us, he ate the least and had only one s'more. "I'd hit you harder, but I'm going into a sugar coma and am losing control of my limbs." Inwardly I was hugging myself. Noah wanted me to stay. Any nervousness I had before had been eroded by the sun, swimming, food, and company.

"We'd better get you to a safe place before that happens," Noah said, standing up. Then he bent over and picked me up in his arms. "Get the door, Finn."

"Yessir," Finn slurred. He'd had many beers with his s'mores. He claimed he hated chocolate and was only able to eat it with copious amounts of alcohol. I wasn't sure if he was serious.

"I was only kidding about the carrying business," I said to Noah's chest.

"You're my guest. I don't want you getting injured. I'm not sure we're current on our homeowner's insurance," Noah joked. I could feel the rumble of his voice through his chest. If I had eaten or drunk less, I'd have protested more, but right now I felt too satiated and happy to argue. If he wanted to carry me out to his truck, I was okay with that. Only he didn't proceed out the kitchen to the driveway. Instead, he started up the stairs.

"Are you trying to work off your s'more?" I asked.

"Nope, I'm putting you to bed."

I started to struggle weakly. "I can't stay here." My protests were half-hearted, though, and Noah merely ignored them.

He carried me down the hall like I weighed no more than a marshmallow and took me into a room on the right. The room was dark and the walls seemed to be painted gray or white. I couldn't tell in the dimness.

A large bed was positioned between two windows. Noah walked straight to the bed and laid me down on top of the gray striped comforter. He went over to a dresser and pulled out a T-shirt that had the letters USMC. "You can sleep in this," he said, tossing the shirt to me.

I took the shirt and held it up to my face. It was cool and smelled clean. I wished it was the shirt Noah was wearing so I could be wrapped up in his scent and surrounded by the warmth of his body.

When I didn't move, Noah said, "Should I help you? You mentioned something about non-functioning limbs."

The offer was a joke, but an invitation lurked underneath. I wasn't ready for that yet. "No, I think I can manage but, um, are you sure I can't just call a cab?"

"Cab service is shit out here, and I don't want you to leave," Noah replied firmly.

I went to the bathroom and put on the borrowed shirt. Noah had also lent me a pair of cotton boxers that were too large in the waist. I rolled the waistband down twice so they settled on my hips, the extra fabric from the turns ensuring the boxers wouldn't fall off. Noah definitely passed the "not fitting into my jeans" rule.

He stood next to the bed holding the covers up for me. I exited the bathroom and slipped under them. If I were braver, with more experience, I'd have reached for him. He'd press his body into mine, and I'd run my hands over his broad back. I'd map the dips and peaks of his ridged chest, the one I'd stared at all day in the pool.

I was restless and unsatisfied, wanting something I knew only Noah could give me. My open expression was easy for him to read. Noah sank down on the edge of the bed and put one arm across my body. His head dipped low, and I saw his eyes darken. His descent was slow and measured, telegraphing that I could stop him at any time.

I must've known the day would lead to this, even if I hadn't acknowledged it consciously. I placed a tentative hand on both of his forearms, braced at my sides. I felt him shudder and for a moment, I was filled with a strange sense of power. I could make him shudder for me.

I slid my hands up his arms and around his shoulders, enjoying the feel of hot flesh over hard muscle. My fingers laced around his neck. The first touch of his lips against mine was soft, almost like whispers of a kiss. His touch wasn't tentative so much as patient. If we went any further, he was saying, it would be at my urging.

So I lifted up and pressed into him, using his body as leverage for mine. And that was enough. His arms swept around my body, lifting me flush against him. His hand came up into my hair and cradled my head against the now hard onslaught of his lips and then his tongue. I felt like he was a marauder, invading my mouth and my senses.

His other hand was braced around my ribs just under my breast. I felt my nipples tighten in anticipation of his touch. But when I thought he would move his hand, perhaps caress my breast, he stopped. He pulled his mouth away and rested his forehead against mine. We were both out of breath, but Noah was panting like he had run ten miles with his heavy rucksack.

His hand tightened in my hair and then let go. He ran his fingers over the strands, smoothing them down. I stared at him, trying to read his intentions, his thoughts, to divine the meaning of it all.

"I didn't bring you here today for this," he said finally. His thumbs were tracing patterns on my face, and it was hard to think or form coherent responses. I just wanted to lie down and draw him next to me. Do my own exploration.

But the separation of his lips from mine brought me a moment of clarity. Taking this path with Noah would make me far more vulnerable than I'd ever been. And suddenly the memory of the ache I had felt upon his rejection was piercing. The warm glow that had been fostered throughout the day and the tender night was snuffed out by the chill of that memory.

"Don't close up on me now, Grace," Noah said. He held my face and leaned down to kiss me again, but I drew back.

"Maybe this is a mistake."

"No, it's not." He sounded firm and convinced.

I took a deep breath. I was going to roll over and show my soft under-belly, but it shouldn't be any surprise to him. He had to know he could hurt me. I hadn't ever had a real relationship before, and I didn't know all the rules and moves to make. I'd never been good at games, and I hated uncertainty even more.

"I thought I did know you, Noah, but I don't. You show up here at Central without a word. You ignore me for two years and then you're everywhere." I waved a hand between us. "You even decide when we start kissing and when we stop."

He began to open his mouth, but I interrupted, "If you really want something to work out between us, I'm going to need the whole story."

He nodded and took a deep breath. "I think I was less nervous the first time I was deployed." He waited for me to smile at this confession, but it was too serious to me for jokes. "There are thousands of colleges I could've gone to, Grace, but I came here because it had you."

"What about two years ago?" I asked, my voice breaking slightly, and I turned away as I could feel my throat close up and the tears begin to form behind my eyes.

Noah sat up and leaned his forearms again his knees. His body was angled away from me, and I couldn't see his face, only his profile. The skin seemed drawn tighter than usual against his jaw. "I went into the Marines when I was seventeen. I hadn't ever lived a normal civilian life on my own. When I got out, I found out I had to apply for school, find an apartment, get a job. All the skills I had been taught as a Marine didn't help in the civilian world." He took a deep breath, and I wanted to hug him then and tell him he didn't need to say another word. But he looked so tense I was afraid one touch would shatter him. I remained quiet and motionless, and he continued.

"I flew to Chicago and rented a car. I was going to surprise you, but when I drove up the North Shore to your home..." His voice trailed off. "Grace, you live behind a gate and the drive was so fucking long I couldn't even see your house."

I didn't understand what my Uncle's house had to do with anything so I stayed silent. This obviously frustrated Noah because he drew one hand through his hair, hair that I now knew was soft as my aunt's mink coat.

"What?" I protested.

"You don't even see how different that is. I grew up very poor. Maybe you got that from my letters and maybe you didn't. But I was some grunt from the Marines and while I had saved money, it wasn't anything like that. I couldn't afford to buy you a house like that."

"I don't want a house like that." The house itself wasn't so bad, but the constant tension of watching your mother move around like a ghost and your aunt run down your best friend until she was afraid to eat was intolerable. I didn't want to live in a house like that, ever.

"But you live a life completely different than mine," Noah said. "Do you even know how much it costs to go to college here for one year?"

I didn't know. I mean, I knew it was expensive, but Uncle Louis paid for my tuition and my apartment. And I was finally seeing where Noah was going with this.

"Ah, the light dawns," he said, with a frustrated undertone. He had tilted his head so he could see me.

"So you didn't want to meet me because you thought I was a snob?" I asked, frustrated myself.

"Okay, I was wrong. The light isn't dawning. You're just going down the wrong tunnel," he sounded angry and a little bitter.

"You insulting me isn't going to make me understand better."

He threw up both hands in a defensive position. "I just wanted to meet you on equal terms so you didn't feel sorry for me."

"I never felt sorry for you! I always thought you were amazing and brave and—" I cast around for another word but failed. "Amazing."

"I just needed some time," Noah said, sounding resigned and tired.

"So here you are, all fixed up and feeling 'equal,' and I'm supposed to just be ready for you?" Our two years of separation was because he felt he wasn't good enough? I wanted to cry at the injustice.

"No, you've always been perfect," Noah protested.

"Well, I'm not. You have all these plans and goals, and I can't even decide on a major." I gestured toward his books on the desk.

"That doesn't matter to me."

"Your money or lack of it doesn't matter to me," I assured him.

"It should," Noah's face took on a grim cast. "My mom died because we didn't have enough money."

"You don't know that, Noah. You don't know if she would've survived if she had better medical care. No one knows that for sure. You should've written me. Or met me and told me. I'd have waited or gone to college in San Diego," I pointed out.

"Yes, well, none of those things really occurred to me back then. I told you I was screwed up."

We were both breathing heavily as if we had engaged in a physical fight instead of just throwing a bunch of words back and forth. Noah blew out his breath and leaned toward me, one arm crossed over my body.

"I was tired of the war, the dust, the desert. Being back in San Diego as a civilian was weird. I missed the adrenaline high of always being alert. I started fighting in a gym and then working and taking classes, and when I was super busy, I felt more normal. The relaxation bit was difficult." He paused and swallowed hard. "I, ah, had to talk to someone for a little while to try to get my head screwed on straight."

I hadn't really thought of this. Noah always seemed perfectly together in his letters, often making jokes. Even now he presented himself as this supremely confident male. I wanted to kick myself for being so self-absorbed and not truly understanding how difficult the transition from enlisted Marine to casual civilian must be for him.

"Grace, I want to be with you. I think you want to be with me. Can't we put it all behind us and start new?" he pleaded softly.

I looked into his face, and I thought about the Noah I knew from his letters. He was funny, generous, and kind. I had fallen in love with him once, and I was halfway there now. I just didn't know if he'd hurt me again.

"You make me nervous," I confessed.

"A good nervous?"

"I'm not certain. I feel like," I sat up, wanting him to understand me. "I'm not seeking any compliments here, but I feel like you're out of my league."

Noah laughed a little like I was joking.

"No, really, I mean it," I said.

He re-arranged his face into a suitably serious expression, all hints of laughter erased. "What do you mean?"

"Noah, you've got it together. You've a plan. You're headed somewhere, and I'm not. I can barely figure out what I'm doing tomorrow, let alone next year. You should be with someone like Lana." I pushed my hands together, threading my fingers. "You fit."

"What kind of bullshit is that?" he said angrily.

"It isn't bullshit. It's the natural rule of the universe that like attracts like."

"There are many things wrong with your theory, Grace. It's a good thing that you don't plan on being a scientist. Who cares that you don't have a major? What about magnetic poles drawing each other together? Where in the laws of crazy Grace universe does that actual scientific fact fall?"

I decided that Noah couldn't actually hear me, so I laid it out for him. "I'm afraid that I'll fall hard for you and that you'll hurt me again. My insecurity would end up driving you nuts and embarrass me." I looked down at my hands that were now clenched together. "While I may not know what I want to be, I'm pretty sure I don't want to be that girl."

"Is your insecurity going to play itself out by you trying out other guys to make me jealous?" he demanded.

"What? No! I'm sure my issues would be more with the clinging and stalking. Maybe overtexting."

Noah laid his hand over my clenched fingers. "Why don't we try it out and see if I get fed up with that."

"And then what?"

"Grace," he brought his hand up behind my head and slid closer to me, forcing me to look at him. "You worry too much," he observed. "You don't have to have the answer for everything right now and today."

"I hate uncertainty," I whispered.

"I can tell," he smiled softly. "Here's what I know. I want to be with you tonight, tomorrow, and for the foreseeable future. Nothing you've said tonight scares me."

"You should be scared. Didn't you guys watch *Fatal Attraction,*, or are you too young for that?"

"Every guy watches *Fatal Attraction* by the age of sixteen. There's nudity in it."

I hadn't realized that Noah had been drawing me closer until I was cuddled up next to his chest. He feathered kisses along my temple and down my cheek. "Will you give me a try?"

"What about the laws of the universe?" I mumbled into the side of his shirt.

"Let's pretend we're magnets. Those fit pretty tightly according to the laws of the universe."

"Don't talk that upperclassman speech with me," I joked.

"Feel free to text me all day. Include pictures and videos if you like," Noah invited.

He leaned down and pressed a warm kiss against my lips. It may have been a goodnight kiss, but it felt more like a welcome. When his tongue swept lightly across my lips, I couldn't help but part them in an invitation for more. When his tongue crept into my mouth, I greeted it with my own. My hands reached up to stroke the strands of his hair and mold them against the shape of his beautiful head.

His arms were braced on either side of my head, holding his body just slightly away from mine, and I could feel their tension vibrate next to me. I stroked my hands down the sides of his arms and felt the flex of muscle under my palm. No other part of his body touched mine, just open mouth kisses where he explored and tasted me like I was more delicious than a chocolate soufflé with homemade whipped cream.

He broke away from my mouth and trailed his lips across my jaw and down the side of my neck. The whispered breath, the scratch of his slight stubble, and the wetness of his tongue set my body's nerves on end. I felt super sensitized, as if I could even feel the dust motes that drifted through the air. As his head drifted downward to nuzzle the expanse of skin above the collar of my T-shirt, my fingers delved into his hair once again. One arm braced at my side and his other moved downward. His hand stroked the skin on my leg, sweeping from the bottom of his borrowed boxers to my knee and up, just below my chest.

I wanted to rub against his touch like a cat, arching into his every stroke. I wanted him to touch me everywhere, and I moved restlessly, trying to position different unattended parts under his sweeping hand. But his movements stilled, and he rested his forehead in the curve of my shoulder. I could feel his breath coming in pants against my chest.

Uncertain now, I simply stroked his back. When the rhythm of his breath evened out, he said, "I'm trying to be a gentleman. I honestly didn't invite you over today for this."

The kissing and the touching had made me feel anxious and unfulfilled. I brought my legs together and squeezed, trying to alleviate the ache, but the motion only made Noah groan. He placed his hand on the top of one thigh and pressed hard.

"Please, don't," he said, his voice slightly muffled. "If you move, I'll…" His voice trailed off. He took a deep breath and pushed himself into a seated position next to me, one arm still caging me in. "I better go."

I didn't want him to. Maybe we weren't quite ready for sex, even though my body screamed for it, but I wanted to sleep with him and feel his body next to mine during the entire night. I hadn't ever slept with anyone other than Lana before.

I took a deep breath and made an offer I knew was dangerous. "You could sleep here with me," I said softly. When he started to protest, I held up a hand. "Trust me to know my own feelings. Don't assume you know what's best for me."

"Okay," he said simply. He undressed without hesitation or embarrassment, and I enjoyed the show more than I thought I would. His shoulders were broad, and I could see definition in the faint light from the bathroom creating interesting shadows on his skin. The indentation of his spine was marked and looked like a perfect trail to explore with my fingers. A dark mark spotted his right shoulder. It was a tattoo, but I couldn't make out the shape or form. Tomorrow, I promised myself, I'd explore it tomorrow. He stopped and left his boxers on, a tight-fitting cotton that extended to the tops of his thighs. I lifted the covers and scooted over, and he climbed in bed next to me. As we laid together side by side like two toddlers in a bed, I remembered one of the last letters I received from Noah.

Dear Grace,

My active duty enlistment will run out in two months. I can re-up, but it would be a longer commitment than I'm ready to give right now. There are good parts and bad parts to being enlisted. It's hard to imagine leaving the guys. It's hard to envision going back home.

When I was home on my last leave, it was like the world had become completely different than I'd remembered. I don't ever remember having that feeling of disorientation after basic. It's not just the weather or the terrain or the lack of people with robes in the streets. Or even seeing pavement where it's usually just dirt. Or no longer worrying that next time I take a step it might be my last. Or maybe it is.

Bo is willing to do whatever I want. If I reenlist, he'll reenlist; if I get out, he'll get out. I think most of the guys in my unit don't want to come back, but some of them are going to try for Marine Force Recon. Another guy in my unit is leaving the Marines to try to be an Army Ranger. That sort of thing appeals to me, I guess. It's like pitting yourself against the best alive, and, if you come out the other end, it's amazing.

But having left my hometown, I guess I finally realized I don't have to go back. That my entire life isn't wrapped up in where I was born, where I went to school, or who my family is. But if I don't reenlist and I don't go back home, what do I do?

The one good thing is that while you are here, you're given a list of things to do and then you do them. We're just the weapons they aim and fire. Go forth and destroy shit, say the commanders.

I don't know if I'm equipped to do anything else than be a Marine at this point or if I even want to be anything else. I'm tired of being here, but the war is winding down. Even if I did re-enlist, I probably wouldn't see combat again. And my guess is that non-combat service doesn't deliver the same adrenaline rush. That's why the guys who are reupping are thinking Special Forces.

I think this is why Odysseus stays away for so long. He's addicted to the adrenaline, and he's afraid of what kind of person he might be when he gets back home. It was easier for him to keep going even though each new mission took him farther and farther away from Penelope. Sure, he said his whole goal was to return to her, but it was easier for him to love her from a distance.

Coming home was his greatest battle.

~ Noah

I had read Noah's letters thinking he was invincible, but he wasn't. For all his outward strength and physical ability and unceasing drive, he was just as human and frail as I was. I rolled on my side and placed my head on his shoulder. He slid his arm beneath my head and curled it around me. I thought I wouldn't be able to fall asleep, but the food and the liquor and the warmth of his body quickly lulled me into slumber.

Chapter Eleven

Grace

An insistent, discordant *beep beep beep* woke me. My head was resting on a rather hard surface that I quickly realized was Noah. I may have started out lying on one side of the bed, but I ended up on Noah's side, sprawled over him like he was my favorite childhood stuffed animal.

Noah must not have realized I was awake because he was trying to gently move out from underneath me. He stopped when I stiffened.

"Hey, sorry, shhh," Noah whispered, turning to me after shutting off the alarm. "Go back to sleep."

It was dark out, and not even a finger of dawn could be seen at the edges of the blinds that hung over the window in this room.

"What time is it?"

"It's four. Can you go back to sleep?"

"Four?" Confused, I asked, "In the morning?"

"Yes," Noah's response came back a little strangled, like he was trying to swallow a laugh. "Just go back to sleep, Grace. I'll pick you up later to take you to campus."

I was wide awake now, and I didn't want to sleep in Noah's bed without him, in this strange house full of guys I didn't know, and who I'd be embarrassed to see over breakfast.

"No," I protested, getting up and looking around for my clothes. "You're going to campus now to work out? You can just drop me off at my apartment."

Noah sat on the side of the bed, rubbing his head. "I don't go directly to campus, exactly." Then he stood up as if he'd made up his mind. "If you want to come with me, I'll take you."

"Um, okay?" I said. I wasn't sure where he was taking me, but it sounded kind of intriguing. Besides, I was up and here was an opportunity to learn something more about Noah.

I pulled on my shorts and went to the bathroom. Noah was already in there, brushing his teeth. He stopped and squeezed some toothpaste on an extra toothbrush for me.

"It's new," he said, his words a bit garbled as he talked around the toothbrush in his mouth. Noah finished brushing and left me to the bathroom. I brushed my teeth, washed my face with his handsoap, and ran my fingers through my tangled hair. I tried not to contemplate why he had new toothbrushes at the ready.

Noah knocked a few moments later and said, "I have a clean T-shirt for you." He handed me a grey tee identical to the one I was wearing. Faded, soft, with the letters USMC on it. No stash of female clothing somewhat ameliorated my pique over the clean toothbrush.

I pulled off the shirt I was wearing and exchanged it for its twin. I folded the discarded shirt and laid it upon the bed that Noah had already made. He was gone. I gathered he was impatient to start his day. Figures. Guys could be up and ready in five minutes.

Picking up my bag, I crept down the stairs. I didn't want to be one of those rude overnight guests that the guys would complain about to Noah. I found Noah in the kitchen with an energy drink. He handed one to me, along with a bagel, and took my bag. "Sorry I don't have a better breakfast for you, but we can stop somewhere."

I shrugged. I wasn't terribly hungry, but I really would've liked a shot of caffeine. "Is there caffeine in this drink you gave me?" I looked at it suspiciously.

"No. I'd make you coffee," Noah said, leading me out into the driveway to his truck, "but I've been told my coffee has killed innocents, and I don't want to harm you with my poor kitchen skills."

I bit into my bagel a bit glumly and climbed into the truck. We drove only for a short five minutes when Noah parked at a small collection of stores just east of the main shopping mall. There was a dentist's office, a yogurt shop, and a running store. Was he getting me coffee? But no, he parked around back of the mall, got out, and jogged around to open the door for me since I wasn't coherent enough to coordinate movements like door opening. Noah seemed unaffected and just shot me a wide grin. "Come on, sleepyhead."

I followed Noah into the back of one of the stores and we entered a small, spotless galley-like kitchen. Four glass-fronted freezers stood on one side. There was a large stainless steel table in the center and several contraptions on the other side. A small desk area was situated toward the rear, by the door we had just entered. I guessed this was the yogurt store.

"Welcome to my finance project," Noah said, waving an arm around. "Can you do your hair up with a hair thingy?"

I nodded, pulled a hair band from my shorts, and wrapped my long, kind of snarled hair up into a pony. Noah handed me a white hair net that I put over my hair. He dropped a white apron over my head and spun me around to tie it. He then did the same for himself.

"Pretty sexy look for you," I commented. Neither the white apron nor the hair net could do anything to reduce his masculinity. If anything, he looked more approachable.

"Had a lunch lady crush, did you?" Noah asked with disbelief.

He went to the freezer and pulled out a flat full of strawberries. "We have to hull and chop these by hand."

"So you run this place?" I asked.

"No, but the owner is thinking of selling and said I'd have an opportunity to buy it," Noah replied, methodically and quickly working through the flat of strawberries.

"Will you do it?" This fit into Noah's empire-building scheme. I loved frozen yogurt and likely would eat all the profits if I worked here. I chopped, but my pieces weren't as precisely cut as Noah's. He didn't seem to care however, scooping my diced strawberries into a stainless steel container with his. We silently moved through the fruit, cutting and hulling.

"I will, but I don't have all the cash I need yet."

I thought of my trust fund that I couldn't access until I was twenty-five. I wondered if Uncle Louis would give me an advance against it. "Maybe I could—"

He cut me off with a quick flick of his wrist. "No. Bo already offered," He put down his knife. "I'm doing this myself. The stupid thing is that if I hadn't bought the truck before I came here, I'd have enough." He sounded bitter again.

"When do you have time to train?"

"I train about two hours in the morning. Go to classes. Come here. Keep moving. Train again at night."

"Is that what the person you talked with told you to do?" I avoided using the word counselor since Noah himself seemed averse to it. I wondered if I should tell him how much therapy went on in the Sullivan family, but decided I didn't want to terrify him. *Hey, Noah, my entire family props up the antidepressant-drug industry. You fit right in.*

He laughed, a short, humorless sound. "Not really. He said I should learn to start taking it easy. But then I caught him smoking outside the VA, and when he was stubbing his cigarette out, he told me everyone has a vice. Overworking is mine, I guess."

"Fighting seems dangerous," I said hesitantly. It wasn't like I hated the idea of Noah fighting, just the idea of him getting hurt.

"Not any more so than what Josh does," Noah replied with some mild exasperation.

"He's not in a metal cage with people kicking at his head. And he never broke anyone's eye socket." But I did worry about Josh quite a bit. A defenseless receiver across the middle of the field could receive crushing blows.

Noah just shook his head. "Let me guess. Mike told you that."

I nodded, and Noah looked like he wanted to drive to the library and break something on Mike's face. "I didn't break anyone's eye socket. I punched the guy in the eye. He was a bleeder and shed all over the floor. It was a fucking mess, and I guess he wore an eye patch for a few days. I think he made up the story to impress some girl and it got out of hand."

"I just would hate for you to get hurt if it wasn't something you truly loved doing," I said, trying to keep the worry out of my voice and be more matter-of-fact.

"The incidences of injury increased in boxing when gloves were introduced. Fists rarely cause the type of injury you're worried about," Noah said, sounding a little annoyed. This was definitely not the first time he had said this.

"Do you do any illegal fighting?" I asked, wanting to know everything I could.

"Is that what Mike told you?" I'd have to make sure that I always stood next to Mike when Noah was around. I could tell he was getting increasingly disgusted with Mike.

"He said something that hinted at it," I mumbled.

"There is a lot of good money in unsanctioned events. They're run by shady promoters but probably still legal. They're just not approved by any of the mainstream management bodies. Then there are the underground fights. Those are all cash and you can pull in a few hundred every night, easy. Sometimes more," Noah admitted.

"So yes?" I pressed.

"Have I? Yes. How do you think I'm going to fund this thing?" He waived his knife around the room.

"But if I or Bo could lend you some money—" I started and Noah interrupted.

"It's not really as dangerous as you think. It's rare that you ever fight someone who's had any training. Usually the guy with the quicker fist or the stronger jaw wins. As a trained fighter going in, you can pick and choose what punch to take, to make the crowd excited, and then when to lay out your opponent. The likelihood of injury is low," he said earnestly. It seemed important to him that I understood this and even supported it.

"What about other trained fighters, like you? It can't be all inept people," I objected.

"Mostly. A lot of underground fighters are like bored businessmen. Some of them are former big men on campus who've just gone to college or got a job and realized that all the high school glory doesn't carry over. Sometimes you'll meet up with another trained fighter, but that's rare because there are more legitimate big money opportunities now with network contracts." Noah went over to the strange contraptions, checked things and moved on, like he was executing a mental to do list.

"So why not just fight underground all the time?" I asked, still unconvinced.

"Not enough paying fights. It's really random. Some guy has to find a place for us to fight and then you have to get three or so fights together to make it worthwhile. And, frankly, it's getting harder and harder to find people willing to fight against me because I've been winning. We're making less money on bets too, because the odds are low."

It was all about the money for Noah.

"So you're like a girl stripping to pay for law school, only you're fighting for money?" I asked.

This made him laugh. "I guess so. Never thought of it that way." Noah set down his knife. "You don't have to worry about me, Grace. I can take care of myself. Plus I'm trying to do only sanctioned events now."

I bit back more dire warnings and instead asked, "Do you have any fights coming up?"

"No. I'm trying to get on the undercard for Vegas. There are some scouts from the UFC supposedly coming to a smoker in October."

Noah scooped up the rest of the berries and placed them in a cooler. After taking off his apron and hair protection, he came over to lean against the table next to me.

"And that is?"

"A smoker is an informal tournament. You're mostly fighting members of your gym or maybe some other gym. Everyone uses protective gear. Most of those who attend will be other fighters, but it'd be okay if you came, if you want," he offered.

"Um, sure." I wasn't sure I was ready to see Noah get punched or kicked. I didn't think it would look good if I was cringing and flinching at every blow. "So what do you do now?"

"Train, study, loiter in the library in hopes that I run into this girl I'm crazy about," he said with a sudden grin. He pulled off my hairnet and reached behind me to untie the knot in the apron, pulling my body lightly against his.

The statement and the contact made me both blush and smile. I tried to change the subject while inwardly hugging the words close. *He's crazy about me.* "Grappling sounds kind of kinky," I teased, turning the subject back to fighting.

Noah laughed. "Yeah, there was a big article in a magazine that said MMA was the gayest sport. A bunch of guys rolling around on the floor wrapping their arms and legs around each other in order to get the other person to submit. Also guys always try to grab your sack."

"I can't tell if I'm getting turned on or off by the prospect of you and another ripped guy feeling each other up," I said, pondering images of Noah rolling around on the ground with another guy, all sweaty and delicious.

"Let me know when you come to a decision," Noah nudged me in the shoulder as he directed me to the exit.

"Oh, I will."

***

Noah dropped me off at my apartment. "I'd kiss you, but then I don't think either of us would make it to class this morning," he said ruefully, opening the door and helping me out. He gave me a quick, chaste kiss on the forehead, and I ran to make my first class.

Later, I met Lana for lunch. When she walked into the QC Café, she looked terrible, which for Lana is usually only one step down from show-stopping gorgeousness. Today she appeared more like a bedraggled kitten left out in the rain too long. Her long blonde hair hung haphazardly around her face, and I could see slight smudges beneath her eyes. I half rose to hug her, but she waved me off.

"What's wrong?" I asked before she was fully seated.

She threw her messenger bag into an unoccupied seat and sighed, "Peter came over last night."

"What did he want?"

"Apparently he wanted to explain how his fling was a meaningless mistake. He is so very sorry and didn't tell me because he didn't want to hurt my feelings over something he had decided was so trivial."

"Did you hit him, or can I do it later today?" I couldn't believe the nerve of this guy.

"I know, right? I told him that I didn't believe him and maybe called him a few names. He said I was a shrew who was more interested in fucking herself than any guy and then it just went downhill." Lana looked disappointed in herself. She didn't like losing control like that. The fact that she did suggested she was more hurt about Peter's infidelity than she had originally let on.

"I'm sorry." It was such an inadequate sentiment. I wanted to do something. "Maybe Noah and Bo could kidnap him, and we could take turns kicking him in the balls."

Lana looked like she was contemplating this, but then said, "No. But I'm making an appointment at the health clinic to see if Peter passed anything on to me. I feel like such a stooge for sleeping with him when I got back to school."

"You couldn't have known," I said and added, "I'll come with you."

"Maybe you should think about getting checked out too," Lana replied.

"But I didn't sleep with Noah," I protested, my voice coming out high and squeaky.

"No?" Lana looked me up and down skeptically, as if she could see I was devirginized just by staring.

"No, I mean, we slept together but we didn't *sleep* together."

"You can say it Grace. S-E-X," she said, drawing the word out for emphasis.

"Okay, fine. We didn't have sex." I looked around to see if anyone was listening to us, but it appeared that everyone was engaged in their own conversations. Our drama wasn't very interesting.

"Did you do anything else?"

"Not really. I mean, we fooled around, and then we slept. I woke up at four in the morning to find out that Noah wants to run a mini empire of self-serve yogurt stores."

Lana's eyebrows rose. "That's, um, interesting."

"Gunner," I said glumly.

"So all is forgiven then? His friend-zoning you after years of correspondence is a thing of the past?"

I really didn't want to reveal all of Noah's private confessions, but I also wanted Lana to like him. I wanted the two of them to like each other. "He came to visit me in Chicago, but was intimidated by Uncle Louis's house and left."

By the look on Lana's face, I don't think she'd ever contemplated that this was the excuse that Noah would provide.

"As explanations go, that's not a bad one. Do you believe him?" Lana asked.

"Yeah, I guess I do. Why would he lie about it? It can't just be to get me to have sex with him. I don't think someone like him has a hard time picking up girls."

"No, you're right. He's prime," Lana said. That his primeness was so obvious concerned me, but I kept that worry to myself.

"Could we all go out some time or do you need some post-Peter downtime?" I suggested. It was important that two people I cared deeply about enjoyed one another's company.

"Yes, let's go out. Maybe we can target Jack," Lana suggested. The idea seemed to perk her up.

"Jack, of the tequila shots with Amy, Jack?"

"Yeah, he's sent some signals toward me, but at the time I was still thinking I'd give Peter the benefit of the doubt," Lana admitted ruefully.

"Where will Jack be this weekend?"

"Not sure. I'll go to the house before dinner and see if I can find out what the weekend party schedule is."

"Okay, I'll ask around, too, although I don't really know anyone who knows Jack," I said. Satisfied with our plans, I left Lana to meet up with Noah to study and then have dinner.

Chapter Twelve

Dear Grace,

It's not that the Marines was my only option. It just seemed like the best choice at the time. My father is an asshole. He's kind of like your Aunt Sarah. Nothing I did was good enough for him. He has a miserable life working a number of odd jobs and getting fired for not showing up or being too hung over and making mistakes.

He wanted me to be beat-down like him. I couldn't afford to go to college, and I didn't want to work construction for the rest of my life. Hence, the Marines. But when I came back during my first leave, after deployment, everyone in town treated me different.

Before, I was just a punk that might knock up their girls or break into their stores. Now I wore a uniform. Old vets saluted me. People who had never said hi thanked me for my service. It was like I had leveled up. But half the time, I think folks were sorry that there wasn't another generation of Jacksons to point to as a cautionary tale. I haven't told Bo yet, but I'm not going back home.

I'm going to volunteer for another tour. I felt more at home at a forward base unit than back in Little Oak, Texas.

~Noah

Grace

Noah and I were eating at a dive off campus that served the best tacos when his phone rang. He ignored it, so I gestured for him to answer when it rang again.

A barrage of words sputtered out of the phone, so loud that I could even hear it. Noah drew the phone away slightly from his ear and flicked the volume down.

He listened for most of the conversation but interjected a few times with "no" and "not yet" and shakes of his head. Then he motioned for a pen and paper, which I dug out for him. He asked, "How much?" and jotted something down.

He terminated the connection and set the phone face down on the table. He looked upset and rubbed his hands over his face a couple times.

"What is it?"

Noah leaned back in his chair, tipping it up slightly so it rested on its back two legs, laced his fingers behind his head, and looked upward. It wasn't a relaxed pose. He slammed down the chair and cursed.

"Nothing."

"You almost ruined that chair. That's a lot of anger over 'nothing.'"

"Nothing you should be concerned about." He turned his attention to his tacos and began sweeping up his uneaten portion.

"What is going on?" I demanded.

"Nothing," he repeated obviously trying to turn my attention away.

"You aren't eating. You're abusing furniture. And you're cursing on the phone," I said, aggravated at his secret keeping.

Noah looked frustrated and unhappy, and I was getting worried too. His poorly-hidden anxiety was contagious. He gestured for the waitress to come over and asked her to bring us the check. He threw down some cash and picked up our bags. It was clear he wanted to leave. I looked at my partially-eaten taco with some sadness. I was still hungry.

"I'm sorry. I'll get you something to eat later," he said. We walked out to the truck, or more appropriately, Noah walked quickly, and I jogged to keep up. Noah handed me in, and I kept quiet until he had started the truck.

"What's going on? I don't understand," I asked again.

When he didn't respond, I said, "Don't shut me out, Noah."

Instead of looking at me, he stared out the window and said, "It was the guy who owns the yogurt store. He has an offer for it, but he wanted to give me first shot at it. He'll give me five days to raise the cash."

"How much do you need?" This sounded like a great opportunity, not one that should evoke anger and unhappiness.

"Ten Gs."

I coughed into my hand with shocked surprise. "God, can you get that in a fight?"

"Not a regular one," Noah admitted reluctantly.

"I could ask Uncle Louis for an advance against my trust," I said. "It'd be a good investment."

"No," Noah said with careful enunciation. "Not your problem."

He pulled into the driveway of his house and jumped out. For once, Noah didn't open my door. I fumbled with the latch and raced after him. He was nearly running through the house. "Where's Mal?" he bellowed.

Finn was sitting in the great room playing a video game and jerked up at Noah's shout. "Office," He gestured toward the front room in the house closed off by double French doors. Mal was already at the door.

"What's up?" Mal asked, opening the door wider for Noah to come in.

"Can you call Rickers and see if he still wants that fight?"

Mal's expression changed from mild curiosity to concern. "What about the UFC, man?"

"I need a ten grand fight tonight, Mal. Can you make it happen?"

"If you need ten grand, I've got—"

"Can you set up the fucking fight or not?" Noah interrupted, his teeth clenched.

"Yeah, no problem. Just let me make a few calls," Mal said.

"Let me help you." Bo, appeared behind us. The whole house was there, listening to Noah, which no doubt infuriated him. He was so private. Now all these rich kids, including me, were standing there telling him he had nothing to worry about.

Noah turned on Bo. "I'll do it this once and be done."

"It doesn't work that way," Bo said. I stood by helplessly, but silently agreed with Bo.

Noah slashed his hand through the air. "It's my decision." He turned and pointed to Mal. "Make it happen." At least I wasn't the only one he ordered around.

Bo moved to say something, maybe forestall Mal, but Mal retreated into the office. "It's his decision, Bo. Let it be."

Noah stormed upstairs, and I was left behind, like an extra in Noah's life. I hated that. I ran after him.

"Who's Rickers?" I demanded, standing inside the bedroom as Noah rooted through his drawers and threw a pair of sweatpants and shorts on the bed.

"I'm going to do an illegal fight against a former UFC boxer kicked out because of steroids," he replied flatly.

"My God, no," I cried.

"You wanted to know, and I'm telling you," he said, proceeding to strip. For once the sight of his naked chest didn't rouse my passions. I was too concerned for his safety.

"It's not that dangerous." Noah tried to placate me. "I've been working with professional trainers for over a year now. I'm a better fighter than he is."

"This is a no-rules fight, though. You could get hurt," I pleaded. When he remained silent and continued to ready himself, I tried a different angle.

"Yes, I know I've lived a fortunate life. But, Noah, if I needed the money, wouldn't you give it to me?" I argued.

"It's not the same." He pulled on shorts and then sweatpants over top. "Dammit. All my wraps are at the gym." He loped to the door and yelled downstairs. "Bo, I need some wraps."

"It is the same thing. Do you care more about the money than me?" I asked.

"Don't make it about you. It's not about you," Noah snapped.

"Don't do this, Noah. You'll get hurt. I have the money. "

"I don't want your money. Did you know that one of the most celebrated fighters in MMA history is a guy who lost by technical knockout? Helio Grace wouldn't give up even after his opponent had broken his arm in two places. He was lionized after the fight for his refusal to submit and tap out. Finally, after his arm was broken twice, someone from his corner threw the towel in and ended the match," Noah went on.

"What does that have to do with anything?" I cried.

"It's about being able to hold my head up. I've got some skill, Grace. I can make something for me, for us, but I'm going to have to use my hands to do it. Take a few knocks. Look at your fucking apartment, Grace, or this place here. This is where you're comfortable, and I'm going to make this my world even if I have to break a few eye sockets to do it."

Nothing I was going to say would penetrate his thick head. Bo appeared at the doorway and handed over some wraps to Noah. We wordlessly exchanged frustrated and worried glances, but remained silent. Noah had set his course and no one was going to deter him. Neither his best friend nor his girlfriend, if that was what I was.

Noah was dressed in sweats, a tank top, and tennis shoes. His wraps and a change of clothing were stuffed in a gym bag. Mal came up the stairs. "It's all set up. We'll meet in an hour at the old zipper factory building south of downtown on East Sixth."

"I'll drive you home," Noah said.

"You will not." I told him. I marched over and picked up his gym bag. "If you're going to fight then any post-game celebrating will be with me." My smart remark broke the tension that had built up, and everyone laughed.

"She told you," Bo said.

"I guess she did." Noah didn't take his eyes off me. "Okay then, Grace, you're with me."

***

"Worried?" Noah asked me when we were back in his truck. He had taken the time to help me up into the cab before going around and getting in the driver's seat, his prior lapse of manners completely unnoticed. It was a sign of how upset he was before and how calm and in control he was now.

"Yes." I didn't want to be, but I had never experienced this before. I didn't want anything bad to happen to Noah.

"Don't be. I'll win. He's a T-Rex."

"What's that?"

"He's got short arms, short reach."

"Nice," I laughed as Noah had intended and then tried to return the favor. "Too bad we are on our way to have you roll around with some guy instead of back at my apartment to wrestle in bed."

"We can wrestle later," he said, preoccupied. He didn't even come back with some sexual comment as he ordinarily would. I gave up.

"Tell me about the fight tonight. Maybe if you explain more, I won't be so afraid," I said, hoping to borrow his confidence.

"As long as everyone keeps their mouth shut, there isn't going to be a problem." Underground fighting, Noah explained, was done by all kinds of men of all different body shapes. He figured most of them had rage issues, and this was a safe place to let them out. One guy he knew fought regularly and did so not to win but for the adrenaline rush from the pain. But he often won because he wouldn't quit. This guy loved to take a punch—the more brutal, the better. Noah contemplated that it was almost a sexual thing for the guy.

"I'm not sure how he explains that at work the next day," Noah admitted. Many of the fighters refused to get medical attention. The more injuries there were, the greater the likelihood that the underground fights would be discovered. Noah said, with a few colorful curses, that this was *the dumbest fucking thing ever.*

The worst were the wannabes, he went on. There were dickhead fight clubs where people brought shit like pillowcases full of rocks and frying pans. "You're just asking for a concussion."

"Really? That seems kind of unfair. Are there other fights?"

"There're all kinds. Stupid suburban kids, mostly jocks, thinking they're the shit. Then there are the felony fights, where they pit two former felons against each other. It's like the Christians versus the lions with the promoter acting like fucking Cesar. Thumbs up or thumbs down. Everyone in the audience thinking they are cooler than shit," he sneered.

"Are there rules or officials?"

"Not really. There is the promoter, who sets up the fight, like Mal, and a couple of people that monitor the bets. You can have a corner, but they can't interfere."

We entered downtown and pulled onto some side street, parking behind a warehouse. It was dark and quiet, but Noah made no move to exit. He leaned against his truck door and turned to me.

"Who are you fighting tonight?"

"DJ Rickers, who got kicked out of UFC for using steroids. I know he feels like he was unfairly singled out, but no one will sign him now because performance-enhancing drugs are ruining sports. He's wanted to fight a UFC fighter for a long time and will pay a lot of money to do it."

"You aren't UFC," I pointed out thinking that maybe Rickers wouldn't even show up to fight.

"I'm an 'up-and-comer,'" Noah said, "and that's enough for Rickers. He knows me and my reputation."

"You think you can win?" I asked hopeful.

"I know I can," was his immediate and confident response.

I nodded, relieved, but I was still a bit upset. He opened his door and gestured for me to wait. I really disliked waiting to have my door opened, but I knew from past experience that this was important to Noah. He helped me down, but stayed my hand when I reached in for my bag. "Don't bring anything in," he said. "You don't need anything."

"What about my phone or ID?"

"No one is carding you, and I have mine." Noah took my hand and pulled me close.

"Noah," I tugged on his hand. "I will feel really uncomfortable without a phone in there and no cash or ID or anything."

"Are you okay with your phone in your pocket?"

I grimaced and wondered if my pockets were even deep enough to hold a phone. He bent down so his face was close to mine. "I'll hold it for now and then when Finn comes, he can hold it. I need your hands free. Stay with me at all times. Don't let go of me. Grab my wrist, my pants, my shirt. It can be crowded, and the people in there will be rowdy. I don't want you to get hurt." He waited for me to assent. I nodded, but it wasn't enough. He wanted oral acknowledgment.

I gave a big audible sigh so that he was aware I found this a bit tedious. "I promise I will stay with you at all times and that I will attach myself like a barnacle to some part of your body."

"Just wanted to know we are on the same page," he said, clucking his tongue in mock admonishment.

I handed the phone to Noah, and he tucked it into his front pocket. I tapped it with my fingers. "Isn't it uncomfortable down there?"

"No, but if you pat me a little to the left, it might become uncomfortable." Ah, teasing Noah was back. He wasn't at all concerned about his fight. I hoped he wasn't being overconfident.

"Is this the place?" I gestured toward the seemingly empty warehouse building.

"No. You can't all park next to the building, or the cops will know what is going on. The building is five blocks from here."

That meant walking in the darkened streets. Kind of creepy. Noah's admonition to stay close and hold his hand really didn't need to be repeated out here. I slid my arm around his back and tucked myself under his arm. I wasn't so foolish as to not appreciate his protection. "This doesn't look safe."

"Safe places are well lit and observed by regular folks. Underground fighting kind of means unsafe and unknown."

"I'm going to pretend we're going to a rave, just so you know."

"Stick close to me, and you won't get roofied."

"That's a pleasant thought."

Noah drew me close to his side and we started walking across the empty parking lot at a quick pace. Noah's jeans rang and he pulled his phone out. "Where are you?" He barked into the phone. He listened for a moment and said, "Mulberry and East 6th. We'll meet you at the entrance. Text me when you get there."

Noah ended the call and tucked his phone away.

It sounded grim and dirty and not at all romantic. "Who will be here? Women?"

"You would not believe the women there," Noah replied, rolling his eyes toward me. "From the suburban mom to the punked-out chicks. They're turned on by the fighting, I guess."

I clutched his hand a little tighter, which caused Noah to lean down. "I'll take care of you."

"I know you will," I said with conviction. "I trust you."

His eyes, lit by the moonlight and the stars, darkened a bit, and he stopped. We both understood I meant for more than for just this one night and one moment. With both hands on my hips, he drew me close so that we were flush from head to toe. "You won't regret that."

His mouth came down onto mine with almost a bruising pressure, as if he were trying to brand his message into my body. My hands clenched around his biceps, and I felt them flex slightly underneath me as his arms folded around my back and pressed me hard against him. When he lifted his head, we were both breathing heavily. Even through our two layers of clothing, I could feel the outline of his hard-on against me.

"No more distracting me," he said, his eyes glittering. His mouth tipping up at the corners.

"No sir," I replied, cheekily. "I won't stop you and force your arms around me again."

"Smart ass." He turned toward a side door of a large brick building that had a dim red bulb above it. No one was standing around outside. Noah rapped out strange pattern on the door. In response, the door opened immediately, and a large man with dirty blond dreads greeted us. "Noah Jackson, what are you doing here?"

"I'm fighting here tonight. Against Rickers."

Dreadlocks shook his head, the tail ends of his hair swinging slightly. "That's bad news. What about the UFC?"

"If everyone keeps their traps locked down, it will be fine. Deke, this is my girl, Grace. Keep an eye out for her. She's precious cargo," Noah gestured for me to enter. I stepped forward and felt my hand engulfed in Deke's giant paw. Noah handed Deke a few bills.

"Nice to meet you, Grace," Deke grunted. After I returned the pleasantry, he pointed down a dark hallway. "Go to the back room. No one wants you to get in trouble. You're our hometown boy." Before Deke could close the door, Finn rushed in.

"Great, I caught you. I can never remember the stupid knock," he panted, clearly having run quickly to make it through before the door was closed. Finn and Deke exchanged greetings and money, and then we all left Deke at the door to venture down the dark hallway.

"I feel like I'm in some bad Halloween movie, and Freddie is going to jump out with his chainsaw at any moment." I shivered under Noah's arm.

"I thought the chainsaw guy was Jason." Finn draped his arm around my back and patted my head.

"Finn, make sure no one mauls Grace tonight, okay?" Noah ordered, pushing Finn's arm away and drawing me closer to his side.

"Will do," he replied, unperturbed that Noah seemed to be creating a pocket of space between Finn and me—as if even his friends were not allowed within a certain distance.

At the end of the hallway, a tiny bit of light seeped out underneath a nearly hidden doorway. Noah didn't bother to knock this time. He just opened the door. Inside were the remnants of an office. Filing cabinets were stacked on top of each other, some perpendicular to the floor, and there was a battered desk with its drawers open and askew, like a lady of the night with her heels kicked off and her pantyhose around her ankles. It was somewhat obscene. Two sofas, with cushions that were nearly flattened by use or age, were positioned opposite the desk. Next to the sofa stood Bo, Mal, and Adam. Bo held out his hand for the bag Noah carried.

He dug in and pulled out the wraps while Noah emptied the contents of his pants pockets and handed my phone to Finn. Noah held out his hands, and Bo wrapped him. "I saw Rickers earlier. He looks like he has trimmed down some, off the 'roids."

Noah gave a short nod. "Have you heard where he's been training?"

"No. Maybe out of town."

"Strategy?"

"Don't let him punch you in the face. He was weak in the stomach before. A good kick should level him. I don't think he's a good grappler, but you're on sand and cement here, not the Octagon, so you don't want to spend too much time on the floor. If I think the fight is getting out of hand, I'm throwing in the towel," Bo said.

"I don't need a motherfucking babysitter," Noah snarled.

"Yes, you do," Bo shot back, "or you wouldn't even be here."

Noah didn't respond to this taunt. After Bo finished wrapping his hands, we went back into the hallway. As we got close to the entrance, I saw another door that I had missed when I first walked into the building. Bo threw it open. The warehouse smelled of old wood and dust. A cluster of people maybe five or six deep stood in the center. Many held bottles or cans of beer. As we approached, the sea of people parted, and I realized it was more like ten deep.

The center wasn't a boxing ring at all, just a crudely chalked out square. Whether from the traffic of feet or the oppression of machinery that once stood here, there was slight bowl in the dirt floor of the warehouse, creating a miniature amphitheater. It was a good setting for a fight—there were no chairs and the dip in the floor made it easier for the people in the rear to see the action.

The sea of people closed in behind us. A barrel-chested man covered in tattoos stood to one side inside the square, shifting from foot to foot and lightly punching one side of his chest and then the other with alternating hands. He looked huge. If this was trimmed down some, I wouldn't want to see him all 'roided up.

I stood at the very edge of the square. Noah turned and said, "Don't move from here. Finn," he directed, "take care of her." Noah moved down to the corner with Bo.

A tall, gangly guy came out to the center and told the crowd they had five minutes to finish up their bets. Five minutes crawled by. Noah pulled off his sweatshirt and sweatpants. He stood with his arms crossed, staring impassively at Rickers. The gangly guy came up to Noah and handed him a white towel. Noah balled it up and threw into the middle.

"Fuck," I heard Finn say softly.

"What's wrong now?" I whispered to Finn.

"Rickers is a masochist. Totally gets off on getting hit and won't stop even if he is seriously injured. He refuses to tap out, and now Noah has rejected the towel," Finn explained. Fuck, indeed.

"This isn't going to end well, is it," I said. It was a statement, not a question.

Finn shook his head, "No, probably not."

The gangly guy went to Rickers' side and talked to him for a minute. Ricker shook his head and seemed to refuse the white towel. Finally, he turned to someone in the crowd, a woman, and gestured for her to take the towel. Part of the crowd groaned at this but most seemed to swell with excitement. From what Noah had said earlier, seeing a fight where no one tapped out was what wet dreams were made of for some of these attendees.

I felt so nervous that I wondered if I should bite my nails to alleviate my anxiety. Instead, I just shifted from side to side so much that Finn finally put both hands on my shoulders.

"Stand still," he warned, "or I'll tie your shoelaces together."

Noah bent his head down slightly so his and Bo's foreheads were almost touching. They exchanged words, serious looks on both their faces, and then Noah held out both wrapped fists. Bo crashed his hands down on top. He slapped Noah on the back and went to the corner.

The skinny guy came out and gestured for the fight to begin.

Noah

The plan was to knock Rickers down and get the hell out of there. I didn't want Grace to see us grappling like animals, further cementing the idea that I wasn't right for her, but damn I needed this money.

Rickers could take a punch and, despite his size, he was fairly light on his feet. But, his short arms were always going to prevent him from moving forward. No amount of steroids was going to change that.

I didn't want to get punched in the face, so I danced backward as he advanced. I had plans with Grace later, and a broken lip would put a serious dent in them.

I could hear the crowd groaning as I ducked and weaved away, wanting more action. Few fighters enjoyed fighting backwards. I figured I'd move around for a minute, catch Rickers off balance, and then attack.

He advanced wildly, eager to make contact. Eager to show me my place. His eagerness played right into my hands. On his next advance, I shot my leg out and round-housed him in the gut. His fist caught me on the top of my head, but I barely noticed. The kick caused him to bend over slightly, and I clipped him with an uppercut. He fell like a shorn log to the ground.

I straddled his body and struck him twice more in the head. I waited for him to tap out, but he struggled upward, trying to throw me off. I held my forearm against his windpipe and waited. Nothing. Fuck this.

I pressed my forearm harder into his neck. Sweat and blood rolled down my forehead, obscuring my vision. I pretended not to notice. "Tap out," I growled. All my energy was focused into my arm at Rickers' windpipe.

He grunted. "Can't. Won't."

This was insane. I'd never choked someone into submission before. I had knocked people out with a fist or a kick, but never deliberately choked the air out of someone's lungs, and I didn't want to this time. This was the motherfucking problem with unsanctioned fighting. There wasn't a referee who would jump in and call a halt to the stupid shit we fighters do. Left to our own devices, we'd choke each until we were all brain damaged.

"You aren't goddamned Helios. There isn't any honor here. This is a fucking warehouse," I ground out, but still he refused. His eyes stared up at me, unblinking.

"I'd take honor wherever you can get it, brother." He raised up slightly, as if he wanted my face near his. I should've drawn back. A head butt would hurt like a son of a bitch. Instead, I leaned forward and heard him whisper. "It's all good." He cracked his head against mine, and at the same time, his hands on my forearm reversed pressure slightly. I don't think anyone around us could see but he was almost pulling my arm into his throat.

Gritting my teeth, I acquiesced to his unspoken command and pressed harder. His grip went limp and the light in his eyes dimmed until they were blank and his eyelids rolled shut like a garage door. I felt his entire body go lax beneath mine. I sat up on my haunches and looked down at Ricker's body underneath mine, laid out like a corpse on a slab.

This was the last time, I thought. The last time I'd ever do this. I had left the Marines because I was tired of the dirt and the death, and here I was, voluntarily rolling around in the dirt in a warehouse fighting some guy practically to the death. I pushed up to my feet and looked for Grace. She was what had brought me out of the war, took me away from my past. My future was with her, if she'd still have me.

Our angry words hung over me, weighing me down like a fighter on my back. I stood up, dizzy from the blow and the head butt, and stumbled toward her. I guess that was all the encouragement she needed, because I could see her run to me, her hand slightly covering her mouth. My vision was clouded, and I felt weak. I stumbled again and before I could fall, she was there, holding me up, pressing her pristine shirt into my chest and getting my blood and sweat mixed up. If I was any kind of decent human being, I'd push her away, but I couldn't. I could never push her away again.

Chapter Thirteen

Dear Grace,

We have been moved to a tiny forward operating base near the base of some mountains in eastern A'stan. A patrol went out in the morning and was hit with small arms fire, mortars, and RPGs. One of the sergeants was shot and killed. The entire FOB felt the blow. Everyone liked this guy. I can't even write his name down. Too painful.

An older NCO who has been on several tours said that the patrols are nowhere near as dangerous as they were even six months ago, and that deaths are becoming rarer. But no one believes him, not when your buddy's corpse is lying in a tent waiting be flown back to Dover.

I probably shouldn't even write this to you. Now I really do feel like I'm contaminating you, like the dust on the letters is carrying all the ill feeling to you. Maybe the ocean can cleanse it.

Yours,
Noah

Noah

I wanted to take Grace home. I was pumped full of adrenaline and flush with cash. There was only one thing that would make this night better, but everyone wanted to celebrate.

Grace had promised her cousin earlier that she would go hunt down some frat boy, and no amount of wheedling would get her to change her mind.

"Why not The Circus?" Grace told me Lana was down there, waiting for her.

"That's a dance club." I shook my head no. I didn't want to dance. I wanted to go have one drink and then go home or to Grace's apartment. I didn't care which one.

"There's a dance floor and music, so if that constitutes a dance club, then, yes, it is," My victory had made her sassy. I liked it. Of course, there was little I didn't like about Grace. Even her earlier worry made me feel good, but I didn't tell her that.

"Grace," I drew her name out slowly. "That's like the seven circles of hell for me."

"What're you talking about? I saw your moves inside the circle." Apparently now that the fight was over, it was okay to refer to it.

"I told you before that dancing isn't my thing."

"I'll ask them to play a marching song," she reassured me, laughing.

"You know why dance clubs are the worst?" I said.

"No, why?" Her giggling made me smile, but I wasn't going to back down.

"Because you girls love to dance, which attracts all kinds of fools, and then I'll be forced to beat them all up." I needed to unwind, not get all worked up again. I might attack Grace on the dance floor, and I'm pretty sure she wouldn't be down with that.

"Then maybe you shouldn't come to the bar with us."

"That's a negative." I shook my head to emphasize my words.

"Oh come on, Noah. It won't be that bad," she wheedled.

"It will be."

"Don't you dance in the ring?"

"It's called the Octagon. And only because I'm trying to avoid being punched in the face. That's not the right attitude to have on the dance floor," I said, impatiently. I wanted to get Grace alone and ask her a very important question about her past experience with other guys. My desire for her coupled with the post-fight adrenaline made me restless and uneasy. I'd settle down once I had her in my bed. Then I could show her how little any guys she'd had in her past mattered.

"You aren't going to talk me out of this because I already abandoned Lana earlier tonight," Grace insisted.

"Why don't we go to the Americana? They have bands. I'm sure there is a dance floor there, because that's where my roommate Adam broke his leg," I offered.

"You know, when you are upset, your accent becomes more pronounced."

"We don't have accents, sugar," I laid it on thick. "It's you Yanks that have foreshortened all the good words, so they aren't even any fun to say anymore."

"Well, cowboy, are you going to meet us out or are you gonna wait with your horses at the campfire?"

"You have a terrible drawl, but don't worry, I'll give you all the tutoring you need." This tutoring would require for us to both be naked and for me to have my tongue all over her body, but I kept that to myself.

After a bunch of texting with Lana, it was agreed. She'd meet us at the Americana.

***

Grace wanted to go home to change. Given that she had a mixture of my blood and sweat all over her, I didn't argue. I drove her home, and she said she'd meet us at the bar.

Bo taped a small cut above my eye that must have come from the weak, late head butt, and I pulled out a T-shirt and jeans that I had thrown in the bag.

While the Americana wasn't a bevy of hot chicks like a college party, there were usually plenty of women here. But tonight it was like a ten to one ratio of guys to girls. Our group, composed of the five roommates and three guys from the Spartan gym, wasn't helping much.

We were all relieved that Grace and her friends were coming.

"Is the band like a bunch of rapists or something?" I asked Adam, who was slumped sullenly in his chair.

"Nah, screamers though. Kind of like Slipknot wannabes." That explained it. Few women were going to want to sit through a bunch of bad headbangers.

"Don't text that to Grace," Bo said, grabbing my hand.

"What am I, twelve?" I shook him off. Of course I wasn't going to text Grace, who wanted to go dance at some techno hip-hop club, that she was in for a night of heavy metal rock. "But you know she isn't going to want to stay long."

"I know. Didn't you say there was a party over on Forest?"

"Yeah. Grace's cousin is trying to hunt down some frat guy tonight and thinks he'll be there."

"The lovely Lana is single?" Bo raised his eyebrows. That was the first interest he'd tossed in that direction.

"Apparently her boyfriend accidentally forwarded a nude picture of some woman he hooked up with over the summer," I explained. The entire table was now leaning in listening to our conversation. I felt like I was in the middle of some goddamn church picnic where everyone got together to gossip about their neighbor while pretending not to really care.

"Ouch," Bo grimaced. "Rookie mistake."

"Who's lovely Lana?" Mal asked.

"Lovely Lana," Bo said, "is a glorious blonde creature."

"You hitting that?" Mal asked.

"Nope," Bo leaned in. I could tell he was going to impart one of his dating philosophies. He had many. "There are only two circumstances in which you sleep with your wingman's girl's friend." He pointed to me. "First, when all you're doing is hooking up casually. Second," he lifted another finger, "when you think you're both going to marry those girls. Otherwise, you dip your wick elsewhere."

"Why's this?" Mal said.

"Don't encourage him," I protested.

"Because when your wingman breaks up with his girlfriend, you don't want to be stuck with the extra baggage." He cocked his fingers at me and pretended to shoot me with them.

"Thanks for the vote of confidence." I didn't really get Bo's objection to Grace and me as a couple. He seemed convinced we weren't going to last.

The door to Americana opened, and I heard the entire bar suck in their collective breath. I didn't need to look at the door to know it was Grace and her cousin. But I looked anyway, because I was hungry to see her. She was dressed up in shorts and heels. It was a good look on her, and apparently I wasn't the only one who thought so. Some asshole detached himself from the bar to greet her. I stood up.

Bo stood next to me. I wasn't sure if he wanted to hold me back or go with me, but I didn't wait. As soon as I started moving, I saw Grace notice me. Her eyes lit up and she smiled. The guy next to her glanced in my direction but didn't back away.

He was talking to her, and she pointed to me and shook her head. I caught the tail of her conversation.

"I have a boyfriend," I heard her say. Pride swelled up in me, along with a fierce possession at her use of the word boyfriend.

"I had tacos for lunch," he replied.

"What?" Her attention swung away from me.

"I thought we were talking about random things of no importance." He grinned like it was the wittiest, bad-ass, motherfucker thing that he'd ever thought of it, but it was a well-rehearsed line that I had heard trotted out a million times at base bars.

She just shook her head. "My random thing of no importance is standing right behind you."

I refrained from baring my teeth at him and instead took Grace's hand and pulled her to me. I bent down. Instead of kissing her on her lips, I pulled her hair aside, exposing her neck, and pressed a hot wet bite to the soft flesh right above her shoulder. Her breath hitched in surprise. I didn't even raise my head, but I turned my face slightly so I could look at the guy with challenge in my eyes. *She's mine*, I told him silently. I wanted to describe how I had choked someone until he passed out, but refrained. He got the message, though, and I watched him carefully until he turned and went back to the bar.

"Um, hello," I heard Grace say. I kissed her neck again and straightened up, brushing her hair down her back. I wanted to mark her, but I knew I probably shouldn't do that in public. I drew her back to the table. In my absence, another table had been pulled up and three more chairs added. I looked behind Grace and saw Lana and Amy, the girl I carried up into Grace's apartment the night of that frat party. When we were out of shouting distance of the bar, Grace tugged me down so she could speak into my ear. "I don't know whether to be grateful that you didn't hit him or mad that you manhandled me. Those are two bad options."

I tried to look repentant, but I wasn't pulling it off. "I'll do better next time?" I offered. I thought that as time went on, and I was surer about everything that maybe I wouldn't react so poorly after seeing some guy hit on Grace in front of me. But probably not.

She gave an un-Grace-like snort and went to the table. Bo greeted her with a hug and shook hands with Lana and Amy. Bo was thawing toward her. Every guy at the table perked up at the sight of two additional women, but the odds were still on the poor side. I slid Grace's and my chairs back a little, so we were out of the line of fire as the guys all geared up to compete for Lana and Amy's attention.

I tuned out whatever they were talking about and instead spent my time admiring Grace's sheer top and the tight fit of the tank top she wore beneath. Tonight I'd like to see Grace wearing just that sheer top with nothing on underneath. I could suck her nipples through the cloth and see the wet fabric cling to her skin. If there were a light behind her, the entire top would be illuminated, both hiding and displaying her curves.

I shifted in my chair, my jeans suddenly a bit too tight on me. I closed my eyes and pictured myself dismantling my rifle instead of disrobing Grace.

A screeching of guitars and a smattering of mismatched drums woke me out of my reverie. The band was getting ready to play.

"Why are we here again?" I asked Adam.

"The lead singer used to be in my band, and I want to make sure he didn't steal any of my music," Adam replied. I nodded to indicate I heard him and sat back. I placed my hand on Grace's back and felt the silky fabric beneath my palm. I rubbed my hand up and down, idly wondering if the delicate shirt would catch on the calluses of my hand. I wanted to reach under the shirt and smooth my hand over Grace's skin. The tank she had on was riding up a little, and I could see the top of the waistband of her shorts. The tank needed just a slight nudge upward, and I'd be treated to a sliver of golden skin.

I wondered if I could get Grace to go the bathroom with me. No, too public. Maybe the truck. My backseat was a bench and I could—I shifted again. Pulling my hand off Grace's back, I took a deep breath. I needed to calm down. Remove the magazine. Empty the chamber. Place rifle on table. Pull the hand guard. Breathe.

She turned to me with a questioning look. "Anything wrong?" she mouthed.

I'd like to lay you across the table and eat you out, and I don't care if the entire bar watches. I shook my head no, but she slid back in her chair and nestled up next to me. My arm closed around her, almost involuntarily. Her nose brushed my neck as she leaned in and I had to suppress a shiver.

"Is it okay that we are here? Seems like we have interrupted a manly convention of drinking."

"Just before you came, the entire table was bemoaning the low chick to dick ratio."

She released another little snort and said, "Nice."

She said something else, but I couldn't hear her because the band had started their first song. It was a lot of screaming, jumping around, and really poor guitar playing. I winced at a particularly bad note and nudged Adam again. "These guys are really bad."

He yelled back, "I said that they were *like* Slipknot, not that they *were* Slipknot."

There was only one acceptable act after fighting and that was fucking. If I didn't get Grace alone for a minute, I was going to explode. Standing up, I pulled Grace up from her chair and led her toward the only semi-private spot in the joint.

The hallway to the bathrooms was dimly lit and there was a small space at the end illuminated only by a faint EXIT sign. The walls provided a barrier against the awful sound emanating from the stage.

I leaned her against the wall and put an outstretched arm by her head.

I rubbed a strand of her dark brown hair between my fingers and then leaned close. "I'm going to kiss you here, okay?" I felt I should ask because it was public, but Grace didn't protest. She only pressed her body closer to mine.

"Because it's the only way to endure the music?" she teased.

As if I needed an excuse. I didn't respond with words, but instead I closed the distance between us. Her lips were soft and a little sticky, remnants of some lip gloss perhaps. I swept my tongue across the bottom of her lip and then pushed inside to taste her.

The cool of a mint still lingered, and I could feel a faint tingling sensation. Dimly, I thought that she must have just eaten a breath mint. She offered no resistance to my touch and instead curled her little tongue around mine, stroking it, welcoming me inside.

My hand tightened in her hair. I clenched my other hand in a fist against the wall even though I wanted to touch her all over. Cup her breasts. Unbutton her pants, stroke her from throat to pussy. But this was a semi-public place, and I didn't want Grace to feel embarrassed by anything she did with me, ever. Public making out seemed to be a good limit. For now, at least.

But that didn't stop me from imagining what it would feel like to have her hot mouth all over my cock, having her suck me like she was sucking my tongue. Then I couldn't resist. My body blocked the view from anyone else. I let go of her hair, pressed my palm just below her breast, and let the plump weight rest on the top of my fingers. When she moaned, I took this as permission and covered her breast, kneading it slightly with my palm and rubbing my thumb across the nipple I could feel even through the sheer shirt, the tank, and the bra she wore underneath.

I wanted to put my mouth on that tip and suck it like the juicy piece of fruit it reminded me of.

My hindbrain was telling me to keep going, to rip the shirt off and pull her shorts down. I pulled my hand off her breast and tore my mouth from hers.

She made a small sound of frustration. *Me too, sweetheart. Me too.* Instead of taking her again, I pulled her in for a hug and held her close, trying to will myself to calm down. "Can we go home or are you committed to a night out?" I asked, pushing strands of her hair out of her face and down behind her ear.

"I can't," she whispered to my shirt. "Lana, she's had a rough week." I took a deep breath and exhaled. I had waited this long, another few hours wouldn't kill me.

"Later, then, tonight?" I hoped she knew what I was asking. Maybe it seemed like we had only been dating for a short while, but our courtship had extended nearly six years. Surely that was long enough.

"Yes, tonight," she promised.

Grace

Noah's response to my agreement was a blinding smile. Shaking my head, I asked, "Why doesn't just being with me generate that kind of happy response?"

"It does. It's just on the inside." He gave me another hug and a kiss on the top of my head. "So let's go find this Jack dude."

"Wait," I said and looked down. Lana had told me I should let Noah know he was my first, so he could be gentle with me. I was embarrassed and wasn't sure how he would take it.

"What is it?" Noah asked, tipping my face up. I must have looked pained because he stroked my face and kissed my temple. "What's wrong?" he asked again.

"I'm, ah," I stumbled around for the words. "I'm not very experienced." I felt his body tense up against me. Was he upset by this? *I should've never told him.*

"Oh baby, really?" he said, sounding a little winded. I nodded and looked down, a little afraid of seeing the expression on his face. He laughed a little and hugged me closer.

"God, this is going to make me a jackass if I say this, because it truly wouldn't have mattered to me if you weren't a virgin, but goddamn Grace, this is amazing."

"So you aren't upset?" I asked him, finally looking up. When I saw his eyes, my breath caught. His lips were curved upward in a smile, but his eyes were blazing.

"No fucking way. I'm glad you told me, but now I'm so hard I'm not going to be able to walk for a good minute," he admitted. "I'm going to make it so good for you, Grace, I promise." He said it so seriously that it was like he was vowing it on his mother's grave.

I gave him a small smile in return. "I believe you." I ran my hands up and down his chest, molding my fingers against the ridges and valleys. I shivered with delight at the idea of Noah teaching me all of the things other, more experienced girls hinted knowingly about.

He pressed me closer and took long, deep breaths that I felt in his chest when he inhaled and against my hair when he exhaled. After at least a minute, Noah stepped back, reached down to adjust himself with a pained grimace and said, "I think we can go back now."

"What time is it?" I pulled up his wrist to look. It was past ten. Surely whatever party the Forest house was holding was in full swing by now. "Do you think the guys will mind if we leave?"

We both looked toward our table. It was nearly empty, as were almost all the tables around the stage. Adam sat in one chair, his legs outstretched and arms folded. Mal sat next to him, texting someone. The rest of the occupants were either by the pool tables in the rear of the room or over by the bar.

"You round up your girls, and I'll see who else is coming with us." Noah instructed. I nodded. Lana and Amy were by the bar with Finn and a couple of other guys from the table. Lana gave me a smile and wiped a finger across her lip when I approached.

"Do I have lipstick on my teeth?" I asked.

"No, but there is some gloss on your cheek." She reached out and smudged it with a finger. Turning my head slightly, she said, "Also on your jaw." I'm sure I blushed because everyone in the group laughed.

"You guys ready?"

"Just waiting for you," Lana replied. I beat back another blush. Apparently Noah and my makeout session had been seen by all. At least our conversation had been private.

Noah came up with the other guys whose names I didn't catch when I came in. "It looks like Mal and Adam are staying here. What about you, Bo?"

Bo drained his glass. "I'm with you."

"Who's good to drive?" Noah asked. One of the unnamed guys raised his hand, but Noah ignored him. "Great, Finn, you drive Eric, Bo, and Tim. I'll take Grace and the girls."

This drew a round of protest from Eric that made Lana and Amy smile, but Noah ignored them and hustled me toward the door. "Let's go, or we could spend the whole night talking about who drives whom." The tone of Noah's voice was implacable, so we just went. He held opened the back door of his truck and helped both Lana and Amy in.

Then he lifted me into the passenger side.

I didn't protest like I normally did. Noah liked doing this, and admittedly I didn't mind either his minor show of strength or his courtesy. These little things made me feel important to him, like I was a treasure. As he was circling around the front of the cab to climb into the driver's side, Amy said, "God, swoon. He helps you into this car? Is Bo like this?"

"I don't know. I've never ridden with Bo," I said.

"Did you ask Noah if he was seeing anyone?" Amy said.

"No, Amy, he was too busy giving her a tonsillectomy." Lana hit Amy in the arm.

"Ouch, I was just asking."

"I'll ask him," I promised. Noah climbed in and started the engine and the heavy metal music he enjoyed listening to filled the air. I immediately turned it down and flipped it to a popular radio station.

He rolled his eyes but didn't change the station.

Amy and Lana chattered in the backseat, but I felt strangely shy. Noah reached over, picked up my hand and placed it on his thigh. It was rock hard beneath my palm. I absently stroked it until Noah halted my motion by placing his hand firmly on top of mine. He turned to look at me. His dark eyes glittered, and he gave me a slight shake of his head. He pulled my hand higher and pressed it lightly over his hard-on and then released my hand.

I hid a small smile, delighted in my ability to rouse this man's body. Noah lifted my hand to his mouth and kissed it and placed it back on his thigh. A hot ache spread through me, and I clenched my own legs together in anticipation and excitement. I felt feverish, as if all my blood was bubbling right under the surface of my skin, and I wanted to run his hand all over my body. Could he ease me just by a touch? I didn't know, but I wanted to find out.

"Swoon," Amy said in the back. This time my smile couldn't be disguised.

Noah dropped us off with a promise to catch us inside after he found a place to park. Bo and the other guys spilled out of Finn's car and walked us inside. The house was charging cover but the guy at the door waved us girls in for free.

Away from Noah, my comfort level took a nosedive. Had I just promised to have sex with him? It's not that I didn't want him. I did. But what did I know about pleasing a guy like Noah in bed? What if he decided I was so terrible at sex that he would break up with me? Or worse, what if I was terrible, but he didn't tell me and kept pretending that he enjoyed having sex with me but instead had to fantasize about Emma Stone or something. Actually, I didn't even know whom he would fantasize about.

I wondered if I could get Lana alone and get some tips from her. What if I needed to pull a Meg Ryan and pretend like I had an orgasm?

Inside, crepe paper streamers were draped along the walls and lit up with Christmas lights. A fake disco ball was strung up in the middle and spun every time someone tall enough went by and slapped it. The place smelled like weed, spilled beer, and sweat.

Either it was too early or the entire crowd was in the back, but the front room was fairly empty except for a few people loitering around the windows.

A table set up at the end blocked the path to the rooms beyond. It was full of small shot glasses filled with amber liquid. A guy wearing a T-shirt that read "FCK" in big letters waived us over. As I neared, I could see that the small print read "All that's missing is 'U.'"

"Two dollars a shot for the guys. Free for the girls. Beer's free back there." He gestured behind him. I rolled my eyes. The Forest house was apparently a party house where the members tried to make money by charging for liquor. The freebies for the girls were to entice the guys to come and spend generously.

I wanted to wait for Noah out front, and I turned to head back out when Amy grabbed my arm. "Let's do a shot," she said. I nodded agreement. I hated whiskey but maybe a little liquid courage would help me in bed. I'd have fewer inhibitions. I wouldn't be so embarrassed at being naked.

"Is that whiskey?" I asked.

He nodded, "Jack."

"Please," Amy pleaded. Maybe she needed some liquid courage to hit on Bo, too.

"You should wait until Noah gets here," Bo suggested, which set off Lana.

"She needs permission from Noah to drink now?" Lana marched up to the table and laid down a ten-dollar bill. "Three shots. This can be your tip."

Shot guy wordlessly picked up the $10, stuck it in his pocket, and pushed three shot glasses forward. I took one of the shots and drained it. As the Jack burned down my throat, I coughed and wiped at my watering eyes.

"Come on, ladies, do a shot with us." Tim and Eric, the guys from Noah's gym, came forward to do their own shots. Bo looked to protest again, but Lana held up her hand. He remained silent but brooding. We all did another shot while Bo looked on like a discontented father. This one went down far easier, as if the first one burned away any resistance. I felt better already.

Tim and Eric wanted us to do another shot with them, but by that time Noah and Finn had walked in. Noah looked unhappy to see us crowded around the shot table.

"Did you have to park really far away?" I asked him.

He laced his fingers through mine and pulled me close to him, placing a quick kiss against my forehead. "No, why?"

"You look unhappy."

"I tried to stop them, brother, but no go," Bo said, clapping a hand on Noah's shoulder. He turned to the shot man, with sarcasm heavily weighting his words, "Did we pay a sufficient toll?"

Shot guy merely held up his arms. "Go on through."

Noah led the way, pulling me behind him. This room had tubs of glass-bottled beer, a luxurious drinking item for college students. Noah stopped and bought drinks for everyone. I tried to remember the rhyme. Was it liquor first and then beer or reverse?

"You look perplexed," Noah said, leaning down to speak into my ear. His breath tickled my lobe and thoughts of our activities in the bar made me squeeze my legs together slightly. Thank god I was a girl. The shots were doing their job. I wondered if there were some dark corners I could take him into.

"I'm trying to remember if I should just keep drinking shots or if it's okay to have beer."

"Liquor first. You're good to go," Noah said and then sighed.

"Do you want to go?" First the glower and then the sigh.

"No, it's all good," he replied, squeezing my hand.

We wandered through to the back deck that was very crowded. There were two kegs out here and dozens of plastic cups already discarded on the ground like abandoned toys.

"Walk through the crowd with me," Lana demanded. I turned to Noah and informed him of our plans.

"I'll be right back," I reassured him.

He nodded and went to hold up a piece of railing with Bo while the other guys delved into the crowd. Amy looked at Lana and me and then back at Bo. "Go forth, young pilgrim," Lana said, winking at Amy.

We began a slow circuit through the crowd, saying hello to the people we knew. Lana was more familiar with the faces than I was. At the back of the yard, someone was handing out paper cups full of Jell-O shots. We were forced to swallow two before we could get out of there. By the time we had done a full circuit, we hadn't seen Jack anywhere. It was early yet, but I felt buzzed.

"Lana," I tugged at her hand, "how do you know when you should fake an orgasm?"

"I don't think you're going to have that problem with Noah," she said, scanning the crowd.

"How do you know?" *Had she slept with him!?*

"No, I didn't sleep with him." She rolled her eyes, sounding disgusted. I must have said that out loud.

"Sorry. It just came out," I apologized.

"Noah can barely allow your feet to touch the ground. He opens your doors. He carries your backpack for you. He makes sure you have food and that you're entertained. Trust me when I say you aren't going to have to fake anything."

Rubbing the side of my face, I tried to add together all the facts. Impatiently, Lana grabbed my hand and said, "He will make sure you are satisfied. Don't hide your reactions. He'll learn from them."

Lana's explicit instructions penetrated a little better. Don't hide. Be happy. Or was the song "'Don't Worry, Be Happy?'" Confused again, I asked Lana, "Is this the point to stop drinking or keep drinking?"

Jack appeared out of nowhere to hand me a bottle and say hello to Lana. "Keep drinking," he offered.

"Are you a genie?" I asked him stupidly. He laughed and tipped his head back to swallow his beer.

"No, why?" he asked, wiping the back of his hand across his mouth.

"We were just talking about you and, poof, here you are," I said, looking at Lana. I didn't want her to bring up my orgasm question in front of Jack.

"Like magic," she nodded in agreement.

"I've got something magical, but I can't show it to you here," Jack replied. Lana rolled her eyes, but I was gone enough that I actually giggled despite his lack of originality.

I felt a warm hand at the nape of my neck and turned to find Noah behind me with a curious look on his face. Like he wanted to take Jack's magic and crush it beneath his size thirteens.

But when he noticed me looking up at him, he smiled that tender sweet half smile that I could tell was just for me. I swung myself around and threw my arms up to his neck.

"Whoa there," he said, taking the beer bottle out of my hand. Apparently my actions had sprayed a little beer out of the newly acquired bottle. He said nothing about his bath and, instead, scooped me up to half walk, half carry me back to the railing, leaving Lana and Jack to discuss his David Blaine tricks.

Amy was still there with Bo, but there were others as well, guys and girls.

"Do all these people want to take Bo home?" I asked Noah. He choked a little on his drink and threw a look of glee toward Bo.

"I don't know, but Bo's pretty open minded, aren't you Peep?"

Bo lifted a finger, but shifted closer to us so I could hear him. "You do know why we call Noah 'Jep' right?"

"Sure, because he knows all the answers on Jeopardy," I recited.

"That and because the only one who'd blow him was a toy he built himself."

"Better the puppeteer, Geppetto, than the puppet. At least I can get it up without the assistance of pharmaceuticals," Noah said.

"You know, when you brought Bo to the movies, Mike thought you were a couple," I confided. This made both Noah and Bo laugh.

Bo leaned toward me. "I have slept with Noah before, Grace. He snores, just an FYI."

I turned to Noah. "Is this true?"

"I don't know. I haven't ever been awake while I've snored. But I wouldn't trust anything Bo says. He'd sleep through revelry played right in his ear."

I turned toward Bo for confirmation.

"True. I was a bad Marine," Bo said. He didn't look too sorrowful about this. Amy used this opportunity to lure Bo's attention back to her by asking when he got out.

Pulling Noah's head down to mine, I boldly told him, "I'm ready to go home." Instead of swiftly carrying me to his truck, he groaned a little and cuddled me closer. I snuggled into him and waited, but nothing happened.

So I pressed up against him a little and rubbed my hands down his T-shirt. When I got to the bottom, I slipped my hands underneath the cotton so I could enjoy the feel of his skin against my palms. Instead of allowing my exploration to continue, however, Noah pushed my hands out and loosely held my two wrists in one of his hands while he bent down to place my bottle on the floor.

He looked at his watch and said, "Time to go?" I nodded eagerly. Don't hide. Be happy. Don't worry. Be happy. He looked over at Bo and said, "You got her?" pointing to Amy. Bo lifted his chin in agreement.

"Alright, baby," Noah said. "Let's get you to bed."

Instead of heading off to bed, though, Noah went over to Jack and Lana. "I'm taking Grace home, Lana, and I'd like to take you home as well. Bo will make sure that Amy gets back safely."

"Um," Lana looked to Jack, and Jack shrugged.

"I'll see her home."

Noah shook his head. "Can't do it. I brought her, and I need to see her home."

"I live close by, mind if I catch a ride?" Jack said.

"Fine," Noah turned. "Ready?"

I nodded eagerly. I was ready. Very ready. I turned and gave Lana a sly wink but apparently everyone saw it because they all shook their heads at me.

Noah

Getting Grace into her apartment would've been easier if she'd been passed out. Then I could have just slung her over my shoulder and carried her to bed.

Instead, inebriated Grace was handsy, dipping her fingers under my shirt and underneath the waistband of my jeans. At this rate, the wood in my pants would be so hard by the second floor that I'd have to rub one out just to be able to make it up to her apartment without being crippled by my hard on.

I figured that not taking Grace tonight would be another of those *Twelve Labours of Hercules.* I had to be close to accomplishing them all by now.

On the third floor, I picked Grace up to avoid her wandering hands, but when she started licking a sensitive part of my neck, I began wondering at my own restraint. Would it really be so bad? After all, Grace was a virgin. Maybe having her drunk would make it hurt less the first time. I could really make it good for her the next day.

I quelled my thoughts. I wanted Grace to remember our first time together. And I would make it good for her that time and every time after.

Lana unlocked the door and stumbled in. Jack followed close behind. I was going to have to kick Jack out, given that Lana wasn't able to walk a straight line.

First things first. I carried Grace to her bedroom. It was the first time I had been in her room, although I saw a brief glimpse of it when I had picked her up for breakfast that first morning.

It was all white, but there were flowered curtains and a huge bed with a white comforter that looked like it had lace or something around the edges. Huge. Like I think I could have fit a platoon in that bed.

"You have a big bed." I stood her up while I pulled back the covers.

"All the better for you to sleep in it with me." Yeah, Grace was really drunk. She wouldn't be so forward unless she had a few too many tonight. I liked it, though. I wondered if, over time, Grace would lose her inhibitions without alcohol. I certainly wouldn't mind her rubbing against me like a cat against a scratching pole if I could actually do something about it.

I laid her down and stroked my hands down her legs to pull her sandals off. I saw that the straps had made red marks in her feet, and I massaged them a little, trying to rub circulation back in. She moaned and said, "That feels soooo good."

I looked at her body and contemplated what exactly I should remove. The sheer blouse was an easy choice. Her shorts? I debated that for about two seconds and said fuck it. I went to unzip her shorts.

Except there was no zip. I rolled her to her back and found only a seam. Did she just pull these on? Women's clothes were mystifying. Grace's hand went to her side and pulled down a tiny hidden zipper. Underneath I saw all-lace, black panties. I broke out in a sweat.

Boot camp wasn't nearly as painful and trying as this. I pulled down Grace's unfastened shorts and placed those on top of her shoes. I looked at her for a full minute, and, yeah, I even stroked her lightly over the lace nestled between her thighs. She liked it. Her legs fell open to grant me easier access, and she thrust up against my hands.

Jesus, the shadowed valley between her legs called to me. The musk of her arousal rose up in the air, and I wanted to fall on her and devour her. I pressed my forehead into her belly and prayed to someone for a little strength.

I took a deep breath, unbuttoned her blouse, and left her in her bra, tank, and lace panties. I deserved a goddamned medal for this.

When I covered her up, Grace leaned up on her elbows. The weight of her body pulled her tank top down so her plump breasts looked bigger and the cleavage looked deeper.

"Noah?" her tone was questioning. "Are you coming to bed?"

"I'm going to sleep on the couch tonight," I admitted.

"What? Don't you want me?"

"Fuck, of course, I do. Jesus Christ, it's all I can do not to fall on you like some crazed beast, but you're too drunk tonight."

"I'm not," she said truculently.

We could play this game all night. I went to the bathroom to get a washcloth and wiped her makeup off as much as I could. There wasn't much, but it must have felt good, because she made another moan.

"That feels so good," she repeated. She reached for me, and I bent down to kiss her freshly cleaned forehead. Her head tipped. Despite her tipsy state, she was able to make contact with my mouth, her tongue tracing my lips. Involuntarily, my mouth opened slightly and her tongue darted inside, sweeping around my teeth and deeper to stroke my tongue.

I managed to pull back. "But why?" she cried.

"I'm going to make you feel so good the first time we make love that you'll want to jump my bones every second afterward. If you don't remember it, my plan will fail," I explained, knowing she wasn't listening to me.

"You and your damned plans," she said and turned over on her side.

"I love that you're drunk and horny, but we'd both feel like shit if I did anything to you tonight," I said. This was a special kind of torture.

There was some muffled response. Possibly a curse word. I heaved to my feet. One last thing before I could crash. Ejecting Jack.

I went to knock on Lana's door that someone had shut. "Time to go, man," I said and pounded again. Jack opened the door a crack.

"What the hell, man? Are you cockblocking me?"

"Don't be that guy," I warned. My patience was thin.

"You're being an asshole."

"At least I'm not the one trying to get in a girl's pants when she is drunk. Put your pants back on and come back tomorrow when you're both not fully lit."

"Just because you are boning her—"

I'd had enough of this dipshit. I covered his mouth with my hand and said, with all the frustration of the night in my voice, "You don't even want to go there. Either you go put your pants on or I throw you out bare-assed. I don't care either way."

My words or menace must have finally penetrated, because Jack came out a moment later, fully dressed, and stomped out the door. He may have wanted to slam the door, but I wasn't going to let him.

I shut the door and locked it. Lana was passed out in her bedroom. I made a mental note to tell her that her taste in men sucked and shut the door. Looking at the hard sofa and then at Grace's bedroom, I muttered, "Fuck it." I was going to sleep in that big ass cloud bed with my girl.

Grace

When I awoke the next morning, I heard the crinkle of paper as I rolled over to find the bed empty except for a note.

Grace,

You looked so beautiful and peaceful, I couldn't wake you. There's a glass of water and two aspirin on your nightstand. Hangovers are mostly dehydration. We're going to have a party tonight at The Woodlands. Don't plan on drinking much. I want you to take advantage of me. All night long.

Love,

Noah

Love, Noah. I hugged the note to my chest.

Chapter Fourteen

Grace

The clanging of pans in the kitchen roused Lana. She opened the door a crack. "Anyone else here?" she asked.

"No, just us."

With the confirmation that we were alone, she opened the door fully and exited her bedroom. Her hair was matted to one side of her head and last night's mascara was smudged in big half circles under her eyes. She grunted a hello.

"Nice look, Sullivan," I teased. "The smoky eye look is really taking over, huh?"

She flipped me off and sat down in the chair. "Why are you so cheery this morning? And where's Noah?"

"Don't know," I handed her a water bottle and she drank it three quarters of the way before returning the bottle to the table.

"Did he kick Jack out?" she wondered. I shrugged again. I had only the note and some vague memories of trying to lure Noah into bed with me. I had a minor pang of embarrassment, but I took comfort in his note.

"Pancakes?" I offered. After drinking the tall glass of water and taking the two aspirins Noah had left for me, I started feeling human again. He had undressed me for the most part and must have even washed my face. When I went into the bathroom, there was a washcloth draped on a towel rack and my face looked surprisingly clean.

He had taken good care of me and, from the indentation in the pillow next to mine, slept next to me as well. I rolled around a bit in the cool hollow left by his body and sniffed the pillow for a good five minutes, trying to capture the faint scent he left behind.

Pancakes, I had decided, would be a great way to soak up any excess alcohol, and I had just started making them when Lana poked her head out.

"Yes, two," she muttered. I served Lana two and myself two and set the rest aside to put in our freezer.

"Can you help me sort through my pictures this morning?" I asked Lana. Her head shot up in surprise.

"Are you finally going to submit to the art department?" she asked, barely swallowing her food before she spoke.

"I am," I could feel my grin stretching my face. I had gone online this morning and looked at Dr. Rossum's office hours. "I sent an email requesting a meeting."

Lana clapped her hands and reached for me. "I'm so proud of you, Gracie."

"In other good news, Noah left me a note that they're having a party at The Woodlands tonight." Everything seemed to be going perfectly.

"Yeah? That sounds like fun." Her enthusiasm was subdued, but she still seemed happy.

"The note also mentioned that I shouldn't drink much because he wanted me to take advantage of him."

"Does that mean what I think it means?" Lana smirked.

I bit my lip to keep from smiling too wide. "Yes, or at least I hope so."

This motivated Lana into action. She hopped up and came around the table. "We need to go shopping!"

"For what?"

"Clothes! Lingerie!" I laughed at Lana's enthusiasm.

"Why not?" I was a little lightheaded with the idea of having sex with Noah. A little anxiety had driven me into overindulging last night, but today, somehow, I felt excited and empowered. Likely because I had acted a little foolish last night, and Noah wasn't deterred at all.

***

"Where do you see this going with Noah?" Lana asked me as we rifled through bras and panties and other scraps of lace and faux satin at the lingerie store.

"Don't know," I lied. I had elaborate visions of where this was going with Noah, but I wanted to focus on tonight. "How about this?" I held up a pair of lacy white boy shorts. It seemed sexy and something that I wouldn't constantly have the urge to readjust.

"Nice, but maybe you should go all out." Lana offered a red one piece full of lace. Pushing one corner of my mouth up in a grimace, I shook my head.

"You have to unsnap it at the crotch to pee. It can't be comfortable."

"This isn't for comfort," Lana said. "It's for sex."

"Please, can you say it louder? Why not just put a dick on my back?"

"It's sex," Lana said more quietly. "You need to remember that."

"What does that mean?"

Lana laid down the red garment and turned to look at me. Her face was very serious and I thought I saw a glimpse of pain in her eyes. "When you have sex for the very first time, you can ascribe a lot of emotional feelings to that one guy. Sometimes it is really hard to set those aside." She put her hand on my arm as if she really wanted me to pay attention. "Noah hurt you and your relationship wasn't even physical. Now he is going to be your first. When he leaves you, it is going to be a million times worse."

When he leaves you. Those were the only words that really penetrated. I suddenly felt so cold. "God, why is the air conditioning so high here?" I asked with false cheerfulness. I looked down at the red concoction of lace and ribbons. In my little fantasies, I hadn't gotten to the part where Noah left me. My heart stuttered a little.

Putting an arm across my back, Lana said, "Enjoy your time with him. He's a great guy, and he's perfect as your first. But be careful. He's hurt you once. He has a bad track record of stringing you along and then backing out once he's got you. Maybe he just likes the conquest."

"Just sex then?" I picked up the red number. I didn't know if I could do that and still guard my heart from him. But maybe the uncomfortable scratchy lace would be a reminder that this wasn't about being comfortable and safe but about trying new and different things. Just this once.

***

Noah came and got me before the party started. He told Lana that he'd pay for a cab for her, but she declined. She was going to play designated driver for Amy and a group of the sorority girls. Noah left Lana with six wristbands. "Give them to whomever you want. Just show them at the gate to get in."

Noah, Finn, and I went to a warehouse store to pick up plastic cups, napkins, chips, bottled beer and liquor. The other guys were in charge of obtaining the keg.

When we returned to the house, Noah went upstairs to lock all the doors. "The locks are pretty flimsy," he explained. "But having a barrier prevents most people from trying to use our rooms." Finn pulled out some yellow crime tape and draped it across the stairs.

"Do you really think that tape is going to prevent anyone from going upstairs?" I asked.

"No," admitted Finn, "but it might deter some, and that's worthwhile."

Their video game consoles and laptop computers were all toted out to Finn's car and placed in his trunk. He and Mal drove away and returned about twenty minutes later in Mal's sports car.

"What is that car that Mal drives?" I asked as I saw it pull into the driveway next to the kitchen door.

"A McLaren. You like it?" Noah asked, coming up behind me and putting his chin on my head. It was a really gorgeous car. Silver, sexy, and low slung. I didn't really know much about cars. Uncle Louis drove a big Bentley, and Lana had a zippy BMW. I didn't have a car because I didn't like to drive. I could count on having Lana or Josh drive me most places I needed to go.

"It's pretty neat."

"It also cost more than hundred grand," Noah said flatly.

"Really?" I guess I knew that there were cars like that but it seemed crazy. "And Mal owns it?"

Noah spun me around. "Yeah. You want a ride?"

I shook my head vigorously. "No. I'd be too afraid I'd accidentally scratch the interior with my finger or something."

He looked at me, his hands on my upper arms. He started to say something and then stopped and kissed me hard. Thoughts of the car dropped away and all I could think of was how much I didn't want to party with anyone tonight. Instead, I wanted to go up to Noah's bedroom and lie down and show him this red teddy, as the saleslady had called it, and see what his response would be.

Instead, Noah stopped kissing me like he had a hundred times before. One of these days, he wouldn't stop, but instead we would kiss and touch and love each other until the sun rose. Maybe even tonight.

Noah lifted me onto the corner counter in the kitchen. The stove sat just to the right of my legs, but I guess that no one would be cooking tonight. The keg was positioned outside on the patio.

The long sectional sofa that usually sat in front of the fireplace and big screen had been carted upstairs. All that was really left was their ten-foot long table and a multitude of chairs surrounding it. The house looked even more cavernous. Even the flat screen had been removed from above the fireplace.

"Three parties ago, the TV suffered a near-miss," Finn explained when I asked him about it.

"Do you guys have nicknames for everyone?" I asked after Finn referred to Mal as "Charles." Charles was short for Charles in Charge, an old show that featured a manny, I was told. Mal had four younger sisters and had taken care of them since he was 14 until his mother married "dickhead" last year and Mal finally moved out of the house.

"Yes, and for everything," came Finn's no-nonsense reply.

"It's part of the guy code," Noah explained, leaning around me to rearrange a tray of freshly poured shots of Patrón. "And since you've been privy to some of our secrets, we're not going to let you leave."

"Oooh, threats," I teased.

Noah looked at me with a serious expression. "Nope, not a threat. A promise."

My laughter kind of died in my throat. I wasn't sure what he was saying to me. I know what I wanted it to mean. I spoke, but my voice was raspy. "I was just joking."

"I know," he replied. "I wasn't."

Finn coughed to remind us he was still present. I changed the subject.

"Do you guys charge for the party?"

"No, charging is for douchebags. If you want to host a party, pay for it," Finn said, throwing a couple chips in his mouth. "Though maybe we shouldn't have gone for the Patrón this time."

"These parties get a little wild," Noah agreed. "Open up," he said and pushed a Jell-O shot in my mouth when I complied.

"Are you trying to get me drunk?"

"No, but I figured one Jell-O shot early in the night wouldn't hurt either of us."

"Our parties are a goddamned debauchery," Finn added, clapping his hand on Noah's shoulder.

"Where's her bracelet?" Finn asked, looking at my bare wrists.

"Don't have any," Noah said. "You and Adam went over to campus. I gave mine to Lana."

"Oh man, I gave them all out at campus. I wasn't even thinking. I tagged about two dozen hotties. I'm going to be morose when you and Bo graduate. No more college—"

"Language," Noah interrupted.

"Ladies," Finn substituted. "Maybe I'll have to audit some classes."

I shook my head. Finn talked a big, dirty game, but I hadn't seen him with anyone.

He went over to the patio doors and asked Adam whether he had any spares left. Finn turned and shook his head at us. "Negative, buddy."

"Are you handing out jewelry to coeds? No wonder your parties are so popular," I said. I pushed lightly against the counter, making a motion to get up. Noah absently pushed me back. He obviously wanted me to stay. He looked down at me, contemplatively, and I quirked an eyebrow up in question.

Then his hands went to his neck and pulled his dog tags off his chest and over his head. He strung the chain over my head. My hand came up to clutch at the metal, warm from his body.

"She's wearing his dog tags," Finn yelled back to the patio. Two heads—Adam and Mal's—poked in the doorway.

I blushed but said, "You guys are worse than sorority sisters having a postmortem after a mixer."

"Is she calling us pussies?" Mal asked.

"She's calling you a pussy, jackhole," Adam said and pushed Mal in the back of the head.

I shook my head. "I take that back. I think you guys haven't graduated from kindergarten yet." But I hadn't removed my hand from the dog tags, and Noah noticed.

***

"We need Grace," Lana yelled, running over to my corner where I sat, virtually unmoving, since Noah had set me here hours ago. I hadn't needed to move. One or more of the Woodland boys were always with me, filling my cup and making sure I was entertained. Finn and I engaged in thumb wars. Fortunately, Adam was doing my Jell-O shots when I lost, because I lost a lot. Adam was well on his way to being trashed—if he hadn't already arrived at his destination.

He had gotten his cast off and was weaving a path from the kitchen to the great room, alternately singing, dancing, and drinking feverishly. I could see why he was in a band. He was a natural performer. His ease with having every eye on him and his charisma that spread like a netting over the room were apparent forty feet away. I could easily envision him on stage in front of a stadium full of screaming fans.

Mal was completely different, more like Noah. They were both quiet and watchful. Finn was the clown, and I wondered, the more time I spent with him, if his funny man routine wasn't a little too forced. Bo was even joking with me, even if he kept a cautious eye out for Noah. But I liked them all. These five thoughtful, handsome guys who all took turns taking care of me, making sure I was having a good time.

Lana was out of breath when she reached me, as if she had been running a mile rather than the space of a room. "Come on and do the Single Ladies dance with us. We need another body." Lana had learned a number of dance routines at her camp. Dancing, she was told, was a good way to keep her body in shape in a healthy way. She forced these routines on me after she returned home. I hadn't the heart to resist her, and frankly they came in handy when we killed at Dance, Dance Revolution, which was about the only video game either of us were adept at. But I didn't want to dance in front of the crowd here.

I shook my head no. "Oh no, not tonight. I'm tipsy and it's been forever since I did that routine with you." I wasn't tipsy at all. I had stayed carefully sober so that Noah wouldn't have an excuse to deny me, but that still didn't mean I wanted to shake my booty in front of this crowd.

Mal was my drinking partner at the moment and looked on with interest. "Routine? Dance? I wanna see."

I rolled my eyes. "I can describe for you what it will look like. One awkward girl who can barely remember any steps stumbling into nine drunken girls. We'll be like dominoes."

"Your description only makes us want to see it more," Noah said, turning up behind Lana. I could see I wasn't going to get out of this without making a big scene. A crowd had gathered. I weighed the choice between being the party downer or making a fool of myself and decided for the latter. If there is ever a time to make a fool of oneself it's while everyone is half-baked and unlikely to remember in the morning.

I allowed Lana to pull me down off my perch. I made a face at Mal and Noah. "I expect repayment in the form of sober embarrassment from both of you tomorrow."

Mal gave me a flimsy salute, and Noah pushed him in the side. But the two followed Lana and me as we approached the great room. Adam was over at the music console, spinning up the song. I almost groaned when it started. Lana took her place in the middle and I attached myself at the end. I didn't remember the moves very well and found myself turning the wrong way a couple of times. Still, by the chorus, muscle memory had kicked in.

Noah watched from the front row, his dark eyes unwavering. I don't know if I've ever felt sexier in my life. When I shook my hair or dipped low, I kept my eyes trained on his. It felt like we were exchanging secret messages I hadn't yet figured out how to decode. My thoughts were jumbled, but I gave over and let the music take me and move me. I danced as if Noah and I were the only ones in the room.

When the song was over, there was a big cheer and clamors for more. Out of the side of my eye, I could see the other girls preening, but Noah was walking purposefully toward me. He grabbed my hand and led me through the crowd to the police-taped stairs. He unhooked the tape from one side, pulled me through and leaned back to reattach it. Then he moved upstairs, pulling me gently but insistently behind him.

Bo appeared at the top of the stairs and gave us a knowing half smile. I flushed with embarrassment and anticipation. Noah's room was dark and somewhat quiet. The pulsating music from downstairs was deadened a bit by the space and the walls of the bedrooms. He paused and looked down at me. "You okay?"

I was okay, and I was ready.

Noah

I walked her into the room. Shutting the door behind us, I locked it and stuck my desk chair underneath it. I didn't want any drunken fools to interrupt us. The room was dark. I had drawn the blinds earlier, and with the door to the hallway closed, it was hard to even make out the bed.

I didn't want to flip on the light, though, feeling that might make Grace uncomfortable. Instead, I crossed to the bathroom, flicked the switch and left the door ajar. The light spilled out and threw shadows over the bed.

I looked back at Grace. She appeared adorably awkward, folding and unfolding her arms as if she didn't know what she could touch. *Everything*, I said silently. I would show her instead.

Crossing over to her in two strides, I swung her up in my arms. She gave a squeak and patted my chest. "Nice," she smiled.

"That's not the only thing you'll be saying about me tonight," I told her with a cocky smile.

"Do you prefer the religious exclamations like 'oh God,' or do you have a bedroom nickname?" she sassed. I liked her when she was teasing me. Placing her on the bed, I knelt down next to her.

"I think you'll be too incoherent to form full words," I taunted.

"Big talk, no action," she countered.

"I'll give you action." I leaned over, kissing her neck and stroking my hand on either side of her throat, down her chest and over the plump rise of her breasts.

I felt the thrum of her heart speed up against the press of my lips against her throat. I opened my mouth and sucked gently at the pulse point. I pushed her shirt upward but instead of encountering bare flesh, I felt the uneven pattern, like the lace of the panties she wore last night.

I pushed up on one arm and raised the shirt higher. "What's this?" It looked like a very sexy undergarment made of lace, a shiny fabric and a ribbon that held the two together. Her fairly demure outfit of T-shirt and white denim skirt hid a very naughty secret.

I urged her to sit up, and I swept the shirt off her body. I barely restrained my urge to tear the entire thing off. Surely that was what they were made for. I took a moment to admire the picture she made. The red lace cupped her breasts and the dark of her nipples could be seen through the fabric.

I bent down and drew one nipple into my mouth. Her hands crept into my hair. Encouraged, I brought one hand up to cup the neglected nipple. I rolled one nipple with my tongue and lips, and plucked and tugged the other with my fingers.

The other hand I placed on her bare, silky thigh. No signs of resistance met me; instead, her legs opened slightly. I accepted the silent invitation to move upward, pushing the denim skirt as I moved to expose more of her tender flesh. The lace fabric between her thighs was wet and the metal snaps gave way to my questing fingers. I rubbed her gently, petting her until she raised up to meet my hand to force a harder pressure. I slipped one finger inside of her.

So very tight. I groaned against her breast. Carefully, I pushed the other finger inside of her. I kissed her then, my tongue invading her mouth with the same rhythm my fingers pumped into her. I curled my fingers upward, feeling for that soft spongy flesh of her G spot.

I knew I found it when her body tensed against mine. When she made to move away from the unfamiliar sensation, I blocked her with my thighs, settling my cock against the back of my hand, rubbing against myself as I stroked her. I teased and caressed her with every skill I had ever possessed. I kissed her with every ounce of energy inside me. I felt her body tense; her thighs closed hard around my hand. Her fingernails dug into my shoulders, and I reveled in the pain.

I could come this way, but I didn't want to. I thought of marching in the desert. Of my finance exam. Of cleaning up after the rager downstairs. I kept stroking her until I felt her release rush down my fingers onto my palm and heard the sweet, soft cries of her orgasm ring in the night air.

"I promise to admire this later, but this thing has to come off," I told her. She nodded mutely at me but didn't move. Her eyes were filled with wonder. *Not just a virgin*, I thought with fierce pleasure, *but no one had ever made her come*. Or at least not that hard.

I wrestled her skirt off and tried to remove the laces. Eventually she helped me push the lace and ribbon concoction off. Her body was flushed from passion. I stroked my hands all over, touching her throat, molding her breasts into peaks for my voracious mouth. I tongued, sucked, and licked one and then the other.

Moving lower until my head rested between her legs, I kissed her and then spread her wide. She made a weak sound of protest that I ignored. I had to taste her. Her lower lips were plump and wet. Remnants of her orgasm glinted in the faint bathroom light. I laid the broad flat of my tongue against her and gave one long, languorous lick. Delicious. I could eat her all night, and someday I would. But tonight I wanted to make her come, just one more time. My hard cock was so ready for her that I feared I would break in two before I could sink it inside of her.

I held her thighs apart and ate at her. Her musky scent filled my nose and her taste on my tongue made me want to spill. I slipped two fingers inside her again, working her with my fingers and tongue until I felt her convulse again. Now she was ready.

Grace

I felt like my mind had splintered into a thousand pieces, like I had become a collection of dust mites, just a hundred particles floating in the air.

Noah shifted, and I heard the crinkle of a wrapper. His fingers slid back down between my legs, circling and pressing until my breath hitched, and I cried out softly in desire. His gaze was wicked now, and he made no effort to quiet me even though there were nearly a hundred people downstairs. As he slid one and then two fingers inside me, I turned my head to the side and bit into the fleshy part of my hand. He laughed and crouched over me. "Afraid someone might hear you?" he whispered in my ear. The hot wash of his breath made me shiver. His fingers kept stroking me and in the quiet I could hear how wet he was making me. He was learning me with each stroke. What turned me on, what made me weak with want.

He pulled my fist away from my face and laced our fingers together, holding them flat against the bed. His other hand was still thrusting and rubbing between my legs. I began to sob softly, wanting so desperately another release. "I don't care who fucking hears you when I make you come," he said. With his words, I did, and a cry escaped me. Noah's lips were sucking on my earlobe, then my neck, biting into my shoulder as I came again. He cupped me until my breath evened out.

He slid his fingers from me, and I could see they were wet, slick with my desire. He rubbed his sheathed cock with his fingers and then dipped inside for more lubrication. His long fingers curved around his girth, pulling hard at his length.

In the dim light, I could see the skin of Noah's cheeks pulled taut. I pleaded with him, not sure if I wanted to be the one stroking him or just wanted him inside me. "Please, Noah, please," I moaned. He was out of reach for me, sitting almost perpendicular to my body in repose.

"Just getting ready for you," he said and then scooted back to position himself between my legs. I opened my legs wider to accommodate Noah's frame. He pushed in slowly, slicked by my release. He placed both hands at my inner thighs, widening me even farther, opening and exposing me to his gaze and to the push of his cock inside me.

"You feel so big," I said, gasping at the sensation. He groaned out loud at this.

"You okay?" he panted, bracing himself above me.

I pulled him toward me and said, "Yes."

He pumped shallowly against me, waiting for me to fully accept him. With each movement, I became slicker and wetter until he had slid home completely. He rested there, allowing me to accustom myself to his thickness, and then, when I lifted my hips, he began thrusting faster. His moans and grunts mingled with my cries and the noise we were making, the wet slapping sounds as he pushed into me echoed loud in the room, mixed with the deep bass the reverberated from the party downstairs.

Right then, there was only Noah and me and a pinpoint sensation at my center that was flooding outward into every extremity until I was one mass of feeling, shaking from the inside out. My toes curled and my head flung back, I allowed that wave of feeling to overtake me like the warm tide and I felt Noah push hard into me twice and then shudder and collapse. I raised my arms and felt the sweat like a fine mist all over Noah's back. I licked at the saltiness of his skin and he buried his face into the side of my neck.

Noah

I was lying on top of her, breathing heavily. This was what I had fought for. Like Odysseus, I had strung my bow and carried my love to the bed that I made for her, the living olive tree at its base.

I slipped out of bed to dispose of the condom and pulled down the covers. I slid us both underneath, and she curled around me.

I ran my finger down her back, tracing the slight slope of the valley formed around her spine. I felt the sharp shape of her shoulder blades and marked the spot mentally. I would want to travel the path with my tongue.

Maybe other guys could give her nicer cars or more money, but no one would ever want her like I would. And no one would work to give her the same pleasure.

Chapter Fifteen

Grace

At Noah's urging, I showed some of my pictures to the guys at the house, pictures that Lana and I had chosen for my portfolio, although I didn't tell Noah that. The lavish praise from Noah and the guys infused me with new energy and confidence. Suddenly I wanted to take my pictures everywhere and show them to everyone.

"Lana, who would I talk to in admissions to take pictures from Old Main's bell tower?" Lana did her ten hours of service in the admissions office, which was housed in the oldest building on campus. It was a traditional brick building with two wings, but the original structure had a bell tower that would be the perfect place to take pictures of the students moving around on campus.

"Not sure, maybe the Provost?"

"Could you ask for me?"

"Sure. Gonna take some pictures up there?"

"Yeah, I think it would be a great setting."

My phone beeped. *Call me.* Josh had texted. I rolled my eyes. Like he couldn't call me. I dialed him anyway.

"What's up, buttercup?" I chirped at him.

"Do you want to make some money?"

"Um sure, do I have to take off my clothes?" I asked to torture him.

"Ha ha. Very funny. Not," Josh replied. "Look, the University PR folks were in here the other day and saw your photo, and they want to use it on some promotional material. They said that they would pay for it."

"Wow, that's cool," No matter what Noah had said before, no one had offered me any money for my photos. "How much?"

"They said if you sold it to them outright, five Gs."

I almost dropped the phone, "What? Did I hear you?"

"For real. I almost swallowed my gum when they told me, but apparently full-color prints like this easily could run in excess of five grand because you could charge a set fee and then only sell them usage licenses."

"I didn't know any of this."

"No worries," Josh said, utterly cheerful. "Nate and I talked with some girls over in the art department. We'll handle it all for a cut of fifteen percent."

"No way! You didn't do anything."

"I got you access to the press box for the game and free tickets."

"Five percent," I countered.

"Ten."

"Five."

"Fine, five percent, but next time we go out, you're paying," Josh conceded.

"Deal," I hung up and gave a squeal.

"What is it?" Lana was standing over me, impatiently tapping her hand on the table.

"State is buying my photo and paying me a lot of money for it." I felt dazed. "I think I need to go lie down." I stumbled to my feet and lurched over to the sofa.

"Wow you must really feel faint if you're lying on my sofa," Lana snarked. She came over and sat on the chair. "Why are you so surprised? Your pictures have always been awesome."

"I guess I thought when people said it could be a career, it was a joke."

"Good thing you're going to meet with Dr. Rossum."

"No, I think I need to be a finance major. Josh was talking about licenses and set fees and stuff I had zero understanding of." I felt dazed by it all.

"Nah, you're the artist. You create. Someone else sells." Lana looked at her fingers and nonchalantly added, "And you've got the perfect person to be able to do that."

I already knew a finance major. A surge of adrenaline spiked through me. "I have to go take more photos. I've always wanted to take a picture of the State capital. I wonder how much it would cost to rent a crane."

"A crane?" Lana laughed.

"So I can get some height," I said. "No wait. I need to learn to take ground level tilt shifts. And maybe do some freeze motion photography." I got up and ran to my camera. "Can I borrow your car? I want to go over to the Botanical Gardens and take some shots."

"Sure. I'll come with you. Remember, I'm your assistant," Lana teased.

As we were walking through the Gardens, admiring the late fall foliage, I told Lana that I had received a response from the head of the program. "I'm going to talk to Dr. Rossum tomorrow about a major in the Fine Arts program."

Lana jumped up and down and clapped her hands in glee. "Yay!"

"I'm excited," I admitted, trying to suppress my pleasure both at my decision and Lana's reaction. "I'm supposed to bring in a portfolio of my work, and he said that he would assess my suitability."

"He'll love it."

"I hope so. I never thought my work was any good, you know? So I told everyone that I wasn't interested in making money off it," I admitted.

"I know," Lana took my free hand and swung it, walking like we were five-year-olds on our first jaunt in the park.

"How so?"

"You were scared and deflecting, diminishing expectations in hopes of avoiding disappointment."

"Do you really think talking like that to your patients is going to be helpful?"

"Too much?" She stopped and turned to me.

"Definitely," I reached over and gave her a hug. "I still love you best."

"Nah," she said, hugging me back. "I think you love someone else best now, but I'm okay with that."

I blushed a little and goosed her in retaliation.

"Speaking of true loves, you telling Noah about your plans?"

"No, not until after I talk to Dr. Rossum. I want to surprise him with the good news."

***

I fingered my prepared portfolio. I had pored over my photos, but there were only a few I felt comfortable showing to Dr. Rossum. One of Lana's sorority sisters was an art major and said that he was notoriously difficult and picky. I wished I had taken Lana up on her offer to come or told Noah about it. They would both be here, holding my hand, if I had asked them.

But I had relied on Lana for so long. I wouldn't even be here at Central if she hadn't surreptitiously sent in my application. Noah could go fight a war, come back, and build an empire. I could face down one college professor.

"Don't hover, Ms. Sullivan. Either come in or leave," I jumped at the slightly nasal command. The door had been ajar, but I hadn't realized he had spotted me.

I rubbed a finger across my nose, took a deep breath, and pushed the door fully open to walk through. Dr. Rossum's office was a disaster. There were two wooden chairs set in front of his desk, but they were overflowing with magazines and papers. A small path from the door to the desk was cleared, but there was nowhere to sit. I inched in, careful not to tumble any of the piles to the ground. I stood awkwardly while he inspected me.

His gaze was so penetrating I felt like he could see all my flaws. That

I didn't know how to draw. That I hadn't taken one art class, ever. That I spent most of my time walking in Lana's shadow and my best friend was a boy I wrote to for four years and had never met, until recently. The organs in my throat seemed to swell, and I swallowed rapidly to try to keep my airway open. *Don't cry. Don't cry.* I ordered myself silently.

Dr. Rossum held out his hand and I laid the portfolio in his hand. For several minutes, I stood as Dr. Rossum silently paged through my pictures. He reached the end, flipped through rapidly again, and tossed it toward me like a Frisbee. I fumbled it and the photos spilled out onto the piles and the floor like refuse. My cheeks were burning as I bent to pick up the trash. Tears sat at the base of my throat, threatening to spill out if I so much as opened my mouth. I mutely tucked all the photos into my portfolio and stood up.

"Your photos look like you are trying out for the high school year-book. Pretty pictures of flowers and trick photography? I hardly think you'd cut it as an art student here at Central. We are not here to train people to win Cosmo contests, but to capture the heart and soul of people through the lens," he sneered the words as if just looking at my photos had begun to contaminate the department. I said nothing in my own defense because what could I say? That I liked pretty flowers and trick photography?

"Art is not about the acquisition of money. It is the portrayal of human suffering and triumph. Your photographs are as plastic as the images you are trying to digitally alter. Go back to your humanities studies." He waved to shoo me out. I fled as if rabid dogs were chasing at my heels. My tears began to fall before I had even crossed the threshold of his office into the hallway.

It was my cursed luck that the FAC building was on the south end of campus, down by the theater and the diner that Noah had taken me to that first time. I ran home, straight down the middle of campus, tears streaming down my face. I heard ugly moaning sounds and, after a min-ute, came to the horrible realization that I was making them.

I had allowed myself to be convinced by my friends that I had talent, but deep down I must have known the truth. I hadn't tried to enter the art program here because I knew I wasn't good enough. A little money and a lot of friendly encouragement had puffed me up, and Dr. Rossum brought me right back down to earth.

I ran up the stairs ready to bury myself in my bedroom, only when I opened the door I was greeted with the smiling faces of Lana, Noah, several sorority girls, and all of Noah's roommates. It looked like a party was in progress. I wanted to die.

Noah

Grace stood at the doorway, her mouth slightly open, tear tracks running down her face. She was breathing heavily like she had run a mile to get here. We all froze in our tracks. And then Lana and I shook off our surprise and moved toward her at the same time. Grace rushed past us into the bedroom. I followed, but found the door locked. I didn't even know these doors had locks. I jiggled the doorknob and then knocked. "Grace." When she didn't respond, I knocked louder. "Grace!"

"Stop it," Lana hissed beside me. "You're making it worse." She tilted her head discretely toward the living room. Turning I could see the entire crowd of people standing and watching the drama. Grace wouldn't want this, but I had to get in there. I didn't know if some dickhead had attacked her outside or if she had terrible news from her family.

Swiftly I moved toward Lana's bedroom. I would call her from the privacy of Lana's bedroom. I didn't ask permission or speak to anyone, but I signaled Bo with a tilt of my head. He responded immediately.

As I was shutting the door to Lana's room behind me, I could hear Bo telling everyone to go home.

"Maybe you should just let her be," Lana had followed me in.

"Do you know what this is about?" She turned away. "Tell me," I grabbed her arm to pull her back.

"She wanted to surprise you," Lana said, getting a little tearful herself.

"About what?" When Lana didn't immediately respond, I pulled out my phone and dialed Grace's number. Through the doors I could hear it ring, but Grace didn't pick up. I hung up and dialed again. No answer. I dialed again. No ring. No answer. Fuck. I'd break down the door. Out in the living room, Bo sat on a chair, bent over with his elbows on his knees. He was tossing a phone back and forth between his hands.

"That hers?" I asked.

He nodded. "She opened the door and threw it at me."

"Motherfucker," I cursed. "Grace, talk to me."

Lana was at my elbow again. "Maybe you should let me do it."

"I'm not leaving until I see she is okay."

"Just go to my bedroom and wait," Lana gestured toward her room across the hall.

"Fine," I ground out. I stomped off, signaling Bo to follow.

"Grace, it's just me. What happened with Dr. Rossum?" I stopped and left the door to Lana's room ajar so I could shamelessly eavesdrop. Bo sat down on Lana's bed, my battle buddy, always having my back. "Dr. Rossum?" I mouthed to Bo. He shrugged. I had never heard of this dude. Was he one of Grace's professors? Had he come on to her? White-hot rage flashed in front of my eyes, blinding me for a moment.

I heard a door open and soft murmurings then a soft sob. Goddamn, Grace was crying. I had never heard her cry. Shit. Was, there anything worse than hearing your girl cry and not being able to do a damn thing about it?

My phone rang, sounding unreasonably loud. Paulie it said. Fuck me. I had to take this. "What's up?" I bit out.

"I have more details on the Halloween fight." Paulie gleefully spilled out a number of meaningless words. I had come over to Grace's apartment to share the good news. The guy fighting the undercard on the next UFC fight had laid down his crotch rocket on the highway in L.A. He broke five ribs and had a crushed knee. He was out, probably for good. An agent who had seen me spar Bo last week called up and invited me onto the card. I was going to fight a legitimate pay-per-view bout.

But none of the details mattered now. I had two objectives as I saw it. The first one was to make sure Grace was okay. "Paulie, I've got something going on right now. I'll be at the gym first thing tomorrow. Send me any tape you have of the guy I'm fighting." I hung up before he could blurt out more instructions.

"Can you call Paulie back and find out what's so important while I deal with this?" I asked Bo. He nodded. "Take my truck."

He hefted the keys I tossed him. "How'll you get back?"

"I'll cab it or borrow Lana's car. I'll figure something out," I told him. We walked out to the living room. Grace's door was open. I viewed that as an invitation. I gave Bo a chin nod and walked into the bedroom.

Grace was sitting on the edge of the bed. She looked ragged, a completely different person than I had left this morning. Her shoulders drooped, and it looked like it was taking a super human effort to even hold her head up.

"It's just one person's opinion," Lana said consolingly, rubbing Grace's back.

"That opinion belongs to someone whose art hangs in the Smithsonian," Grace replied, almost too softly for me to hear.

It all made sense now. Dr. Rossum must be the head of the art department and he must have rejected her hard. "State U isn't going to pay five grand for pictures that suck, Grace," I said, trying to keep the anger out of my voice, I felt my body tense up into fight mode. I'd like to go and beat this Dr. Rossum into a bloody pulp.

I didn't expect a response. Grace was too far gone inside her own head right now to listen to either Lana or me. I bent down and picked her up. She stiffened against me at first, but then collapsed against my chest.

At her surrender, I felt a flood of relief rush through me. Lana quietly shut the door behind her as I laid Grace on the bed and followed her down.

"Tell me," I urged, holding her close. Her body felt like ice.

"Remember when I asked you what your greatest fear was?" Her head was on my chest and I could feel the faint movement of her jaw as she spoke.

"Yeah, it was water. The Marines beat it out of me."

"My greatest fear wasn't spiders like I told you."

"No? Do you like them, then?"

That didn't even elicit a laugh, only a short shake of her head. "My biggest fear was that I wasn't ever going to succeed at anything. Lana's super beautiful and smart. Josh is great at sports. My Uncle Louis invented some great software program, which is why we live in a house you can't see from the street. But me? I wasn't anything. I'm a follower, Noah. The biggest chance I ever took was on you." Left unsaid was that I had fucked that up by rejecting her advances because I was too screwed up to be around normal people when I got out.

"I always said I didn't want to pursue photography, that it was just my hobby, because then it would never be judged as lacking," she continued. I could see where this was going and my heart began to ache for her. I had pushed her into this. My goddamned big mouth about pursuit of money and success.

I felt the nod against my chest. I hugged her close. I tried not to give voice to the thousand platitudes that pushed against my tongue. My assessment of her work wasn't going to matter right now because she was flayed open by the criticism of this Dr. Rossum, but I couldn't keep quiet.

"Your vision of the world, Grace, of making the boring and simple objects seems so interesting, is part of what makes you so amazing. If other people didn't view your work as unique and special, no one would be asking you to take pictures. No one would be paying you real money. Real money, Grace, is the currency of criticism. Not words."

Grace remained quiet. Only the soft hiccupy sounds of her breath could be heard in the still room.

I didn't know how to fix this. I wasn't going to convince Grace that she was awesome at photography, so I did the one thing that I knew how to do.

Her sorrow had exhausted her. She watched me with big eyes, wet with her earlier tears, as I undressed her. I swept my hands in long, soothing motions down her body until I could hear her breath quicken and see her body flush in response. When she moved to reach for me, I looped her wrists lightly in my right hand. "Let me do all the work, honey."

I slid down her body, running my mouth over her soft, rounded belly and lower still until I rested between her lush thighs. "I promise you won't even notice the time passing." Then I was too busy doing other things with my tongue and mouth to say another word.

Grace voiced no complaints. I knew that this was just a temporary fix, but it was all I could offer.

***

Leaving Grace sated and sweaty in bed, I padded to the kitchen to rummage around for something to eat. Grace's apartment was the antithesis of our house. It was quiet and clean. At my house, the television was always on and there were always random people moving in and out to drink, play cards, or just hang out. Grace's place was a sanctuary. I wanted to provide this kind of atmosphere for Grace and me; a place like this that could be a haven for both of us. I'd do anything to make that happen.

Chapter Sixteen

Grace

The next day, I felt wrung out, like day-old bread. All the soothing concern that Noah had lavished on me seemed to have dissipated with the rising sun. He didn't want me to be alone that day and insisted that I go with him while he trained. I packed my books into my messenger bag and left the camera backpack lying in the corner. I wasn't sure if I would ever feel the confidence to wield it again.

"Do you miss the Marines?" I asked, fiddling with the radio. I wondered if I would miss my camera. Sometimes I would forget I was even carrying it, since it was such a natural extension of my body. This morning when I picked up the camera bag, it felt like it weighed as much as a cement block. I could barely drag it into the closet. My portfolio was lying on the desk, and sitting on top was a mint tin emblazoned with the tilt shift photograph I had taken of the Alpha Phis. Lana must have left it for me last night. I assumed it was one of the many rush-related paraphernalia they had produced. Maybe it wasn't true art, but I couldn't deny a surge of pride when I looked at the tin with my photo printed on the lid.

"Sometimes, but not today," he said, interrupting my reverie.

"Why not today?"

"Today is Field day. If I were still in the Marines, I would be cleaning today. Shining my shoes, cleaning the barracks. Everything."

"But if today weren't Field day?"

"It's nice not to have every aspect of your life under someone else's control. I don't miss walking in the desert and disrobing in order to take a—well, you know. I don't miss getting shot at. But I miss my brothers. I think that's why Bo and I enjoy living with all the guys. There's a sense of community there that we had in the Marines. Plus, you know, you were paid to shoot stuff up. It's unreal in some ways. But every day was like a challenge, a competition between yourself and the elements or the insurgents."

***

The Spartan gym looked like its name. There were mirrors along one wall, but there were no machines like you would see at a health club. Bags hung from the ceiling, old huge tires were stacked in one corner, and long ropes coiled on the floor. Racks of free weights lined the wall opposite of the mirrors. The place smelled of sour sweat.

Noah led me through the front room where everyone seemed to stop what they were doing and stare at us. In the back was a larger room that resembled the warehouse where Noah had fought for his ten thousand dollars. Except this room had large fluorescent lights that hung down over a raised boxing platform. To one side sat a long bench like you'd see in a schoolyard. Noah led me over to it and gave me a hard, long kiss that left me blushing from the tips of my ears to the soles of my feet.

"Be right back," he said.

When he returned, he and Bo were dressed only in loose shorts. They climbed into the ring and a couple of other guys came to help them suit up with protective gear, red on Noah and blue on Bo. They looked a little like the kid's game of Rock 'Em Sock 'Em Robots. My trigger finger twitched involuntarily. If I stood up on the rafters and looked down, the bright colors contrasting against the dull gray walls would've made an amazing photograph. Dr. Rossum's jeers about my trick photography killed the thought off quickly. I shook my head to rid myself of his taunts. I didn't want to dwell on it. I resolved to just live in the moment.

A crowd of thickly muscled men filtered in from the front room and soon it seemed like everyone was standing or sitting around the platform.

This was different from the warehouse fight. Bo and Noah circled each other, their arms outstretched as if measuring the distance between them. When one moved in, the other feinted. They danced like that for a minute before Bo sprang toward Noah with a punch across the jaw. Noah's head snapped back, but he responded with a quick kick to the side that pushed Bo away.

For two friends, the blows they exchanged seemed fierce. A flurry of punches, kicks, and parries followed, and a few of the blows elicited shouts of delight from the audience. Noah was on his back with Bo atop him, Noah's legs snug around Bo's torso.

With a quick movement, Noah rolled Bo onto his back, his arms around Bo's neck and his legs around Bo's arms. Bo tapped his hand to the side and Noah let go immediately. He rose easily and leaned down to help Bo to his feet. They hugged each other. When someone came to remove Noah's helmet, I could see him grinning.

Noah said he fought for money, but it was clear by the expressions on both faces that they enjoyed this exertion of testosterone quite a bit.

Noah was breathing hard when he came to the edge of the ring. Leaning on the ropes, he motioned me over. I resisted the urge to look behind me, but I did see out of my periphery about a dozen heads swivel toward me. I have to admit the feeling that welled up inside me wasn't pretty or nice. It was possessive, with a tinge of pride. Yes, that guy up there all sweaty and gorgeous who just fought the crap out of the other guy? That guy was gesturing toward me.

Someone, I'm not sure who it was, gave me a boost at the same time Noah reached down to grab my hands. I stood on the outside with the ropes of the boxing ring between us. They were soft and springy.

"What'd you think?" Noah asked me, holding my arms so I didn't fall backward. "Different from the other night?"

"I'm a little afraid of what I think," I admitted.

"Oh," he said, one eyebrow rising.

"It's very primitive," I said, "and it evokes a primitive response."

He laughed low, and I felt my stomach tighten in response. "I don't think this is the place for the discussion I'd like to have. Let me shower and change, and we can get out of here."

"Shower," I said plaintively. I wanted to finger paint the sweat all over those defined muscles from his chest down to his low-riding gym shorts. His hands tightened on my arms, and I wondered if he was going to haul me over the ropes. He just looked at me, his nostrils flaring.

"Don't push it, sister," he said, growling a little. "Pull up on the top rope." And he ducked under the raised rope and came out on my side. He jumped down and held up his arms for me. I leaned forward, and he effortlessly lifted me down.

"Why is your nose still unbroken? Or your face rarely bruised?" I patted his face.

"It's the face masks, but sometimes I can get a bloody nose. Bo wasn't aiming for that, though."

"Aiming?"

"Yeah," Bo's voice came from above us. He jumped down from the ring to land softly beside Noah and me. "Noah has a glass jaw, so I couldn't hit him too hard, or I'd mess up his photo shoot."

"I don't like getting hit in the face, so I try to avoid it," Noah admitted.

"Does that mean if you get hit in the face you're knocked out?" I asked.

"Nah, it just means I can't take too many of them. And I've developed very good duck and jab instincts."

"So this is like the swimming thing," I said to Noah. "Exposure is like an antidote."

"You told her you were scared of the water?" Bo asked, surprised.

"He wrote to me about it," I replied. Bo gave Noah a strange look and then slapped him on the back.

"Let's get you cleaned up," he said and took Noah off to the locker room.

The mini high that I had been on faded, and discomfort set in as I looked around the room as it emptied. A big, barrel-chested man who had been standing in Noah's corner during most of the fight came over.

"Paulie," he said, holding out a giant hand that could have engulfed two of mine.

"Grace." I watched as my hand was swallowed up. Where Noah was lean and muscled, this man's physique screamed steroided body builder. I shrank away at the menace in his gaze, but he didn't release my hand.

"My boy Noah's got a chance to be a big name in this sport. You gonna help him or mess with his mind?"

"Um, I think Noah decides what he wants to do without much input from others." Paulie must not have had a good understanding of Noah's mentality if he thought I was going to influence Noah one way or another.

"There're two kinds of girls for a kid like him: The hometown girl and the ring girl. One is going to do everything she can to propel her man up the ladder to the title."

"I'm guessing I'm a hometown girl." I tugged at my hand and he finally let it go.

"Yeah and you hometown girls have a lot of ideas about what your men should do. Uptight chick like you with money written all over her probably thinks she's too good for this place. Maybe you should let go now and hook up with your own kind."

Right, like I was going to take lessons from a guy whose neck had been swallowed by his shoulders.

"Leave her alone, Paulie," Noah demanded. He had returned from the locker room. "Let's go," he directed to me.

"Bo?" I asked.

"He's got his own ride," Noah ushered me to his truck. His hair was wet from the shower and laid flat against his head, like a silky brown cap.

"Bo mentioned you had a photo shoot? What's that all about?" I asked when we got into the car.

"I've been offered an undercard fight on Halloween," Noah said.

"My God, is that why you were all at the apartment the other night?"

He nodded. "Yeah, I came up to tell you the news. Lana was making spaghetti, and we just dumbly invited a bunch of people over."

"God, I feel like an idiot. I ruined your big news."

"Nah, it's all good, Grace," He turned his head slightly, and I could see a smirk on his face. "The evening ended just right."

"What happens now?" I asked, slapping him lightly on the arm.

"It would be great if you could just get into the Octagon and fight. But there is a ton of BS involved. The publicity you're required to do. The constant monitoring of your diet. The working out constantly. They make me wear my cowboy boots to public appearances." Noah's voice started to take on a whiny quality.

I stifled a laugh at his side.

"I can feel you laughing," Noah accused me.

"I'm sorry," I giggled a bit. "Cowboy boots? I've never seen you wear those!"

"Yeaaahhh," he drawled. "And they want me to talk with a twang and use loooong vowels."

This time I couldn't contain my laughter.

"Being successful in the UFC isn't just about being the best fighter; it's about being a personality. Making people want to either cheer for you or against you," Noah complained.

"How do you get chosen for the fight?" I asked.

"Money," Noah said flatly. "It's all about how much money I can generate. I've got a perfect record, but there are a lot of low level guys with perfect records. We all earned them against gym chum."

"Gym chum?"

"Yeah, for smaller gyms, they drag in guys off the street, promise them money fights, and then throw them up against more experienced fighters so that those fighters can build their records."

"You aren't making this sound very savory."

Noah shrugged. "Anything where there is a lot of money contains unsavory things."

***

Sleep came easily each night with Noah's attentiveness, but each day I awoke with a sense of dread. Noah needed to spend more and more time training. And I felt like I was just marking time. Mike asked me to cover for a classmate who was struggling with midterms and I said yes. I had nothing better to do. I hadn't picked up my camera since the debacle with Dr. Rossum, and other than the one time at the gym when Bo and Noah were fighting, I hadn't had the urge.

Ironically, it wasn't the money that killed off my hobby. Getting paid for it was exciting. Instead, it was knowing that what I was doing was fake, a trick, no more worth gracing the cover of a magazine than a bowl of fruit. I wished I had the nerve to tell Dr. Rossum how much State was paying me, but money probably didn't matter to him. Noah had said that real criticism came in the form of dollars exchanged and if someone thought my work was worth paying for, then it didn't matter what a million Smithsonian artists had to say. I wanted to believe that was true more than anything, but I was having trouble convincing myself—or at least of getting the courage to return to Dr. Rossum. One visit to the firing squad was enough for me.

"Have you thought about coming to Vegas with me?" Noah asked during one of the rare moments when we saw each other.

"I can't," I told him, twisting my face up in disappointment. "I thought I told you I was going to cover someone's shift who was study-ing for midterms."

"I thought you were going to turn down the trade?" Noah asked.

"I was, but this person was really desperate."

"Why are you taking all these hours on at the library? It's hard enough for us to see each other."

"You're so busy, and I'm just trying to keep myself occupied," I explained.

"With Mike? I thought you said your insecurity wouldn't manifest itself by making me jealous." He wasn't looking at me at all. Instead he just tapped his pen against the desk, fast and hard. I wondered if he would break the pen or gouge the desk first.

I wasn't sure where the Mike accusation came from, and I wasn't trying to make him jealous. The accusation did hit close to home. I complained incessantly about the ring girls to Lana. She told me to go to Vegas already if I was so worried.

There were girls everywhere, and Noah was so fine with so much drive and potential. I knew that there were dozens of them on this campus alone waiting for him to tire of me. My indecision must have shown on my face because Noah threw down the pen and swore at me, which he rarely ever did.

"Goddammit Grace, you don't need money from the work study. You can just sit at home."

Sit at home and wait for him like I had for four years? I had waited for him, and only when he had decided it was time, did he come. Now he was telling me I could just wait some more until he had time for me? I felt a sudden and unexpected rush of anger toward him. "I just can't sit around and wait for you to show up after you're done with your activities."

"Why not?"

"Because I'm not that girl," I spit out. Maybe I was, but I didn't want to be. I was tired of being Josh's little sister, Lana's cousin, and now Noah's girlfriend. I had to start stepping out on my own, even if it meant just working at the library for more hours. Before, when my confidence was buttressed by my black metal case full of lenses and mirrors, maybe Noah's absence wouldn't have been so noticeable, but the divide between us seemed greater now than ever.

"I'm doing all of this for you, you know." He threw out his arm, gesturing into the air. I had no idea what he was talking about.

"How is your fighting for us?"

"It's too low-class for you, is that it?"

"No!" I shook my head vehemently. I felt like we were talking two different languages. "I don't fit with you, Noah. You know where you're going and what you're going to do. You've put actual plans in motion. I can't even pick a major, and I dither over what classes to sign up for. My—" I couldn't bring myself to say it, to give voice to my greatest failure. To admit that I was actually terrible at something I loved.

"You have plenty of time to experiment with what you want to do and decide later."

"Don't play father knows best here and tell me that because you're four years older than me, you know what I'm feeling. You don't. You've always had a plan. "

"Grace, you're killing me here. Don't throw away this thing between us over some ridiculous idea of what you think I want. I want you," he said flatly, as if the conversation was over and done.

"Thanks for calling my concerns ridiculous."

"Don't do this, Grace." He sounded disgusted.

"Or what? You'll fuck some ring girl?"

He reared back like I slapped him. "Don't curse."

"Don't curse? You curse all the time. FUCK! FUCK! FUCK! FUCK!" I screamed. Noah stood up.

"I'm not going to sleep with any ring girls. Calm down or just come with me. Then it isn't even an issue."

"Well, it isn't an issue if we aren't dating, is it?" I spat out. All my anxiety, frustration, and worry spilled out. I stomped over to the entry and threw open the door.

Noah picked up his bag and, with one motion, swept all his materials into the opening. He shouldered the backpack and stalked toward me. "Fine. If this is what you want."

No, no, it really wasn't, but what else could I say at this point without actually looking like a crazy person? I nodded, unable to speak, knowing that if I did open my mouth a million sorries would pour forth and I would be back to where I was before. In someone's shadow.

"You'll regret this," he threatened. His face was dark like a thundercloud. I remained silent, and he stepped through the doorway. I waited half a heartbeat and closed the door with a slam. I didn't hear his footsteps right away, and I thought about opening the door. But he took off a beat later, running down the steps.

I ran over to the living room window. At the corner of the street, I saw two coeds stop him. I shouldn't worry about hurting his feelings. There would be any number of women ready to take my place. I felt like these past weeks had been borrowed time anyway. Like the magic clock had been broken and midnight was delayed. Only now the clock was fixed, and my time was being ticked off as the golden hour approached steadily. Inexorably.

***

The library was bursting with people during midterms, but everyone walked around like silent ghosts. Worry marked many faces, aging us past our years. I tossed Mike's red ball around by myself and stared down at the library entrance from the balcony. I focused on the monitor's desk, purposely trying to blur the edges. People slowed down, moving like windup dolls, as I mentally took their photos. A girl with a bright red jacket walked in. She would've been a great subject.

My heart ached, missing Noah, missing my camera. He hadn't called me or texted me. He didn't show up around campus after class or even here at the library. Given that he had pursued me so hard in the beginning, his lack of effort now spoke volumes. We were done.

I began to dimly understand why my mother couldn't face the world and hid behind a veil of prescription drugs. Being a zombie from too much Xanax was vastly preferable to feeling hollowed out by pain.

My text message alert sounded. I swung away from the balcony and rolled my chair to where my phone lay on the desk. *Call me.* Josh.

"Yes, Master Josh, what can I do for you, Master Josh?" I asked, dutifully calling him.

"Can you come up here for homecoming?"

"I can't. I traded with someone, and I'm supposed to cover their shift on Saturday."

"Trade again." He sounded impatient. "Get your student supervisor to cover. Tell him you have a family emergency."

"Is Mom okay?" I asked, instant concern making my voice a little screechy.

"It's with me, you dumbass."

"Are you okay?"

"Better than. Guess what?" He continued without giving me a chance to guess. "The Athletic Director was down here the other day and saw your photo."

"What photo?" I asked dumbly.

"The one you took of me looking awesome. What other photo would I be calling you about?"

"I already got paid for that one." Maybe I wasn't art major material or good enough for Dr. Rossum, but someone liked my stuff enough to pay me a substantial sum of money.

"Right, so anyway, the AD loves the photo and wants you to do one for every sport on campus. They're gonna pay you to do it, of course. I'm negotiating your fee," Josh said, sounding so proud of himself, almost as proud as when he talked about his athletic accomplishments.

"Seriously?" I was stunned.

"For reals, baby sis."

"Why do I have to come up for homecoming?"

"They want you to take pictures of homecoming too. The parade and then the game. Whadda think?"

"I'll get someone to cover." I hung up on the sound of Josh's laughter. Mike had no problem covering for me when I explained my situation.

***

Homecoming was more fun than I had anticipated. It was good to get away from Central. Noah had left for Vegas without a word. Lana came with to serve as my assistant. I was grateful for her help, as this time I really did need assistance, having to keep track of where I was supposed to be and when. I didn't get to see much of the game except through the camera lens. This time, I stayed up in the press box for the entire time. Lana sat and charmed half the sports writers.

By the time we landed at Josh's apartment after the game had ended, I was mentally and physically wiped, but I hadn't forgotten that Noah was fighting that night in Vegas.

Josh pulled me aside after pizzas had arrived.

"Noah's fourth on the card so he'll probably fight around 8 pm or so. I've bought the fight. But he's a huge underdog and he's likely to get crushed, so maybe you want to miss it anyway?"

"No, really?" Dismay and fear chased down my spine.

"Yep, according to what I've read on the Internet, the original challenger hurt himself. So Noah is filling in. It's not a title match or anything, but it's a fairly big deal because the opponent is undefeated, and in order to make the fight worth the pay-per-view money, they had to find another undefeated middleweight."

I felt sick to my stomach and refused all offerings of food. Noah had never once expressed any concern about his fight, but then I never gave him the chance. The crowd in Josh's apartment had blossomed. It was homecoming, after all. I claimed a place in front of the TV and refused to move.

The first match lasted all three rounds. Both fighters were bloodied and exhausted. Their blows were more like grabs, and they spent the last four minutes grappling on the mat. The blood from cuts on their faces was smeared on the floor.

Noah had once told me that the grappling portion could look very provocative, and he was right. The one opponent was lying on top of the other in some weird sixty-nine position. As the announcers narrated the events, the terms they used had more sexual innuendo than Cosmo's front cover.

None of the men in the crowd were turned off by this. Apparently sweaty man on sweaty man in a sexual position was exciting if their intent was to hurt each other. After the fight was over, a decision was made, anointing the red shorts guy as the winner. I had no idea how they arrived at that decision.

The two looked completely exhausted with bruises and cuts all over their face and arms and chest. One's guy nose looked broken and cotton had been stuffed up it to stem the flow of blood. I felt sick that this was what Noah would look like at the end of his match. After the commercial break, the announcers started talking about Noah's fight.

Noah's strength, according to the announcers that I could barely hear over the din, was in his legs. He had powerful legs, and his kicks had knocked people out. His weakness was grappling. No one mentioned his glass jaw. Maybe that was a weakness only known to him and Bo.

His opponent looked just as powerful. Noah's fight was a little anti-climactic after I worked myself up to believe that he would be choked or struck into unconsciousness and carted off on a stretcher. Scenes from the night in the warehouse flashed through my mind. Instead, the first round consisted of the two grabbing each other around the neck and circling. There were a few blows exchanged, and Noah took his guy to the floor only to be thrown off. Neither looked too damaged after the first round.

The second round ended about twenty seconds in, after Noah kicked his opponent in the face and then drove his knee into the opponent's abdomen about ten times until the opponent collapsed and tapped out.

Despite the shortness of the fight, I was wrung out and went to lie down. I didn't need or want to see the big title fights. I missed Noah terribly. He looked great tonight, and there were all those girls ringing the fight, ready to attack him the minute he stepped out of the Octagon.

And he had every right to take them up on their offers, because I had so stupidly told him to get out.

"You okay?" I hadn't heard Josh come in nor seen him because my arm was thrown across my face in an attempt to keep my stupidity from leaking out and infecting others. I felt him sit on the side of the bed.

"What's more important in life, Josh? Knowing who you are or just being happy with what you have?"

"I don't know that you can have the latter without the former."

"Right."

"Is this about Noah?" Josh asked gently. "Because the guys and I think—"

I groaned and rolled over away from Josh. "Why are you always gossiping about my life?"

"Nothing better to do. They keep canceling our favorite soaps. But seriously, Grace, you can have both. There's no reason why you can't enjoy yourself with another person even while you're searching for direction."

"I just think that I can't focus with Noah around. He makes it so easy for me."

"That sounds kind of contradictory. If Noah eases your way, doesn't it mean he gets rid of all the clutter so that you can focus on finding your 'direction'?"

"What's with the scare quotes? I can hear you emphasizing that word with derision," I mumbled into his pillow.

"Because, Grace, you have this rosy and very wrong picture that everyone else around you knows what the hell they're doing. I'm probably not going to get drafted, and I don't know what I'll do if I don't play football, but I've got to figure it out. You don't think Lana wonders whether the life choices she has made are right? Everyone has moments of uncertainty. You have to give yourself room to fail, Grace." Josh pulled on my arm and rolled me back over so he could look at me. "I know you've been lost since Dad died. And I've been a shitty brother, at times, but not moving forward with your life isn't going to bring him back. And it wouldn't have kept him alive."

The tears I had tried to keep at bay were sliding out of my eyes and dampening the pillow. Josh reached over to wipe them away. His own eyes were a bit wet. "I miss Dad every day, especially on game days. While I'm not a fan of the idea of my little sister dating, this Noah guy seems to make you happy. I'd rather have you happy and with him than miserable and alone."

I wiped at my tears. "God, I'm like the poster child for every emo, sad-sack girl out there. I'm letting down my gender."

"At least you admit it. Now dry those tears and come out. The fight's over, and the guys are going to want to impress you by doing keg stands."

"You make it sound so enticing," I mocked.

"I know. This way they will be so disgusting, you'll take a decade to want to date again."

"You're so clever." I patted him on the chest and pushed off the bed.

Josh was right. Watching a bunch of players do keg stands and then puke did turn my stomach. I was glad to go home the next day.

***

I waited until I was sure Noah had returned to campus.

"Aren't you going to tell me I'm doing the wrong thing?" I asked Lana as we were picking out the clothes I would wear to lure Noah back to me. I had, through some sneaking around, figured out that Noah was going to be at his gym tonight doing some kind of post mortem. Maybe planning for his next fight.

Lana was silent for a minute, and when she spoke, I could tell she was choosing her words carefully. "I thought you'd fall apart if you and Noah broke up. But even though you've been a mess emotionally, it's nothing like you were when he wrote you and said he didn't want to meet you."

I was stronger, emotionally and mentally, than I was two years ago. Even though I had been torn up inside about Noah being with another girl in Vegas, I was still functioning. I could be alone and survive, even though I was happier with Noah. He might have slept with a girl in Vegas. He might have done two dozen of them. But Noah had written to me faithfully for four years. He had come to Central College, thousands of miles away from his base in San Diego. Josh was right. Everyone's life had uncertainty. But my future wasn't completely unknowable.

I had my camera. My family. And, if all went my way, Noah.

He had no one in his life but Bo. And me. He could have me if he wanted me.

I pulled up the bus schedule on my laptop. The bus service was nowhere near The Woodlands but it did go to the Spartan gym. I had showered and shaved every part of my body.

I pulled out the shirt Lana had bought for me the first night I saw Noah at the fraternity party. It wasn't gym appropriate, but I knew Noah had liked it. He told me once that he had wanted to untie those bows with his teeth.

I considered putting on the silicone cups that Lana had given me to wear with this top but decided I would go without. It was an overtly sexual message, but I wanted there to be no misunderstandings.

It was cold out, and I threw on a pair of skinny jeans and a cashmere shawl. I flatironed my brown hair so it hung like a silk curtain down my bare back.

I inserted a pair of wide hoop earrings in my ears and carefully applied some mascara and eyeliner. I didn't try too much because I knew I wasn't the artist that Lana was with the makeup. I outlined my lips in rose and ran a tinted lip gloss over the top, making my lips look bee stung and wet.

Popping two mints in my mouth, I stuck my ID and debit card in my pocket along with my lip gloss. I slid my wedges on and double checked the bus route I stored on my phone. I'd need to make one stop and get a transfer and the second bus should take me within three blocks of the Spartan gym. Lana had wanted to drive me, but I wanted to do this all on my own, no safety net.

Both buses were sparsely populated. When the driver stopped at my destination, he warned me, "This isn't a night club, girlie."

"I know. My boyfriend is a fighter."

"You best hustle inside, then, else he'll be using those fists of his."

Thanking him, I hopped off. It wasn't just cold; it was freezing. I hurried the three blocks west of the bus stop to the Spartan gym. The lights above the gym were dimmed, and for a moment I had this terrible thought that the place was closed. I checked my phone. It was 7:30 and the gym didn't close until 10:00. I pulled at the door, and it opened easily, a bell like sound occurring when the door opened. The sickly sweet smell of antiseptic and sweat assailed me, and I took a moment to acclimate myself.

There were the sounds of metal against metal as burly guys lifted bars heavy with weights. Another person was watching himself do curls in front of the mirrors. No one stopped me, although it seemed like everyone was looking.

I took a few more steps inside the gym, clutching the shawl around me. For a moment I wondered what the hell I was doing here at this nearly all-male enclave of muscle and sweat.

"You lost?" I heard a familiar voice call out to me, and I spun to my left and saw Bo standing there. He was shirtless, and he was unwrapping a long cloth from his hand.

"No," I answered, straightening my shoulders. "I know exactly where I am."

We stood there for a minute as he weighed my response against his own love for Noah. I must have passed, because he jerked his head toward the back room that held the boxing ring. "He's back there."

"Thanks."

As I was walking toward the back room, I brushed by him and heard him say, "Don't make me regret it."

I saw Noah almost immediately, sitting on a bench against the wall. His elbows rested on his knees and his shoulders were hunched forward. Noah had always appeared solid and in charge, but in this moment he looked burdened by the weight of something.

My cork wedged heels made almost no sound as I walked toward him on the rubber mat floor that covered the expanse of the gym. It wasn't until my feet were nearly under his nose that he even noticed another person was in the room with him.

"Not interested, babe," he said without raising his head.

"You haven't heard what I'm offering," I said. His head jerked up and for a moment I saw a strong emotion blaze in his eyes. Relief? Love? I knelt down in front of him and placed my hands on his.

"Congratulations on your win. It looked fairly—" I cast around for the right word "effortless."

"It wasn't exactly effortless, and my body still hurts more than usual, but it was a good win. I'm surprised you watched it," he admitted.

"I couldn't not watch it. I'll definitely believe anything you say about the other guy looking worse than you."

Noah shook his hands a little restlessly but didn't move them out from under mine. "Did you really come down to the gym to tell me congratulations?"

I took a deep breath. "I need to ask you an important question. One bigger than whether Converse sneakers are better than Keds. Or what the best super power is."

"Yeah?"

"Yeah," I paused and took a deep breath before plunging ahead. "Do you think magnetic polarity can be reversed?"

"All of those questions sound interesting, but I think we both know the answer to one of them," Noah replied in a serious tone.

My heart sank. "So that's a no?"

"Every sane person acknowledges that Chucks are the superior sneaker."

I managed a weak smile. "Indeed."

This time he turned his hands palms up and gripped mine. "Magnets can be reversed. But, for some, their attraction is so strong that they can't be kept apart."

"Not even by stupid words and stupid actions"? I said softly, looking at our entwined hands. I could feel mine getting sweaty, and I wanted to pull them away and wipe them on my jeans.

"Not even."

"I picked out my own clothes and rode the bus here," I blurted out.

This statement was met with silence. Then he said, "You're the strangest girl sometimes. Let me help you, Grace: 'Noah, I miss you, and I forgive you for being an asshole.'"

I looked up at him, wanting him to see how earnest I was. "Noah, I've missed you," I didn't repeat the last part calling him an asshole, but I was glad that he knew the mistake wasn't all mine. "I was afraid of what you made me feel, and it was easier to push you away than accept it. I'd like to try again if you're willing."

He let go of one of my hands to sweep my hair back and tuck it behind one of my ears. His big hand cradled my face. I leaned into it and turned to kiss his palm.

"I've just been waiting for you to come around instead of forcing myself on you," Noah said softly. He drew me closer to him with his one hand, still holding my face with the other. The kiss that he gave me was more tender than passionate, but it still curled me toes and made me want to drag him down on top of me.

"I was never interested in Mike, you know. You're the only one for me," I vowed.

"I didn't sleep with a ring girl in Vegas. I've never wanted anyone but you." He tipped my head up, his face suddenly vulnerable. "We all right?"

"Yes, forever," I breathed out. He swept me up against his body. Neither of us cared that his sweat was staining my top. He could rip it off me later, and I'd keep a piece in my memory box as a remembrance of our reconciliation, tucked in next to all his letters and notes.

***

The next morning, I told Noah my plan to submit a different set of photos to Dr. Rossum. The one with the girl on the bench. The gravesite of my father. The picture I took of the front of our house the one time Josh and I returned for a visit after we'd moved to Chicago to live with Uncle Louis. And another tilt shift photography piece—the one of Josh looking awesome. Someday I hoped the portfolio would include Noah fighting.

"After class today, I'm going back to see Dr. Rossum," I said, pouring Noah a cup of coffee.

He made a face, but I knew it was about my announcement. I made good coffee. "Why Grace? Do you really need an art major to take pictures for a living? You said before you just needed more practice."

"No. But I can learn a lot about perspective and composition and self-expression." I took a sip of my own coffee. "It would make me better at photography."

"Then I'll go with you," he announced.

"You can, but you have to stay outside the building." I had anticipated this and wanted to set early ground rules. If Dr. Rossum was mean again, I could see Noah barging in and punching the professor in the nose, which would result in Noah getting suspended or worse.

"No way. I'm coming inside," Noah insisted.

"You aren't the one applying for entrance into the art program," I replied calmly, sipping on my coffee. He wasn't going to win this argument.

"No, but I'm not going to sit on my thumb while someone tears you a new asshole."

I tried a different approach to reason with him.

"Let's assume that at some point in the future, I'm working for a newspaper or magazine and I have a problem with the editor. I need to be able to work out these issues on my own," I explained.

"No, you really don't." He looked so serious that I tried to keep from smiling at the absurdity. "I'll come and break his face and then your problem will be solved."

"What if you're gone on a fight?"

"When I get back, I'll come and break his face."

"Noah, be serious. You can't go around breaking people's faces in order to protect my feelings," I admonished him. I couldn't tell at this point how much was teasing bluster and how much was serious threat.

He heaved a huge, put-upon sigh and took a long drink of his coffee. "Is it okay with you if I'm mentally punching their lights out?"

"Yes, perfectly. And I want you to describe the action in great detail after."

***

Noah was waiting for me, just like that first day, slouching against the wall. This time I didn't hesitate at the door but ran to him. His arms came around me immediately and he kissed me, uncaring of the students around us.

"Ready?" He asked, tenderly moving a little hair that had fallen forward and tucking it behind my ear.

I nodded and lifted up my black portfolio.

We walked silently across the campus, holding hands. The fallen leaves from the trees crunched under our feet. The fall air was getting cooler, but it would have to be much closer to freezing before the students would pull out jackets and jeans. I couldn't recall a time I had felt more content and just generally pleased with the world. I knew that even if Dr. Rossum hated my work again that I'd be okay.

I'd still be able to perfect my photography skills without classes. What I had told Noah before still was true. Nothing was better for me than actual practice, which meant experimentation and, yes, failure.

I'd learned so much from trying and failing. It's something I wouldn't fear again.

Funny how facing down your greatest fears actually made you stronger.

"Are you sure I can't come in?" Noah asked as we reached the steps of the Fine Arts building.

"Yes, I'm sure," I reached up on my toes and pressed my lips against his. "Your love is so strong I can feel it even upstairs."

I grinned at the sudden redness appearing in his cheeks. "I do, you know," he said softly, "love you very much."

"I know, and I love you," I said. Pleased with myself, I pushed him onto a bench and ran inside the building. Even walking up the stairs, I felt different. Last time I was tentative, as if I was going to my own execution. This time, I took the stairs swiftly and confidently.

I marched right up to Dr. Rossum's assistant and gave her my name. "Grace Sullivan," I said. "I have an appointment to see Dr. Rossum."

The assistant's blue eyes twinkled at me. Could she recognize the difference too? "Go right in," she said.

"So you're back?" Dr. Rossum's flat voice met me at the doorway.

"I am, sir," I said. The sound of his voice made me falter a bit, and I recalled the harsh words he had flung at me before. But I shrugged the memory off and entered the messy room. There was still no place to sit and barely any place to stand. Noah had said to imagine a steel rod from the base of my foot into the floor to keep me steady and focused. I visualized instead a long metal chain that hooked me to Noah, my rock, and mentally grounded myself.

"Do you have new material for me?" He held out his hand wearily as if this meeting was too tiresome for life.

"I do," I said and stepped forward, handing him my portfolio. He paged through quickly, as he did before, and then stopped at the photo of the girl on the bench.

"Why did you take this picture?" he demanded, his demeanor a little less tired.

"She reminded me of my mother," I admitted.

"Your mother wears poorly-fitted cardigans and ugly shoes?" he mocked.

"No. My mother's eyes are dead. Her spirit was snuffed out when my dad died. This girl's eyes show the same thing. No life. Something killed her inside. Nothing is growing there yet. Not now. Maybe not ever," I said flatly. I didn't relish dredging up my old pains; by including those pictures, I was offering up a piece of me. I'd look foolish trying to deny those feelings to Dr. Rossum.

He looked at me sharply and gave me a short nod. "It's not like I can really keep you out of the program."

I didn't say the obvious, which was that he could. Instead, I waited for the official verdict and tried to keep the triumph off my face. Probably an impossible task. Noah and I hadn't practiced that. It was enough that I was still on my feet.

Dr. Rossum tapped the portfolio against his hand. "Do you know why I am hard on students, Ms. Sullivan?"

I shook my head. *Because you're an asshole?* I thought, hoping my thoughts weren't blazing across my face like a neon sign.

"Because," Dr. Rossum instructed, "if you plan to be an artist you need to learn how to take criticism and stand up for your work. If you don't love it, no one will."

There were better ways of teaching, in my opinion, but I wasn't going to voice those to Dr. Rossum, I said nothing.

"Nothing to say for yourself?" he finally asked.

"No, sir. I plan to let my art do my talking," I replied, allowing a little snarkiness to leak through.

"You have a lot to learn, Ms. Sullivan."

"I hope that the art program will teach it all to me," I said. This time I couldn't prevent a smile because we both knew I had won.

Dr. Rossum grunted and tossed the portfolio to me. This time all the photos remained safely tucked inside. "Leave your email with Ms. Grant. She will send you the admissions papers, and you can start classes in the spring."

After I did as Dr. Rossum instructed, I sped down the stairs to Noah.

He saw me running from inside and caught me as I flew out of the doors. "I'm in," I cried with happiness and showered kisses all over his face.

He threw back his head and shouted "Ooooorah!" which made me laugh like a loon. People stopped and stared at our spectacle, but I didn't care.

"I knew it," Noah laughed and carried me down the stairs, setting me down when we had reached the bottom.

"Oh you did, did you?" I teased, slapping him lightly on the arm with my portfolio. He grabbed it and carefully tucked it into his backpack.

"Yup," he said, cradling me under one of his arms as we started the trek back across campus toward my apartment. "Either you were going to get in, or I was going upstairs to break Dr. Rossum's legs. It was all good."

I snorted and said, "Well I'm glad I could save us both with my superior skills, then."

"How so?" Noah queried, grinning down at me.

"Because otherwise you'd be expelled, and I'd be a humanities major, if not for my photographs."

"I've always known you were superior," Noah said, all sign of humor vanishing. "You're too good for me."

"Bullshit," I said, in a no-nonsense voice. "We're just right for one another. Let's go home and celebrate."

His eyes lightened. "I know just the thing."

"Does it involve us being in bed together?" I recognized that look. It's the one that he gave me before my clothes ended up on the floor. It was one of my favorite Noah expressions.

"Yes. Why do you even ask?" He looked at me like I was just being silly. I was.

"I thought celebration was dinner and drinks?" I teased him.

"No. Why waste our time doing that when we both know what we want," he somberly told me.

"All right, Noah Jackson. Let's go home and you can show me how to celebrate things the right way." I was totally in the mood for anything he had in mind.

"You know, you're very sexy when you tell me what to do," he grinned, teasing again.

"Really?"

"Yeah." This one word was growled at me, sending a shiver of excitement down my spine.

By the time we reached the apartment, we could barely keep our hands off each other. Our mouths were fused together as if we could only keep breathing through each other.

He picked me up and carried me to the bedroom, throwing me on the bed. I bounced once and tested out his earlier suggestion.

"Take off your shirt," I ordered.

He stopped short and grinned at me. "I like this." He reached behind his back with one arm and pulled the shirt over his head. I admired his bare chest, the rock hard muscles, the golden skin, the thin trail of hair that marked the path from his belly button into his jeans. His erection was clearly defined behind the denim and seemed to grow larger as I stared at it. "What now?" he asked.

I had forgotten what we were doing as I took in his obvious masculine beauty. "Um, now the jeans."

He shucked those quickly, too. I pulled off my denim skirt. His hardness was now tenting the thin cotton of his boxer briefs. I motioned for him to come sit on the bed, and I climbed on top of him, rubbing myself against him.

He ran his hands up my sides, eager to touch me. "And now?" he murmured.

"My shirt," I said breathlessly, "take off my shirt."

He did so slowly, the calluses of his palm and fingertips lightly abrading my sensitive skin. He rubbed the flat of his palms against my breast, pushing the shirt up and over the lace-covered mounds and then lifting the cotton over my head. I ground down against him, and he groaned audibly.

"I want you to kiss me," I moaned.

"Where?" he drew me close to him, his breath whispering over my skin.

"Here," I said. I lifted my breast to him.

"What do you want me to do?" he asked me, moving down so that his mouth was positioned just over the crest of my breast. "Lick it? Suck it? Bite it?"

I was panting now. "All of it."

He didn't require more instruction. Through the lace, he mouthed my breast. I fumbled at the bra, wanting to feel his wet mouth against my skin. He understood and released the bra closure, pushing it down my arms, all the while licking and biting and sucking on me. I rubbed harder against him.

"Do you want me to touch you anywhere else?" he asked, his lips moving against my breast.

"Yes," I said. Oh yes. I wasn't even conscious anymore. I was lost in his touch and in the flame of our desire for one another. I grabbed his hand. "Touch me here, Noah," I placed his hand between my legs. "I'm so wet for you."

His forehead was resting against my chest as he stared down at his fingers dipping inside my panties. "Jesus, Grace, I love how hot I can get you." He pressed the flat of his palm against me and rubbed his fingers against the soft flesh between my legs.

I started to say something more, but he brought his hand up to my mouth. "Not another word, or I'll come in my shorts. Your dirty talk is too much for me." He looked up ruefully and dropped his hand away.

I gave him a pained smile. "Then take the wheel."

And he did.

Noah

I must have fallen asleep after our celebration because the next thing I knew was that I was alone in Grace's bed. I swept out a hand and it hit the crinkle of paper. Grabbing it, I sat up, flipped on the nightstand, and began to read.

Dear Noah,

Don't let this go to your head, but you were right to not come for me two years ago. Neither of us was ready. We both had to face down our greatest fears.

I know your fear isn't of water anymore. I know that your greatest fear is that you aren't good enough. But you are. You are the best kind of person, Noah. The best kind of friend, the best kind of supporter, the best kind of lover.

I will never want more than I have in you. The journey may have been long, but it was oh-so-worth it.

You are even better than Odysseus because he was an imaginary character dreamt up by some writer. You are real. And amazing.

I love you and will always love you.

Your Grace.

P.S. The weather is always really hot around you, for some reason.

Epilogue

Noah

"Really?" I looked down at the circular shield with the red, white, and blue circles that Finn had handed me. "Who put you in charge of costumes anyway?"

Finn clapped me on the shoulder. "Take it up with Bo. He insisted."

Bo waved his sword at me while Lana and Amy helped buckle him into his chest plate.

"If I'm the only one wearing tights in this photo shoot, someone is going to be having a hard time walking tomorrow," I yelled out. No one was listening to me. I felt the press of a familiar set of fingers along the top of my ass. I guess someone heard me.

"If it makes you feel better, your costume is kind of a turn-on."

"How much of a turn-on?"

"Post-fight, can't wait to get out of the car, turn-on?" Grace whispered against my back. I lowered my shield to cover my groin as I felt my body tighten in response. Tights were not very good at disguising a guy's reaction to the woman he loved, particularly when she was stroking a sensitive patch of skin on his low back.

"I, ah, think you need to take two steps back and to the side." But when she listened to me, I immediately regretted it. I swept her close to me and placed my shield at her back.

She pushed out her lower lip, which I took as an invitation to bite.

She drew back, and I followed to give her a firmer kiss, but she placed her hands against my upper arms.

"No more kissing or we'll end up giving everyone a free show."

"Like I care," I pressed her closer to me. Never a fan of PDA, I really couldn't get enough of Grace. I admit I liked having her within arm's reach, preferably with her amazing rack pressed against my chest and arm. My eyes crossed a little at the thought of licking down the line of my dog tags that disappeared into the valley that her v-neck T-shirt exposed. I contented myself with laying a hard, wet kiss across her mouth.

When she parted her lips, I swept in, allowing the hoots and laughter of our friends to serve as the soundtrack to our happily ever after.

The End

Contact Me

Look for Bo's story in September 2013. You can read an excerpt at JenFrederick.com.

If you enjoyed this story, please consider leaving a review at Goodreads, Amazon, Barnes & Noble, or any other reader site or blog you frequent.

I love hearing from my readers, so drop me a line at jenfrederick@gmail.com. You can also find me on Facebook (http://facebook.com/AuthorJenFredrick) or Twitter (@jensfred).

Author Notes

I took a few liberties with the facts of reality in telling my story. It is highly unlikely that Noah and Bo served three deployments in row, particularly after 2011. One of the longest concurrent deployments on record was the eighteen months served by the Iowa National Guard. Ordinarily, you would have to get a special dispensation from the Department of Defense to serve that long in a war zone.

It is also rare that Grace would not be able to attend some classes in the art department, even if she did not have a major in art. I made up that part of the story to provide the dark moment of Grace's life. I hope you'll forgive me for taking the artistic license.

All other errors are, of course, mine.

Acknowledgments

No book ever reaches the publication stage in solitude. This journey would be stalled on my laptop if it weren't for a group of people who encouraged me and provided faultless guidance.

To my beta readers: Brie, AW, Daphne, Elyssa, and Kati, this book would have been a sad and sorry product without your input.

To my editing team: RL, Daphne, and AW, each pass gave this rough rock a wonderful polish.

To the ones who know more about self publishing than I may ever learn: Jessica and Elyssa.

To Meljean Brook for the amazing cover.

To Sean for all the help with the military aspects. All errors are mine, of course.

To my friends: Gretchen, Chris, the MGL email group.

Made in the USA
Charleston, SC
08 May 2013